Undead of Winter

——————

Sarah E. Glenn, Editor

Mystery and Horror, LLC
Tarpon Springs, FL

Dedication

Undead of Winter is dedicated to Noah Gray. He stepped into the realm of the undead for the cover of this book. While we at Mystery and Horror, LLC are grateful that he turned himself into our cover zombie, we are also grateful that was able to come back to the land of the living.

Thank you, Noah, for an image that captures the cold bleak sadness we were looking for in this anthology. We hope seeing our cover gives you a laugh. You are much more handsome smiling, particularly when you are not green...

Undead of Winter

Sarah E. Glenn, Editor

Mystery and Horror, LLC
Tarpon Springs, FL

TABLE OF CONTENTS

Abandoned

By Neil Davies

The ghosts of the abandoned chattered through the trees as the winter rain overflowed the afternoon and poured into evening. Gunnar and Leif huddled in their rain capes in the slight shelter of an old, broad tree and listened. They knew the sound of the rain, the hiss as it hit the leaves, the rapid tapping as it dripped from branches, but behind the familiar were the ghosts, chattering, rushing back and forth, agitated, looking for something, or someone.

"We'll freeze if we don't move soon," said Gunnar, the older of the two brothers.

"But the ghosts. What about the ghosts?"

Gunnar breathed deeply, calming the fluttering in his stomach. Just back from three years of university, living in the city, he was too intelligent, too wise to believe in the old folk tales of his grandparents. And yet he was afraid. There was no such thing as ghosts, in the woods or otherwise. He knew this. It did not take his fear away.

"The ghosts are just noises," he said, determined to show Leif that his time away from home had changed him. "Nothing more. Just sounds. Sounds can't hurt us, but the cold can. We need to get home."

"We shouldn't have walked through the wood," said Leif, shivering from cold and fear. "It's Halloween for God's sake! Everyone knows bad things happen on Halloween."

"Yes Leif, bad things happen. Kids knock on your door and ask for candy. People dress up in stupid costumes and the shops are full of plastic crap that's meant to look somehow scary. *Very* bad things." Gunnar laughed. It helped cover the slight tremble in his voice that gave the lie to his show of bravado. "Now, come on."

They pushed away from the shelter of the tree, wincing against rain whipped to a bitter cold fury by a sudden wind.

"It's all right for you, Gunnar," said Leif, following behind his brother. "You got away from the village. You didn't have to live through the last few years. Things have changed."

Gunnar stopped, despite the rain in his face, and turned to Leif.

"The village? What are you talking about? We live on a suburban estate in England, not some rural hamlet in medieval Norway. Our grandparents may have been born back there, but everyone since is English, born and bred."

"But I'm telling you things have changed," insisted Leif. "It's not just the grandparents. Everyone is talking about the old ways and how things are returning to them. Even Mrs. Dahlby at number 58 has stopped going to church on Sunday, and you know what she was like with her Virgin Mary statues and crucifixes all over the place. She's gone back to worshipping the old gods. They all have."

Gunnar hesitated. He could see the genuine worry, even fear, in his brother's eyes and yet he could not believe that a whole community on a housing estate could throw off the civilized ways of the modern world and return to barbaric, earlier beliefs. He'd noticed nothing when he returned home the previous week, except that, now he came to think about it, the small crucifix that his mother always kept on the sideboard "just in case a prayer was needed" was not there. And Sunday morning had been extremely quiet. None of the usual car doors slamming as people drove off to church.

"Come on," he said to Leif, determined to ensure his civilized and educated way of thinking would not be overwhelmed by superstition and folklore. "Let's just get home."

"Coming through the wood was a mistake."

"Well, to be fair, we didn't know it was going to pour down then."

"No! I mean, the wood isn't safe."

Gunnar once again saw the fear in his brother's eyes. He struggled to believe that the carefree, confident teenager he had left three years ago had become the frightened, superstitious, *gullible* person before him now.

"How do you mean not safe?" he said, hoping that he could calm Leif down by getting him to talk, explain. Then it might be possible to put all these irrational fears to rest.

"Can't you hear the ghosts in the trees?"

"I hear wind and rain and all sorts of other noises you would expect in a wood on a rainy night," sighed Gunnar. "There are no ghosts."

"I can hear them talking," said Leif. "Whatever you say, I can hear them. They're calling the *Mylings*, the *Utburd*, to jump on our backs and make us carry them to the graveyard."

"You're talking the kind of old folklore nonsense Granddad used to tell around the fire on Halloween to scare us when we were little," said Gunnar. "It's no more real now than it was back then."

"He told us at Halloween because that's when the barrier between the dead and living is at its weakest. And tonight is Halloween."

"Will you stop with the Halloween bullshit!" snapped Gunnar angrily.

He paused, gathered his thoughts and calmed himself. It would do no good to start a shouting match with Leif.

"Listen," he said, his voice calm and in control. "If you choose to believe old legend and folklore that's your business. But even if you think it's all true, my memory is that *Myling* were the ghosts of unwanted children, abandoned straight after birth in the woods to die. Now, surely you're not telling me that people on our estate have been killing babies, are you? I mean, surely you can see how ridiculous that is."

Leif looked up at his brother with tears in his eyes.

"Gunnar, until Mum and Dad left her out in these woods, we had a sister."

Sister?

3

In stunned silence, Gunnar stared at his brother. Somewhere behind the wind and rain he thought he heard slight, brittle laughter but he dismissed it. Just another noise caused by the weather in the trees. What else could it be?

"Mum got pregnant about a year after you left," said Leif, continuing in a low voice that Gunnar strained to hear. "It was a baby girl, a sister, but Dad had wanted another boy. He said a girl was of no use to him or the family, that with you gone we needed another boy to continue the line."

"No one told me," said Gunnar, his voice cracking. "Why didn't anyone tell me?"

"I was forbidden. I don't know why."

"Forbidden? What the fuck is going on in this place?" Gunnar's voice rose as anger replaced disbelief. "You could have emailed. Mum and Dad would never have known. You could have sent me a text, anything!"

Leif glanced quickly behind him. Was that movement between the trees? Something flitting from trunk to trunk, hiding behind the rain and the darkness?

"Gunnar? We need to get out of these woods."

Gunnar ignored his brother as he struggled to bring his anger under control, to understand. It was difficult.

"Tell me what happened when the baby was born."

Leif, his fear growing, his conviction that something was nearby strengthening, shook his head, blinking stinging raindrops from his eyes.

"Gunnar..."

"Tell me!"

Leif hesitated. Was that laughter or wind in the branches? Did something just duck behind the trunk of that tree or was it rain stirring the leaves?

"The baby was born. It was a girl. Dad got rid of it. What else is there to tell?" His voice trembled with fear, grew high-pitched with desperation. "Please, we need to go."

Gunnar refused to move.

"How did he get rid of it? It's impossible. There would be hospital records, doctor's notes, all kinds of stuff."

4

"No hospital, and the doctor's from the village. He's one of them. He helped Dad bring the baby out here and leave her to die."

Gunnar shook his head, struggling to understand, to believe.

A pale shape darted between the trees behind Leif, the movement catching Gunnar's eye. He stared and his fear returned, fighting his anger for dominance. He could feel the civilization of the previous three years being stripped from his mind, layer by layer. Desperately he held on.

"Who's out there?" he shouted, making Leif jump. "Stop messing about and show yourself!"

Leif glanced around fearfully. The voices behind the wind were amused, laughing. "What...?"

"Someone's running around back there," said Gunnar, pointing over Leif's shoulder. "I'm not in the mood for all this."

He waited a few moments more and, when no one came out from behind the trees, wiped the rain from his face and sighed.

"Let's just get home. With a bit of luck whoever's out there will get hypothermia."

He turned, preparing to continue their walk towards home, and stopped. A figure stood on the path, rain-sodden and barely dressed in a ripped and tattered nightdress. A little girl, no more than six years old.

"Gunnar..." began Leif, his voice strained and quiet.

"Don't even think it," said Gunnar angrily. "Our sister would be a little over one year old. You're being stupid. Now, get on your phone and call for help."

His voice softened as he smiled at the girl, wondering if perhaps she was the victim of an attack or had just wandered off from home.

"What's your name?" he said. "Mine's Gunnar, and this is my brother Leif. Don't be frightened, we won't hurt you."

"I can't get a signal," hissed Leif. "Nothing."

Gunnar continued to smile at the girl.

"What are you doing out here? You must be cold. Here."
He quickly pulled off his rain cape and held it out to the girl. She
did not move.

"Will you take me home?"

Her voice was soft, almost lost in the hiss of the never-
ending rain, yet it seemed to be echoed through the trees all
around them.

"Of course we'll take you home," said Gunnar, still
holding the cape towards her. "Where do you live?"

"Will you carry me?"

The echoes were stronger this time, causing Gunnar to
glance quickly around, wondering if there were more children
hiding in the darkness. But that just wasn't possible, he told
himself.

He could hear Leif behind him, breathing heavily,
obviously frightened. He guessed he heard the echoes too.

"Are you tired?" he asked the girl, suppressing his own
fear, telling himself it was stupid superstition and all the talk
from Leif that was getting to him. Nothing else. "Of course I'll
carry you if you're tired."

"Will your brother carry my brother too?"

The girl raised an arm and pointed over Gunnar's
shoulder. He turned and saw Leif staring, wide-eyed, at the small
boy who stood nearby, as pale and emaciated as the girl.

"How many of you are there?" stammered Gunnar, trying
to recover from the surprise of seeing the second child. What the
hell was going on in these woods?

"Just the two of us, for now," said the girl. "It's enough.
Will you carry us?"

Gunnar shuddered, wondering if it was just cold and
damp that caused him to react so, or whether his fear was taking
control. He wasn't sure he could tell any more. Nevertheless, he
was a civilized man and here were two children in obvious need
of help. He looked at his brother, saw fear in his eyes but knew
he would, ultimately, feel the same. How could they refuse?

"Of course we'll carry you."

He didn't even see the girl move. She was simply no
longer on the path and he felt the sudden weight of her on his

6

back, fingers pressing into his shoulder, legs gripping around his waist.

"Careful," he said, stumbling under the unexpected burden. "You're hurting..."

Her fingers burned through the polyester of his jacket and dug deep into the flesh of his shoulders, melting into the muscles. He screamed with the sharp, withering pain. The clothing on his back blackened, flared into small gouts of flame and became ash. His flesh bubbled and popped as the girl's body fused to his.

Even through his pain he wondered about Leif. Had his brother managed to escape? Was he even now on his way to get help? But then he heard the screams, the laughter of the small boy, and he knew his brother suffered too.

He fell to his knees, the searing pain in his back spreading through his limbs, into his neck, his head. His whole body screamed at him to lose consciousness, to escape from the agony for a little while, but he did not pass out, *could* not pass out.

"You can't go to sleep," said the girl, mocking, in his ear. "If you sleep you cannot carry us."

Gunnar tried to focus through the pain, to make some kind of sense of what was happening. But there *was* no sense to the way the girl's body had melted into his, how her bones scratched at his spine with each movement, how her skin stretched and became one with his own.

"What do you want?" He managed to gasp the words out through gritted teeth.

"You promised to carry us," said the girl, the sing-song tone of her voice edged with menace. "You can't break a promise."

He tried to turn his head, to see Leif, but his neck would not move with the extra burden of the girl's head, resting on it.

"Leif!" His throat stabbed agony through him as he shouted, his voice weak, broken.

For a moment there was no sound save the soft under-breath giggling of the thing on his back. Then he heard his brother's voice, strained, near breakdown.

"He's on my back Gunnar... *Myling*... Lord help me... it hurts!"

Myling!

Could Leif have been right? Gunnar's educated mind railed against it, but he could not explain the thing on his back. Did the old superstitions have some basis in truth? He could not deny the evidence.

"Are you *Mylings*?" He whispered the question, but his throat still felt as though it were lined with razor blades.

"It is a name," said the girl. "Some say *Utburd* in memory of how they made us. We call ourselves none of these. We just are. Now, carry us!"

Gunnar climbed to his feet, roaring his pain out loud, no longer controlling his own legs. The rain strengthened, its hiss answering his pain, two raw sounds of nature crashing head-on in the wood.

"Where are we going?" he said, fighting the flesh-stripping agony of his throat to ask the question.

"Don't worry, we know the way."

He walked, unable to feel, let alone control, his feet as they took step by step through the wet, clinging leaves on the ground. He managed one more word before the blood filling his mouth made him choke and spit and grow silent.

"Why?"

The girl laughed, an almost sweet sound in the dark and the rain if he had not known what it came from.

"Why? To see your sister of course!"

Soaked through, rainwater spat out with each gasp of breath and forced to trudge onwards with no control over their own legs, Gunnar and Leif suffered their journey into depths of the wood they did not know existed. The things on their backs, parasitic children, in turns giggled and hissed, spat words of encouragement and sudden Tourette-like outbursts of vitriol against the people who had abandoned them.

Gunnar's faith in logic, in modern science, was shaken. Through the tight tugging of merged skin and the scratching of exposed bone he tried to fit these things that had attached themselves to him and his brother into the world view he had adopted since leaving home. But they refused to fit. The only place they *did* fit was in the archaic superstitions and beliefs of his ancestors.

Mylings. Utburd. One which is taken outside.

Could he really believe that his family, the whole estate, most of whom had been born in this country, had turned to the ancient gods and were guilty of infanticide? Why was that any less believable than the impossible creature that had leeched itself to his back and drove him towards a sister he never knew he had?

Behind him he could hear Leif moan, suffering the pain in his throat to mutter prayers, Christian prayers, under his labored breath. For a moment Gunnar envied him his faith, but he quickly discarded the thought. He would not abandon his non-belief through fear. There were no gods, ancient or otherwise. His only belief was in science, in logic, in proof and evidence. He could not deny that the creature on his back was strange and completely unknown to him, but his ignorance did not make it supernatural.

The melted, merged skin and scratching bones screamed otherwise. It was difficult for him to ignore them.

They reached a clearing and, with the control over his legs suddenly released, Gunnar fell heavily to his knees, staring with disbelief at the scene before him.

Children filled the clearing, most dressed in rags, some naked, huddled together on the ground or simply standing, staring at the new arrivals. There was a strange buzz in the air, an electric interference type buzz, a faulty fridge buzz that reverberated in Gunnar's head.

With an agonizing tearing of flesh, muscle and bone, the children on Gunnar and Leif's backs detached themselves, dropping lightly to their feet and running, skipping almost, to join their fellow lost children, the other *Mylings* in the wood clearing.

Gunnar could feel the hot, wet sensation of blood running from the open wounds on his back, yet he was alive. How could he still be alive?

As though reading his thoughts, the *Myling* who had been on his back spoke.

"You will be surprised how quickly your wounds heal. You carried us to our destination as we asked. We are not savages. You will live."

All pretense at disbelief gone, Gunnar stared at the *Mylings* who filled the clearing.

"There are so many," he gasped, his throat already beginning to heal itself. "How long has this been going on?"

Leif, his brother, struggled to shuffle forward to his side.

"I don't think it ever stopped."

The *Mylings* stepped back without warning, opening a pathway to the stump of a lightning struck tree. On the stump sat a small child, no more than one or two years old. A girl. She stared at them with open curiosity and a small smile twitched on her lips.

"This," said the *Myling* who had rode Gunnar to the clearing, "is your sister. Abandoned but rescued by myself and my friends."

Gunnar could not take his eyes off the girl. Nor could he deny a family resemblance. He no longer doubted the story Leif had told him of the pregnancy, the birth and the attempted infanticide.

"Is she *Myling* like you?" he asked, his voice weak but slowly returning.

"She was still alive when we found her. She is still alive now. No, she is not *Myling*."

"What do you want us to do?" Leif asked the question, also unable to take his eyes from the girl. There was no doubt in his mind that this was the child his father and the doctor had brought out to the wood and abandoned to die. Despite his pain and terror, he almost laughed at the thought that they had failed.

"Take her home," said the *Myling*. "She does not belong here. She is *Utburd* but she is not *Myling*. She needs to be with the living, with others of her kind. With her family."

Gunnar said nothing but simply nodded. It was the only decent thing they could do.

Gunnar and Leif staggered through the wood, finally back on the path towards home. The unceasing rain pounded on their uncovered heads, their ripped clothing, their exposed, scarred but healed backs. In his arms Gunnar carried a small child, wrapped in a blanket. She rested her head close to his chest and he did his best to keep the rain from her. She was precious. She was unique. She was a survivor.

"What do we tell Dad?" said Leif, keeping pace with his older brother, sometimes looking and smiling at the child. She smiled back.

"We tell him the truth," said Gunnar through clenched teeth. "We expose his crimes, confront him with the horror of what he has tried to do. Then we tell the police, social services, anyone who will listen and who can put a stop to this ridiculous mania that seems to have taken over the people here."

"But our parents could go to jail," said Leif, an uncertain whine in his voice. He had never left home, never left his family. The bond was strong despite his disgust at what they had done.

For a moment Gunnar said nothing, continuing to push his way through the rain, the wood, the pain in his legs and back. Then one word was spat from his mouth with venom and barely controlled rage.

"Good!"

Brander Evenson was sitting in his front room, comfortable in his armchair, reading the evening paper, when Gunnar and Leif finally reached home. Wet, tired and in pain they stumbled through the door into the narrow hallway and were greeted by their mother, stepping from the kitchen at the sound of the door.

"You're soaked." Hilde Evenson wiped her hands on the dishcloth she had been using to dry dishes, concerned at the bedraggled appearance of her sons.

Gunnar said nothing, pushing straight into the front room, the child still cradled in his arms.

Leif tried to smile at his mother but it was difficult. Eyes downcast he followed his brother.

"Where have you been?" asked Brander Evenson, carefully folding his paper and placing it on the arm of the chair. "You're late." He saw the blanket wrapped bundle in Gunnar's arms, peered at it suspiciously. "What's that you've got?"

Gunnar carefully put the girl on the floor where she sat, still wrapped in the wet blanket, staring at the old man in the chair.

"We've brought our sister home," said Gunnar, his voice low with suppressed rage. "Your daughter. The one you tried to kill."

There was a gasp from their mother in the doorway, but Brander said nothing. He simply stared at Gunnar, not at the girl. After several moments during which neither broke eye contact, he said, slowly and clearly, "I have no daughter."

"Then I have no father!" Gunnar spat the words, hatred and disgust in every syllable.

"Gunnar!" cried Hilde Evenson from the doorway. "How can you say such a thing?"

"He tried to murder his own daughter, and now he dares to deny she ever existed!"

Brander stood, facing his eldest son. When he spoke, his voice shook.

"That girl cannot be my daughter. My daughter is dead."

"You failed, you and the doctor," said Gunnar, his voice low, almost a whisper. "You left her to die but she lived, rescued by... others."

"It's true Dad," cut in Leif. "They saved her life. The *Myling*."

Brander glanced towards his younger son but made no reply. He turned, instead, back to Gunnar.

"That child is not mine," he said. "She can't be. If you really want the truth about this, the child that was born in this house died in this house. Doctor Mathisen made sure of that."

"But..." Gunnar stumbled over his words, caught off-guard by the unexpected confession. "They said they found her alive in the wood, where you left her."

"We took the body into the wood, yes," said Brander, his voice cold, unemotional.

"Brander," said Hilde from the doorway. "No."

"He wants the truth, he can have it," said Brander, without taking his eyes from Gunnar. "Do you want the truth?"

Gunnar regained his composure, his anger.

"Just tell me."

"We took the body, myself and the doctor, into the wood, to a clearing the doctor knew from other times, other families."

"Other families?" Gunnar shook his head in disbelief. "You're all mad."

"In the clearing," continued Brander, "we burned the body, cremated it, and scattered what was left about the clearing. So you see, this child cannot be my daughter. My daughter, your sister, is dead!"

Confused, Gunnar glanced down at the little girl. She looked up at him. There were tears in her eyes. She reached a hand up to him and he took it in his. He was no longer sure who she was, even though he felt he had seen a family resemblance, but she was still a child that needed his help, his protection. His parents, the people on this estate, were monsters. They needed to be stopped.

"I'm calling the police," he said, his determination returning as he reached into his pocket for his mobile. "You're all going to jail for this. The whole fucking lot of you!"

Brander punched Gunnar in the stomach, forcing his son to stagger backwards, losing his grip on the little girl's hand.

Gunnar, winded by the blow, pressed his hand to his stomach and was surprised, when he brought it away, to see it covered with blood. It was only then he saw the bloodied blade of the short knife in his father's hand.

"You're not bringing this family down," said Brander, the gleam of madness in his eyes. "The gods will not allow it."

Gunnar looked pleadingly towards Leif who stood, stunned and immobile, nearby. The younger son turned towards the doorway, towards his mother, not knowing what to do.

"I'm sorry Leif," said Hilde as she dragged the serrated blade of the bread knife across her youngest son's throat. "But your dad is right."

Leif tried to stop the spurting blood with his hands but it spat from between his fingers and ran in rivers down his coat front. He fell to his knees and was dead before his head crashed into the coffee table.

Gunnar, staring at the body of his brother, struggled to stay upright, already feeling weak through shock and loss of blood. He gave no resistance as his father stepped closer and stabbed the blade once, twice more into his body. He stumbled backwards, his knees hitting the edge of an old wooden chair. He sat and, turning to look once more at the small girl he had carried from the wood, died.

Brander and Hilde Evenson stood together and looked at their dead sons. Hilde shook her head.

"It's sad, but they would never have accepted the old ways."

Brander nodded. "Sooner or later it would have come to this." He took her hand and smiled. "We can always have more sons."

"But who's the girl?" said Hilde, and they both turned to stare at the little girl who still sat, wrapped in her blanket. She had not moved.

"I don't know who she is," said Brander. "But we need to get rid of her."

He gripped his knife tighter and stepped towards the girl.

Except she was no longer a little girl.

Her face, so soft, so angelic a moment before, had hardened and twisted into the face of a demon. Her teeth were sharp, like razors lodged in her gums. Her fingers, so short and plump, were claws with curving talons.

Brander and Hilde Evenson screamed as the *Myling*, finally home, sought its revenge.

Neil Davies was born in 1959 and has found everything else to be an uphill struggle. He currently lives in the North West of England with his wife and two children. Any spare time he can find he spends writing horror and science fiction. At present he has five novels, a novella, a stand-alone short story and two short story collections to his credit. For more information please visit his official website - http://www.nwdavies.co.uk

Phantom Pains

By Stephanie Stamm

Was it the howling that woke me or the cold?

I winced as I pushed myself up to sitting, the pain in my arms, legs, and torso, as well as the throb in my head, suggesting that trying to get vertical could be a mistake. My hand went to the back of my head, and I winced again as my glove made contact with a lump. Slipping off the glove, I touched instead with bare fingers and found both a goose egg and a gash. The hair around the wound was thick and tacky with blood, cold but not frozen, and the bottom edge of my wool cap was stiffening as the blood on it dried.

I remembered standing on the edge of the ravine, searching for the best way down. The previous night's snowfall hadn't been heavy, but enough snow covered the rocks to make for treacherous footing. I didn't remember reaching a decision or taking a step, but I guessed I must have slipped. I certainly felt like I'd tumbled over 200 or so feet of rocks.

I looked around me, a frown forming between my brows. A fall would explain the bruises and the head wound, but it wouldn't account for my current location. I seemed to be in a cave of some sort. Light and cold air filtered in from the opening to my right. No tumble down the ravine would have rolled me through the hole, or placed me on the pallet of dried leaves and grasses that rustled beneath me.

My frown deepened as another scan revealed that aside from the pallet—and me—the cave appeared unoccupied. No sleeping bags or camping gear littered the cave floor or leaned against its sloping walls. No gear, no pack—including my own.

The opening in the cave wall beckoned. I tried to push to my feet, but I collapsed with a groan as my right ankle gave beneath me. I gritted my teeth against the pain, the action mimicking the grinding I'd felt in my ankle bones.

Walking might be out of the question, but I could still crawl. I made it to the hole on hands and knees, each movement jarring my broken ankle. Resting against a rock near the opening, I stretched my leg out in front of me. My foot hung at an unnatural angle. I repositioned my foot with my hands, sweat beading on my forehead despite the cold as the bones in my ankle slid against each other.

A few sticks and small branches lay on the ground around me. I broke the sturdiest branch into four pieces. Tugging off my gloves, I loosened the laces of my boot and nudged the pieces of wood between boot and sock on either side of my ankle. Then I retied the boot, pulling the laces as tight as I could around the swollen ankle with its makeshift splint.

Drawing in deep breaths of the cold air, I leaned back against the rock and pushed my shaking hands into my gloves. I let my head roll to the side without lifting it from its rocky pillow and looked through the opening.

Snow blanketed the ground, and more fell from the gray sky. It had been falling long and heavy enough to fill in any tracks that might have been left by whoever had brought me here.

Doing my best not to shift my right leg, I leaned and scooped up enough snow to compress into a loose snowball. I took a bite and let my head rest against the rock as the snow melted on my tongue.

I nearly dropped the snowball when the howling started again.

I searched the area visible through the cave opening, but I could see nothing except snow-covered ground and trees. The wolves weren't exactly at my door, but from the sound of those howls, they weren't all that far away.

I ate the rest of the snowball, then made another and ate it too, while I tried to think of any solution to my current problem.

16

From the angle of the light, it looked like night was fast approaching. With my broken ankle, there was no way I could make it home before night fall. If I had, in fact, fallen down the ravine, it would take me hours to make my way back up, wounded as I was. There was no point in even thinking about leaving until morning.

No food, no water, no sleeping bag, no means of building a fire. Well, there were a few sticks and that pallet I'd lain on. But even if I could get a fire started by rubbing sticks together, the remaining sticks and the pallet would burn out in a matter of very few minutes. At least, the cave blocked the wind, keeping out the worst of the cold. And I still had my winter gear.

I sighed. Maybe whoever had brought me here would return, and we could come up with a plan together.

I crawled back to the pallet, where I curled into a fetal position to conserve my body heat. I waited. No one came.

The cave darkened as night fell. I wasted some mental energy worrying about the wolves, but when their howls moved farther away, I managed to relax enough to fall into an uneasy slumber.

I drifted in that place between sleep and waking. Strange images filled my head but wouldn't resolve into anything I could describe. I lay on my back, unmoving. I felt sharp teeth gnawing at my wrists. Had the wolves found my cave, after all? The howls came from so far away. Though the teeth punctured my skin, I felt little pain. The sensation was almost pleasurable. Not wolves. But, if not wolves, then what? I don't know how long the surreal world of semi-consciousness held me captive before releasing me to the oblivion of sleep.

I jerked awake, heart pounding. Unsure what had startled me, I looked around the cave. Bright morning light shone through the opening. Apparently, yesterday's clouds had been banished. Otherwise, nothing appeared to have changed from the night before.

No, one thing was different. I wasn't wearing my gloves. One lay on each side of me. I frowned, remembering the sensation of gnawing teeth that had filled my sleep-fogged brain. Even as I chided myself for being ridiculous, I pulled up the edges of my coat sleeves to expose my wrists. No teeth marks. No wounds at all. Of course not. I must have yanked the gloves off in my sleep.

Forcing my stiffened limbs into movement, I crawled to the cave opening and looked out on a white world that sparkled in the sunlight streaming from the clear blue sky. I scooped and ate a few snowballs as I contemplated a plan of action. First I had to figure out where I was. Then I had to do my best to get back to the cabin before nightfall. And, with any luck, Mike would be there waiting for me.

Holding on to the rock I'd propped myself against and the wall of the cave, I managed to stand, weight on my left foot, right knee bent and foot lifted. There were some trees not too far from the cave opening. If I could use a branch as a kind of cane, I would be able to hobble. Between that and scooting on my ass, I could conceivably make it to the cabin in a full day. My hike out had taken significantly less time, but I'd had a compass and two working feet.

I fell once on my way to the closest stand of trees. Not a surprise given the several feet of nothing to hold on to between the hillside and the first tree, and me trying to hop through six or eight inches of snow. Plus, I was weak after a day of no nourishment apart from snowballs.

Relief filled me when I found a branch that looked sturdy enough within reach. Now I just had to figure out how to detach it from the tree. Swinging on it, both legs off the ground, didn't work. I searched my clothes. My gear had been in my pack, but maybe I'd stuffed something of use into one of my coat or pants pockets.

Victory. The fourth pocket I checked revealed a Swiss Army knife.

The branch I'd chosen was fairly thick, because I needed something that would support my weight. It took a while to cut through the wood with the knife's small saw blade—especially since I needed to take breaks, to rest both my hand and the left leg that wasn't accustomed to bearing all my weight, and to catch my breath. My weakness was even greater than I had thought, and seemed out of proportion to my injury and lack of nourishment. But what did I know? I'd never been trapped outdoors overnight with a broken ankle and no food before. When the branch finally gave, I sat down on the rock I'd dusted off for my earlier breaks and started trimming the twigs from my future cane.

While I trimmed I also scoped out my position. As I had suspected, I was at the bottom of the ravine. From the looks of things, the cave that had sheltered me was a few hundred yards to the east of the lip on which I'd stood the morning before—as well as about 200 or so feet down. Getting back up to the lip would have been difficult with two good legs. With only one to stand on, the going would be way more than tough. I planned to ease my way up the steep slope on my ass, pushing with the one good leg and the tree branch cane.

My progress out of the ravine went about as well as I expected. For every couple of feet I'd manage to push myself up, I'd slide back down a few inches. And I had to rest more often than I would have liked.

I began to wonder if making it to the cabin before nightfall was a realistic possibility. Spending the night in the great outdoors without so much as a sleeping bag for shelter held little appeal. But my choices were limited. I might die before I made it back to the cabin, but I was even more likely to die if I didn't try. If whoever had put me in that cave had intended to come back for me, they would have done it by now.

What felt like hours later, I'd dragged and pushed myself almost halfway up the slope. And it was getting steeper as I got weaker. A few feet to the right, the slope looked a little more gradual. I angled myself to slide sideways, dragging with my right hand and pushing with the cane in my left.

The cane slipped on the snow covered rocks, and I went sliding. Without thinking, I tried to stop myself with my right foot, and the pain nearly blinded me. I screamed a curse and kept sliding. I felt the impact when my head hit another rock, but I was out before I could scream again.

When I opened my eyes, my head was throbbing and the light was dim. And I was lying on my stomach on the pallet in the cave. How in the …? I pushed myself up to roll over.

"Don't move too fast. You hit your head."

"Mike?"

I sat up and leaned back against the cave wall, staring through the dimness at the reason I'd been standing on the lip of the blasted ravine in the first place.

"What the hell, Mike? What are you doing here? You didn't come home."

"You came looking for me?"

"Of course, I came looking for you."

"Without a pack?"

"I'm not an idiot. I had a pack, but I must have lost it when I fell down the ravine."

"I didn't see one anywhere near you."

"Not this time. Before. The day after you disappeared."

"But I just left the cabin yesterday."

I stared at him, jaw slack. "What? No, that's not right. This is the second evening I've been in this cave."

"You hit your head. You're confused."

I had no response.

"Just rest. Tomorrow, when it's light, we'll get out of here."

I lay down, closed my eyes. "Mike?" I asked. "Where's your pack? Your sleeping bag?"

"Go to sleep."

Again the drifting in sleep's hinterlands. Flashes of light and sound. Voices murmuring. Wind whistling. Wolves howling. Teeth tugging at my wrists and throat. I have to find Mike. He didn't come home. Mike standing at the top of the ravine, the sun at his back. Teeth in my flesh. Wolves howling.

It was a relief to wake.

"Mike?"

No answer.

I looked around the cave. Just like before, it was empty except for me and my pallet. But I had seen Mike. He had brought me here the day before, after I'd fallen back down the ravine. Or, according to Mike, after I'd fallen down the ravine for the first time.

20

I frowned. I'd gone looking for Mike, fallen, and he'd found me? And that had all happened yesterday? Was my sense of timing really so screwed up that I thought two days had passed instead of only one?

Mike had also said we'd get out of here when it was light. If the sunlight filtering through the cave opening was any indication, it was morning. Where was Mike? He wouldn't have just left me here. Would he?

Would Mike have left me? Why would he leave me? The questions rattled around in my mind as I crawled toward the cave opening and the light.

My right ankle barely hurt anymore. It must have gone numb. Probably not a good sign.

I leaned against the rock at the opening, realizing I didn't feel nearly as weak as I had the day before. Odd, after all the exertion, and the second fall. Or was it the first fall—the only fall? Did I try to climb out of the ravine yesterday? Or did I fall down it for the first time? When had I come looking for Mike? When had Mike left me?

Holding on to the rock and the cave wall, I stood—again more easily than I would have thought possible. For some reason, I put my right foot on the ground—and it held my weight. I felt lighter somehow. I chuckled. Light-bodied. Light-headed.

I took a step into the snow, figuring it would cushion me when I fell. My ankle held. I stopped, stunned. Had Mike been right? Had I imagined the first fall and the broken ankle? Had I imagined making a tree branch cane and pushing myself up the side of the ravine only to tumble back down again? Had I imagined Mike's presence in the cave? Had he been any more real than my dreams of teeth gnawing on my wrists and throat?

Images and sensations from the preceding days spun in my head. And I couldn't tell real from unreal, memory from dream or hallucination. Mike leaving the cabin. Mike standing at the top of the ravine. Mike kneeling beside me. Pain in my head. Pain in my ankle. Pain throughout my body. Blood on my glove. Teeth at my wrists. Me in the cave. Mike in the cave with me. Pain. Blood. Teeth pulling the flesh from my hands and arms, my throat, my abdomen.

Reeling from the hyperactive slide show flashing in my mind, I stumbled forward through the snow.

I was almost on top of it before I saw it.

The body. The blood. Clothes ripped and flesh torn away, bare to the bone in places.

But still recognizable. If only because of the clothes.

I knew that coat, those pants, that hat, those gloves, those boots. My coat, my pants, my hat, my gloves, my boots.

My body.

My pack lay a few feet away. It had also been ripped apart. Probably because of the food I'd carried.

I dropped to my knees in the snow, only now noticing that I made no impression. Turning my head, I looked back over my path. I had left no footprints.

I looked from my open body to the top of the ravine. Like snow when the wind dies, the maelstrom of images settled. And I remembered.

Mike and I stood at the top of the ravine. We'd left the cabin together, had hiked out in the snow. We were looking for the best way down the ravine.

Pain in my head, the pack I'd been holding in my hand flying free and tumbling end over end as I pitched forward, my body rolling down the side of the ravine.

Mike standing at the top, a bloodied rock in his hand.

Mike kneeling beside me, checking for a pulse, making sure there wasn't one.

Mike leaving my body for the forest to feed on.

He'd counted on the coming snow to cover our tracks.

As I knelt there in the snow, beside my body, remembering my death, I didn't think to ask why. The reason was irrelevant. The what was all that mattered. That, and the who.

I let the truth settle into my mind, as the cold settled into my insubstantial bones. I let them both numb me, form me, recreate me as a creature as frozen as the winter that surrounded me.

And when I'd knelt there long enough, when the cold and the snow and the truth had instilled in me their icy reality, I pushed to my feet. And I saw that I could make an impression if I willed it so.

I turned my back on my body. The forest and its inhabitants could take whatever remained.

Then, leaving my cave behind, I ascended the ravine and headed toward the cabin to find Mike.

Technical writer by day, creative writer by night and weekends, Stephanie Stamm is the author of A Gift of Wings, *a YA/NA fantasy and the first volume of her Light-Bringer Series. When she's not writing, her favorite occupations are reading (both traditional books and e-books), cooking (preferably with local produce), walking (and generating writing ideas), playing with or snuggling her two cats (individually or together), or hanging out with family or friends (sometimes while also doing one or more of the above). She is currently working on the second volume of the Light-Bringer Series,* A Gift of Shadows.

The Lean Season

By Shenoa Carroll-Bradd

We make sure to boil whatever we catch. Makes the stringy meat taste even worse, but we figure it's the safest way.

Our mama taught Katie and me the importance of preservin' food and not wastin' a thing. One of my earliest memories is of sittin' on the kitchen counter while she cut the mold offa strawberries to make jam. I threw a berry on the floor, just to see it squish, and received my very first hand slap. It stands out in my mind as the moment I realized Mama could offer pain as well as protection.

"No," she had said, eyebrows comin' together like mergin' storm fronts. "That's a bad girl, Jen. We do not waste food in this house."

I think I probably cried from the shock of being slapped, but her lesson hit its mark, and when Katie came along three years later I was first in line to pass along the wisdom (complete with hand slap, because what else are sisters for?).

On the day our mama died, the three of us were busy in the kitchen, turnin' the last soft autumn apples into apple butter. The air swam with a perfume of cinnamon and cloves, spices strong enough to negate the tell-tale tang of turnin' fruit.

Daddy was busy in the back, addin' log after split log to the mountain of firewood behind our house. He'd heard the radio reports: we were in for a hard winter. We already knew it would be a lean season. The last hog had been sold and the ground yielded nothin' now but snow and stones.

Mama was prepared though, and we had all we needed down in the cellar: glass jars of pickles and vegetables and jam and stew, prettier than any queen's jewels.

I'll always remember how lovely she looked that day. The heat of the stove turned her cheeks pink and curled her dark hair into wispy corkscrews at her temples and neck. She never wore makeup, our mama. She was a lady of humility and substance.

I came up to her shoulder, but Katie only came up to mine, so she didn't see the stumblin' shape out in the snow that caught our attention. Katie kept up her stirrin' while Mama and I froze, starin' out the frosted window as the shufflin' shape approached our front gate.

Mama wiped her hands on her apron and her mouth went flat. "Looks like Mr. Haven's drunk again. Damn fool's gonna freeze to death out there." She went to the door and put on her heavy coat, then wrapped a thick muffler around her face and pulled on her gloves. "You girls stay here. I'm gonna go see if he needs helpin'." She looked silly, all bundled up like a quilted snowman. Mama pointed a gloved finger at us. "Don't you dare let that apple butter burn."

"We won't," I told her.

Even if we did, she wouldn't throw it out. Mama would just dose it with some molasses and call it her "special dark recipe". Never wasted a thing. She was a bit of a genius that way. Everything had its place in our home, and once it did its job, we found it a new one. Dresses became skirts, skirts became rags, rags became dolls, and eventually dolls became either kindling or compost.

Mama shook that gloved finger at us one last time, then turned and waded out into the snow.

"What is it?" Katie asked from her footstool by the stove. "What's she talkin' about, Mr. Haven?"

I took the spoon from her hand and hoisted her up onto the counter top, where Mama would certainly say she was too big to be, but was in no position to scold. I took up the stirrin' duties

26

as we both watched Mama trudge through the snow toward the figure that must have been our closest neighbor, Mr. Haven.

He stumbled up against our fence and nearly toppled over, reachin' out for Mama like a drownin' man clutching at boards.

"What's he doin'?" Katie murmured.

"He's drunk too much, that's all. Grownups do that, then they get sick and go to sleep, and when they wake up, they're all better," I told her. "Unless they catch a hangover, which is kinda like the flu."

Katie looked at me with big doll eyes, bathin' in my endless knowledge.

I always felt real smart around her, but that's 'cause she was a baby and never knew anythin'. Movement caught my eye through the window, and I lost interest in trying to educate my sister. "Hey!" Panic prickled up my arms, all the way to my scalp. "Hey, they're fightin'! He's tryin' to bite Mama!" I thrust the spoon into Katie's hand and ran for the back door, burstin' out and skiddin' on the packed snow, calling for Daddy.

He came joggin' up from the splittin' stump, ax still in hand. "What is it, Jenny bean? Why are you out here without a coat?"

The icy air burned my lungs and shrank my voice as I told him what was happenin' at our front gate.

Daddy's face grew hard, and the ice crystals collectin' in his beard made him look like an angry frost giant. "Get back inside," he said as he started to sprint around the house. "Keep your sister in there, and don't look out the windows!" He called the last over his shoulder as he disappeared.

Flakes began to swirl down from the darkenin' sky.

I was glad to return to the warmth of the kitchen, and to the sweet smells of apple butter, but worry shook my hands and made me sweat. I took Katie down from the counter top and resumed stirring duties, trying to focus on keeping the butter from burning.

"Where'd Daddy go?" Katie pestered, pokin' my side and tuggin' on my sleeves when I didn't answer. "Why isn't Mama back? Why won't you tell me what's goin' on?"

I shushed her, but that didn't work worth a damn. Daddy had told me not to look, but I just couldn't help myself. I turned my gaze out the kitchen window.

The snow was falling harder, and the world outside had grown a couple shades darker since I came back in. I could just make out the shapes by our front gate, three vague forms locked in a violent struggle. And, every now and then, I saw the rise and fall of an ax. The darkenin' night slowly turned our window into a mirror, and my own pale face grew to overlay the scene.

"Be quiet, Katie. I don't know any of the answers to your questions."

That shut her up. I always knew the answer to everythin'.

Eventually, the snowy evening grew so dark I couldn't see anythin' but a parody of our kitchen. I stopped lookin'. Katie and I said nothin' for long minutes, just listenin' to the gentle bubble of the apple butter and the soft scrape of spoon against pot.

After what felt like an hour, we both lifted our heads, alert to the growin' sound of shufflin', uneven footsteps. I turned off the stove. "You can't ask any questions when they come back inside," I told Katie, not entertainin' the thought that it might not be them comin' through the cabin door.

Katie turned her little face up to me. "Why?"

I cupped a hand over her mouth as the door creaked open. The shufflin' footsteps entered, and I released the breath I'd been holdin'.

Two pairs of feet. Mama and Daddy.

Katie pried at my hand with sharp little nails, but I held her next to me until Daddy came into view. Dark blood splattered the front of his coat, and the arm not supportin' Mama still clutched the smeary ax. I felt Katie go still behind my hand.

Daddy looked at us, but his eyes didn't seem to focus.

Mama didn't look at us at all. Her head hung like she was ashamed, and the softly curlin' hair I'd admired earlier was tangled into a frazzled, wet knot.

"Jen," Daddy said, his voice strained and rough, "run and get the first aid kit."

I released Katie and did as I was told, skirtin' past our parents. As I went by, I couldn't ignore that the blood on Daddy's jacket stank. It didn't smell fresh. It didn't smell right. If that blood had been left over from sausages, I think even Mama would have tossed it out.

When I returned with the kit, Mama sat in one of our dining room chairs, head still down. Her tattered coat sprawled on the floor like twice-flattened roadkill.

I handed the first aid kit to Daddy and tried to catch his eye, to ask a silent question, but he refused to look at me.

Katie still stood beside the stove, her eyes big as boiled eggs. I waved her over and held her close, my arms crossed over her shoulders. She shook against me, and it was no mystery why.

Mama was bleedin'. From...everywhere. Blood matted her hair, crisscrossed her arms like chicken scratch, and soaked the left shoulder of her blouse.

Daddy spoke softly to her as he cleaned and bandaged her arms, like you would to a dog you're afraid to spook.

Mama didn't respond to him. She didn't even react when he swabbed her scratches with foamy hydrogen peroxide, the kind that always makes me wince.

Daddy didn't say a word to us while he fixed her up, except to ask for water or towels, or a clean shirt. I'd never seen his big, rough hands be so gentle. When he finished, he brought out a trash bag and filled it with all the bloody swabs and cloth.

Mama looked so pale. She murmured somethin' we couldn't hear.

Daddy leaned in. "Wouldn't you rather take a bath first?"

She shook her head slowly, then turned to point at the pot of coolin' apple butter.

"The girls will see to that. You need to rest." Daddy slung an arm under hers and helped her stand, guidin' her to the stairs.

She stopped at the bottom and shook her head again, pointin' to the livin' room couch.

Katie squeezed my hand.

I squeezed back, tryin' to keep my breathin' regular because little kids are like dogs. They can sense when you're upset, and it just winds them tighter.

Daddy helped Mama settle onto the couch with pillows and blankets, fussin' all over her, plumpin' and tuckin' and

29

smoothin'. I felt like I could see into the past then, could see how sweet the two of them were before Katie and I came along.

Once Daddy was done with her, he turned to look at us. "Isn't it time for bed, Katie?"

My little sister started at her name and skittered up the stairs to get ready, leavin' Daddy and me alone in the kitchen.

I squeezed my hands together, workin' up my nerve as I looked at Mama's still form on the couch. "Daddy? What happened out by the gate?"

He turned his head to me slowly, like it weighed a great deal. "Mr. Haven...went crazy," he said carefully. "He attacked your mother, and I...defended her."

Without my consent, my gaze went behind him to where the ax leaned against the wall. "Didja kill him?"

Daddy's face went fierce. "Don't you ask me questions like that."

I nodded, avertin' my eyes again. "What are we gonna do?"

He let out a long breath through his nose. I thought I could hear it whistlin' between his whiskers like the wind in the forest. "We're all going to sleep on it, and see how things look in the mornin'." He ran a hand over his beard. "Then I'll call the sheriff, once we've decided what we're going to say."

I nodded again, but I didn't really follow. If Mr. Haven had gone crazy, then what was there to say? Daddy had acted in self-defense.

He ran his hand over his beard again, then looked at the pot on the stove. "Better get that into jars, Jenny bean. We're going to need every ounce, especially once the doctor comes and takes a look at your mama. House calls ain't cheap." He hugged me then, and I wanted to fight him, but I didn't say a word as he pressed my face into that bad blood smell on his coat. After the hug he opened up the cellar door for me, then went to check on Mama. He smiled down on her, looking sad, and stroked her knotted hair before gesturin' to me. He held a finger up to his lips, then put his hands together in prayer and turned them on their side under his wooly head.

I gave him a big nod. I got it. *Keep quiet. She's sleepin'.*

I started cannin' the apple butter, listenin' to his big footsteps clomp up the stairs, joined by the light patter of Katie's steps. Their voices came to me like bird song, high and faint, and free of meanin'.

The window still reflected the kitchen and myself, but I could see the soft motion of snowflakes beyond. I paused in my labors to cup my hands to the glass and stare out. Fat flakes drifted through the air, and through them, past the yard and the gate, where sick Mr. Haven's body was frostin' over, I saw movement. Someone walkin' through the snow, takin' a leisurely stroll in the freezin' night. I shivered. More creaks came to me, and the hush of shifting fabric. I screwed on all the lids, then loaded up an armful of apple butter jars and turned to take them down into the cellar.

Mama stood there, between the cellar door and me. Her head was up, but her skin was the color of turned milk, and her eyes were wrong. To this day, that's the only word I can find for them. Just wrong.

I shifted my grip on the jars. "Mama? How're you feelin'?"

Her pretty lips peeled back, showin' me all her teeth. She weren't smilin'. The scratches Daddy had cleaned up looked black, and as she moved toward me I caught that smell again, that awful smell. The bad blood, like on his coat.

The apple butter dropped and shattered at my feet as I screamed for Daddy.

Mama came straight for me, gnashin' her teeth and reachin' in that half-hungry, half-desperate way Mr. Haven had.

"Daddy, help! It's Mama!" I stumbled back against the stove as she continued forward, steppin' on the broken glass like it weren't even there.

I heard his heavy footsteps moving toward the stairs, but too late. He wasn't gonna reach me in time, and her hands were so close...

I reached behind me and grabbed the apple butter pot, swingin' it around and slammin' it into her chest.

Mama's nails raked right past my face as she slid backwards on the spilled apple butter and tumbled into the open cellar. I dropped the pot with a mighty clang and put my shoulder to the cellar door, heavin' it closed just as she reached for me again.

Daddy came rushin' down the stairs like a baby elephant, his eyes wild as they ran from the mess on the floor, to the empty couch, to me. "What the hell's happenin' down here?"

I couldn't speak. I was shakin' too hard. The tears came as I pointed to the tremblin' cellar door, where the thing that wasn't my mama shrieked and hammered against the wood.

Katie appeared at the top of the steps, crouchin' down like a little monkey to watch the commotion.

Daddy looked at the couch again, the dropped blankets that trailed halfway to the kitchen, and back to me. He looked like he knew what was going on, but wouldn't admit it. "Jenny bean, where's your mama?"

I pointed to the cellar again. That seemed like all I could do. Point and cry and wonder when I'd be wakin' up.

He rushed to me, grabbin' my arms. "Did she hurt you?" He shook me when I didn't speak. "Did she bite you? Damn it, answer me!"

I shook my head so hard I thought my neck might snap. "No, she didn't get me, but she tried. Daddy, she tried!"

The beatin' on the cellar door paused for a moment, and we all listened as the delicate sounds of smashin' glass began. The thing down there was flailin' around, breakin' all our stores.

He pushed me behind him and pointed for the stairs. "Go to your room. Take Katie and go to your room."

I scampered past as he went to the front door and picked up the stained ax.

"You keep the door closed, and when I'm done here, I'm gonna knock three times. If you don't hear the knock, you don't open up. Got it?"

I nodded, snortin' back snot and tears. He turned a wild look on me and I nodded harder, forcin' the words out. "Knock three times. I got it." I went up the stairs and grabbed Katie around the waist, haulin' her to our bedroom.

She twisted and fought me, askin' all her pestery questions, but I ignored her. I closed the door like Daddy said, and pulled our dresser in front of it.

He said Mr. Haven had gone crazy. Then Mama had gone too, so bad she didn't recognize her own daughter.

We sat on my bed, knees drawn up, arms around each other as we heard the thing's shrieks, and Daddy's bellows, and great thumps and crashes from downstairs.

What if Daddy caught the madness?

After a moment, the sounds all stopped. We held our breaths as the cellar door thumped closed, and then came footsteps, slow and heavy, marchin' up to meet us. If Daddy had caught the madness, we were done for. A dresser wouldn't stop him, even without the ax.

Katie turned and buried her face in my bony chest.

I cradled the back of her head and closed my eyes.

The footsteps reached our door and stopped.

Daddy knocked once. Twice. Three times. Then his sad, heavy footsteps moved off down the hall, to his own room.

Katie fell asleep in my bed, all tangled up with me like roots around a stone.

I never told her, but I heard a sound that night more lonesome than a coyote's howl, more hauntin' than a train whistle in the dead of night. I heard our Daddy cryin', and it made me proper scared. My world had stopped makin' sense.

Descendin' the stairs the next mornin' was like the opposite of Christmas. My chest felt heavy, and my throat was too tight. I rubbed my eyes over and over, but they wouldn't stop stingin'.

Daddy sat at the kitchen table with a cup of coffee, starin' out the window at the fresh snow. It must have kept fallin' all night, 'cause the powdery level was almost as tall as Katie now. He looked up when we came down, and his face looked ten years older than it had when we went to bed. I don't think he'd slept, but the cellar door was closed and covered, and the floor looked freshly scrubbed.

Katie slipped her cold little hand in mine.

33

I had to be the brave one. "When are we gonna bury Mama?"

Daddy looked down into his coffee cup. "We can't. Not until the ground thaws, at least. For now, she's just gonna rest in the cellar."

I chewed my lip and debated whether it was smart to ask about callin' the sheriff.

Katie let go of my hand and went into the kitchen, where Daddy had stacked up a pile of cans and jars on the counter. "What's this?"

"That, my dear, is all I could salvage from the cellar."

My heart dropped. All those smashin' sounds, the breakin' glass and tearin' bags...I started to cry.

Daddy turned on me. "Jen, stop it. Stop cryin'."

I couldn't, and I didn't until he slapped me. It shocked the tears back.

He didn't look mad, he looked just as sad as me. "We're not goin' to cry about this. We're goin' to be adults. We're goin' to think hard and make the best of the situation. Understand me?"

I nodded, wipin' the tears away with my palms and snifflin'.

"But what are we going to do?" Katie asked in a voice like snow slidin' off the eaves.

"We're goin' to think of a solution," Daddy said. "And we're goin' to ration very carefully."

What remained after Mama's fit only lasted us five days, even takin' into account how much we watered everythin' down, turning most of our meals into bizarre and unsatisfyin' soups. I did my best to supplement that with biscuits and cornbread, but with no eggs or milk, they mostly resembled rocks and lumps of clay.

In that time, we discovered that the phone lines were down, likely from the heavy snowfall.

We also saw three more shamblin' shapes out in the woods around our property, and one that came right up to our front fence, where the fresh snow had covered all evidence of poor Mr. Haven. Whenever one passed, Daddy had us hold still and play silent. I guess they didn't see the smoke from our chimney, or were too dumb to know what that meant.

On the sixth day, Daddy drank sweet, hot coffee in place of his meals, and Katie and I made syrupy tea. It gave us a little energy, but that was jittery and fleetin'.

Around lunchtime, the sun poked out between clouds, and Daddy sent us out to clear a path between the back door and the woodpile.

I asked if I could take the ax, in case someone tried to hurt us, but he said no.

He told us to shout if anyone came near, and to whack 'em good with our shovels until he arrived to finish the job.

I thought it was a real mean thing to do, sendin' two little girls out into the snow when they hadn't had a real meal in days and there were crazy people in the woods, but we didn't argue. The path we made was narrow and sloppy, but it was the best we could do with weak and shakin' arms.

By the time we finished and went back inside, our fingers were stiff and numb, and I felt on the verge of faintin'.

Daddy stood at the stove, stirrin' a pot of soup.

I slumped into a chair and just stared at him, too tired to ask, but Katie went right up and stood on tiptoes, tryin' to peek over the side. "What's that?"

"Lunch. Set out the bowls."

Katie did as she was told, but her eyes lingered on the pot. "Okay, but what is it?"

The air smelled...not good...but meaty. There was a definite food smell, but not one I recognized. My stomach grumbled. It didn't care.

"Lamb stew. I found a couple jars in the back. I must have missed them on my first sweep."

My head still felt light from shovelin' and lack of food, but I tried to hold it steady. Somethin' didn't line up.

Daddy ladled us each a big bowl and settled at the table.

Katie blew loudly on hers, specklin' it with spit.

Daddy's spoon hovered over his bowl for a moment, then he took a deep breath and dug in.

I sniffed the risin' steam and twirled my spoon, stirrin' up the chunks at the bottom. "How did you not see these before? We all know the cellar layout, there's no hidden corners or anythin'..."

Katie slurped her soup, not carin'.

Daddy's eyebrows lowered. "Eat your lunch and stop askin' questions, Jenifer. Otherwise you can go back to tea and your sister and I will finish the soup."

I saw somethin' dark in his eyes that I'd never seen before, and it scared the spoon right into my mouth. The soup was thin and weird. If one of Mama's stews had been the base, it was watered down past recognition, but my body rejoiced at consumin' anythin' other than tea and my cement biscuits. There were even bits of meat in it, lamb Daddy had said, though they were boiled and stringy, and tasted like dirty weeds. I shoveled it in, tryin' not to care about the taste, just eager to feel full again at last.

The first cramp struck me halfway through the bowl. I'd picked out the good bits and was slurpin' down the broth when my stomach suddenly seized up. I stiffened and froze, afraid to breathe. It felt like someone had stuck a giant needle through my guts, and every movement twisted it deeper.

Daddy frowned. "Jen, what are you-" he ended the sentence with a grunt and bowed over his bowl like he was prayin'.

"Daddy, I don't feel so good..." Katie's fingers gripped the table edge until they went white as the little drifts along our windowsills.

"Oh God," Daddy answered through gritted teeth, and that was all he said for a while. Just, "Oh God, oh God, oh God..." and then, "Jen, take your sister upstairs. You girls...go lay down for a while..." He leaned so heavily on the table, I thought for sure it would collapse.

I grabbed Katie's arm and pulled her along up the stairs. She didn't take her hands from her stomach, so the going was slow and awkward as I tried to drag her, and tried to ignore the feelin' of somethin' clawin' my belly up from the inside. I looked back when we reached the top of the stairs.

Daddy had gotten up to follow us, but only made it as far as the bottom step. He hung on the railin', pantin'. His face was pale and sweaty, and he clutched his belly same as us. His wide eyes rolled up, and he panted though his beard. "I'm sorry, babies. I made a mistake." He swallowed hard, like he was keepin' back a flood. "I made a real bad mistake."

Katie groaned and tried to sit down, but I hauled her upright.

"S'okay, Daddy. I know you meant it for the best."

Katie went dead-weight on me then, so I didn't say nothin' else to Daddy, focusin' instead on getting her into bed without an incident.

"Jenny," my little sister said, curlin' up tighter and tighter on her bed, clutchin' her stomach with hands like little possum claws, "I feel like I've drunk too much, like Mr. Haven."

"Hush up," I grunted. "You ain't drunk nothin' but soup."

"I know. But it's like you said. I'm feelin' sick, and I think I'm gonna take a nap now. And then...then when I wake up I'll be all better, just like you said..." Her little voice drifted off as she turned and buried her face in the pillow.

I held my own stomach. I don't know why, it sure didn't seem to be helpin', but I hugged myself anyway. "That's right, Katie. We'll take a nap, then we'll be better." A twinge hit me in the middle of the word better, but I spat it out. "Try to keep your mouth closed while you sleep though, 'less you want to catch a hangover."

Through slitted eyes I saw Katie clamp one little hand over her mouth, the other still around her stomach. She looked about ready to puke, but within moments I saw her breathin' slow down and her muscles relax.

I closed my own eyes and brought a hand up over my own mouth. I'd heard Daddy complain about hangovers before, and I wasn't keen to catch one. He'd said it felt like dyin'.

As I fell asleep, I couldn't help but wonder: if a hangover felt like dyin', then what was I feelin' now?

When I woke up, Katie's bed was empty. I sat up, ready to feel like death all over again, but I didn't. I felt...fine. Hungry as Jesus's followers before he brought them loaves and fishes, but otherwise fine.

Daddy and Katie's voices came up the stairs to me. I found them sittin' at the table, eatin' more soup.

I stopped on the next to last step and crossed my arms. "What are you doin'? Y'all are gonna get more stomachaches."

Daddy looked up from his soup and stood, comin' over and pickin' me up off the stairs in a bear hug. He surprised me so bad, I made a little mouse squeak. "Oh Jenny bean, I'm so happy to see you up and walkin'." He put me back down and returned to his soup.

I rubbed my belly with one hand. It felt more empty than it'd ever been, and the soup smelled much better than before. "I'm glad to be up too."

Katie smiled at me, a dribble of broth shinin' her chin. "No hangover for anybody!"

Daddy laughed and shook his big, beardy head. No one seemed to have the cramps anymore.

I took a bowl to the pot on the stove and served myself a portion. The soup tasted...better this time. Finer, richer, more appetizin'. Though, it didn't seem to take much edge off my hunger. I still felt it crawlin' there in the pit of my stomach, buzzin' around like angry hornets.

While we finished the pot, I noticed Daddy castin' looks at the covered cellar door, and could see that he and Katie felt the same as me.

The soup was good, but it wasn't enough.

"Girls, go get your coats and boots on. I'm gonna see if there's any more stew I missed, and I need you to..." Daddy's gaze roved around the cabin, then out the window, huntin' for somethin'. "I need you to check the barn."

Katie scrunched up her face. "The barn?"

"You heard me young lady. Go get your gear on." When we didn't move, he clapped his big hands together like a rifle report. "Hop to it!"

Katie and I scurried off to get dressed. When we returned, Daddy was refillin' the pot with water.

"What are we checkin' for?" Katie persisted.

Daddy's head popped up like he'd forgotten we were there. He waved a hand in the air, a gesture I'd seen when Mama asked him somethin' he didn't want to answer. "Just check to make sure the snow ain't gettin' in. Check inside and out, and be real thorough." He bent to light the stove. "In fact, you keep checkin' 'til I tell you to stop."

We did as we were told, but neither of us had much energy or enthusiasm as we dragged our feet through the snow.

Katie kicked up clumps and made little snow balls.

I ignored the first two, until wet snow slapped my ear and fell into the neck of my jacket. "Quit it," I hissed. My stomach hurt so much I couldn't focus. Even after all that soup, I felt like I hadn't eaten in days.

She stopped throwin' snow, but switched to draggin' her feet along at a cold snail's pace.

I stomped back to where she was and grabbed her arm, tuggin' her forward.

Katie let out a little scream and tried to shove me away, but I wouldn't let go, and all she accomplished was pushin' my sleeve up. When she saw she couldn't escape, my sister dropped her head and bit me.

I saw her little face scrunch up as she closed her teeth on my arm, but it felt like watchin' someone else get bit. I shook her off and stared at the jagged little teeth marks. They were reddenin' already, but didn't really hurt, and barely even bled.

Katie's eyes were huge. "I'm sorry," she said, holdin' her hands to her belly. "I didn't mean to bite you, you just made me so mad..."

I swung my hand back, ready to smack her 'cross the face, but before I could, Daddy stuck his head out the window.

"Girls, come get more soup!"

I pushed her instead, and we trudged back to the house.

Daddy served up a bowl of soup for each of us.

Katie prodded hers with a whine. "I don't want more soup, Daddy. I'm too hungry for soup."

I picked up my spoon and dipped it into the cloudy broth, stirring around the pale chunks of…whatever it was. I was so hungry I didn't care. Even if it didn't fill me up, it would at least warm us through. My first spoonful of broth tasted like nothin'. Salty snow. But when I scooped up a lump of soft, whorled meat, it filled my mouth with the most amazing flavor and richness, better than liver, better than cheeseburgers and fries. I thought it must have been what lobster was like, pale and sweet and heavenly. I hurriedly chewed and swallowed the piece, then picked out another.

Katie watched, wide eyed, then dug in.

Daddy followed without a word.

When I'd fished all the chunks out of my soup, I picked up my bowl and drank the broth in three swallows. The others finished theirs in a similar fashion, and we all shared a look around the table.

"Is there more?" I felt awake again, fully charged and snappin' with energy.

Daddy shook his head.

Katie started lickin' her bowl.

I cleaned my spoon, then ran a finger inside the bowl, collecting the last drops. "Can we make more?"

Daddy set his spoon down and laced his fingers together. "Yes, Jenifer. We can." He turned to Katie, who still lapped at her bowl like an ill-mannered pup. "You stay here and wash the dishes while the adults go out." He winked at me when he said adults, and my face flushed. Me. A real-live grown up.

Katie collected our bowls without so much as a question.

Daddy held my gaze. "Get your coat and follow me. No arguments, no questions, all right?"

I pretended to salute. My whole body buzzed with giddy energy, and I couldn't keep a smile off my face. My first smile since Mama'd gone crazy. I pulled on my coat and followed Daddy out to the shed, where we grabbed a coil of rope and his huntin' gun.

40

My arm itched where Katie had bit me, but I tried not to scratch it as Daddy led me out through the gate and into the frosty woods, where grey shadows shambled back and forth.

He raised a finger to his lips, then waved me forward after the nearest figure. We followed, sneakin' up as if we were playin' freeze tag, and the wind was cold enough we could have. He stopped just a few yards shy of it.

"All right. Once I shoot it we'll have to hurry, because the sound is sure to draw attention. You're going to rope it, and once we get it home I'll take care of everythin'."

The truth of the last 24 hours solidified inside of me, buildin' a crystal of sharp clarity. I looked at my Daddy and thought of the soups, the furtive glances at the cellar door, our depleted supplies. Instead of makin' me feel sick, the sudden certainty warmed me through. The hogs were gone, but hope wasn't.

I tied a loop in the rope and nodded. "Promise we won't tell Katie what's really in the soup?"

Daddy looked at me for a second, then extended his hand like he would to an equal, or a business partner.

I shook it.

The report from Daddy's gun shook snow from the nearby trees, and the thing's knees exploded in a mist of black.

I looped the rope over its shoulders on my third try.

More figures moved through the woods, drawn to the sound.

We dragged the squirmin' thing back home, and I kept Katie distracted while Daddy hauled it to the barn for butcherin'.

That was three weeks ago.

Things will be harder in the summer, when the meat begins to bloat and spoil, but for now, the cold preserves them well. When we catch one fresh enough, Daddy will strip the carcass, but their meat doesn't sate our hunger. It's like drinkin' glass after glass of water, when what you really want is a steak dinner with baked potato and pie. I think we keep it up because eatin' the meat seems normal, compared to the sweetness we really crave.

41

Either way, we make sure to boil whatever we catch.
Just in case.

Shenoa Carroll-Bradd lives in Southern California with her brother and dancing dog. She writes whatever catches her fancy, from horror to fantasy and erotica. Keep up with her progress at www.sbcbfiction.net or join her fan page at www.facebook.com/sbcbfiction .

Under the Hood of Winter

From the Casebook of
Detective James S. Peckman

By Alex Azar

I wish I could say I hate winter, and I'd have every right to, what with the smoking making my lungs feel like they're caught in a frozen vise. And due to an old football injury, my knee sounds like dead branches being trampled by a horse. Snow and rain are preceded by a dull ache in my arm and chest from a gunshot to the shoulder, but damn I love the cold. Feeling the cold in my bones brings a smile to my face, even if it is occasionally broken with coughing. Hearing the crack of my toes after a night of sleep with no socks is one of the little joys in life.

Unfortunately, those little joys aren't always enough to force away my personal demons. Such is the case waking up one morning in Morton, Washington.

I.

I don't know how anyone can handle death well, but you'd think with all the loss in my life I'd be more desensitized. Sadly, that's far from the truth.

Following the death of Elizabeth Gomez, my business partner and former lover, and the resulting fallout with our other partner, Thaddeus Coleman, I closed the doors to our detective agency. Three months later, I've yet to return. I aimlessly traveled the country trying to lose myself, only to find myself here, perhaps even led here subconsciously, to Elizabeth's hometown of Morton.

I haven't been here since the old man first sent me here to recruit Elizabeth. Now I'm back in the very same hotel room, waking up to the cold I love, but unable to appreciate it because of the weight of the task at hand. I returned to Morton to inform Elizabeth's sister, Victoria, of her passing.

With no immediate time frame, I let the urgency of the situation slip as I dawdle in my morning routine: a habit I've found myself in since everything that happened in Chicago. I lose myself in thought with the rhythmic sensation of brushing my teeth. The cascading water flowing from the shower head washes away all desires of completing the very reason for my being here. But eventually reality sets in and, after getting dressed, I prepare a breakfast of instant coffee and a cigarette for the road.

It's not until I'm waiting for Victoria to answer the door that I make the connection of her and Elizabeth being named after British queens. For some odd reason the realization brings a smile to a face. A smile that unfortunately misleads Victoria, who opens the door at this inopportune time, into thinking my presence at her doorstep is for a social visit.

"Hi! Wow James, good to see… Where… Where's my sister? James, where is Elizabeth?" The almost maternal connection she has with her younger sister allows Victoria to understand without words what Elizabeth's absence means.

"You son of a bitch, you promised me you'd take care of her," she cried, falling to her knees with streams of tears rolling down her cheek. "I told you this would happen, but you were supposed to protect her."

I reach my hand down to touch her shoulder and open my mouth to apologize. "Don't touch me, and don't you dare say you're sorry. You don't get to be sorry." Once again rising to her feet, Victoria slams her fist against my chest but her emotions sapped all of her strength, "You piece of shit, this is your fault. Why did my sister have to die while you're still here?"

I want to answer her rhetorical question with tears of my own, tears that haven't been shed for anyone since my wife and daughter died, but I know Victoria wouldn't accept my pain or

44

my sorrow. I take a step back and look at my feet. I'll wait here as long as it takes, but Victoria has to make the next move.

The next two minutes of Victoria crying feel like an hour, but I'm determined to wait her out. Eventually, she sits on the steps behind me, and without looking up at me asks, "Did she die helping someone?"

"I can say with no hyperbole that she died saving the entire world." I begin to go into details, but Victoria cuts me off with a wave of her hand, still refusing to make eye contact.

"One more question before I tell you to get the fuck off my steps. You hear about what happened to the miners about a dozen miles from here?"

"Can't say that I have, but if it's about a case, I have to admit, what happened to your sister was a real wake up call. I don't think I'll be doing any more detective work anytime soon, especially none of the supernatural variety."

"Bullshit! You don't take my sister away from me after I practically raised her, her entire life, helping her cope with the side effects of her abilities and introduce her to this whole new world of horrors and decide to back out now that she's gone." Finally turning to look me in the eyes: "You're going to find out what happened to those miners, some of whom we grew up with, for me. Then you're going to go back to New Jersey and do this until you're the one that dies, while thinking of my sister every day. Now get the fuck off my steps."

With that Victoria reenters the house and with regained strength slams the door with enough force to rattle the windows. I'm left to contemplate my next move, standing in the cold I love, so lost in thought I don't even register the temperature.

II.

It didn't take me long to discover what Victoria had been talking about. All I had to do was turn on the news or look at a local newspaper to find out. Around ten days ago, an entire coal mining crew working in the mountains were found slaughtered on site, by an unknown assailant or assailants. They were completely decimated by crude cutting instruments, also of unknown origins. At this point officials had no clues or leads and were finding it difficult to even find plausible motivation.

Thankfully their cluelessness is making them sloppy; they've left the now vacated caves unguarded, allowing me uninterrupted searching time, or they would have if I had come prepared. With no additional source of illumination, my cell phone light won't allow me to venture too far. I can't even get deep enough to locate where the murders took place, which might be for the better. Five minutes alone in these caves can get to a person. Through my past dealings with the paranormal, I've become a good judge of which cases require my specialized talents and which are just unexplainable while still within what's considered 'normal' boundaries. Everything I can gather about this case makes my skin crawl like only the paranormal can cause. Sadly, this could just be another side effect of everything that happened, just me needing to feel useful after Victoria's verbal barrage.

I head back out while making a mental checklist of what I'll need when I return. Topping that list is a thicker jacket. Even as a fan of the cold, those caves are too much. They gather the freezing air for an effect opposite of hot boxing.

III.

After completing my shopping list, I decide to grab dinner at a local diner. I'm quickly reminded that New Jersey diners are unparalleled. A fact this Washington diner proves in spades. In need of a pick me up, I revert to my standard comfort food, disco fries. Following a blank stare from the waitress I clarify, "French fries, topped with gravy and mozzarella cheese."

Answering in between open mouthed chews of her gum, "All we got is uh-jew sauce."

"You mean 'ah jus', no gravy? Never mind, I'll have the chicken fingers with fries and honey mustard." What arrives fifteen minutes later is chicken nuggets drizzled in mustard with a packet of honey.

Finishing my meal, I promise myself not to judge all of this state's eateries on this experience. I immediately followed this with a vow to finish this case quick enough to never have to eat here again.

I pay for the food and as I'm waiting for the waitress to return with my credit card, another patron approaches me asking if I'm here to find out what happened in the caves.

"I am; how did you know?"

"You look like a cop, but we know all the cops around here." He says 'we' with a shake of his head, motioning towards a table of three other men, all similarly dressed in flannel, jeans and well-worn boots. I'd imagine in comparison, me dressed in my favorite tan pea coat, black slacks, and newly bought winter cap and scarf hiding my shirt and tie, I'd look like an out-of-town cop to most people. "We'd be mighty grateful for anyone who can find out what happened to those guys, even one from the south such as yourself."

It takes me a moment to realize that 'south' here means California, unlike the rest of the country. "I'm Detective James S. Peckman, and I'll get to the bottom of this but I'm not from California; I'm from New Jersey."

Flicking the puff of my cap with a smile, "You're not used to this kind of cold huh?" I politely chuckle and joke that I thought I liked the cold before spending time here.

Breaking my vow from the previous night, I return to the same diner for breakfast. I'm served by the same waitress and see mostly all the same customers, including the gentleman that approached me and his friends.

Upon noticing me they invite me over to their table. Typically, I'd kindly refuse, but with virtually no clues about what I might be walking into, I take a seat between Gus and Chuck, the one I spoke with last night. Sitting across from me are Mike and Michael, identical twins.

These guys, along with the rest of the male workforce of the town, mine the caves. More importantly, they've all at one time or another worked with those who were killed. Chuck tells me that the entire community revolves around the caves, and that no one in the area would benefit from this. They just broke new ground deeper within the cave.

Mike chimes in that the whole community gets excited whenever miners explore deeper or find a new cave. "It's like clockwork; every five years the foremen choose a new cave to begin work in, or explore previously un-mined areas. The town has a festival, and all around it's good for the economy."

"Is there anyone that would benefit from preventing this economic boost?"

Michael argues that "there's no 'Big Business' in these parts that want us failing." He continues to defend his friends' stance, returning me to the conclusion that there was no natural solution to this case, but a supernatural cause.

I announce to the table that I'll be heading to the caves now, and withdraw my wallet when Chuck grabs my hand. "Now you stop right there."

With steel in his eyes, and the grip of a python, he rises to his feet. "We can't have this." Not sure of what he's talking about I step back defensively. "You come out here to look into the murder of our friends, there's no way we're going to make you pay for your meal with us." He emphasizes the last word with a firm pat on my shoulder while never letting go of my wrist.

After a round of 'goodbyes' and 'good lucks' Gus warns me to be careful up there, "Parts of those mountains are covered with snow year-round, making it easy to get lost. Strangers die out there every year."

IV.

Exiting my car at the mouth of the cave, I'm still unsettled by Gus' parting words, unsure if they were a warning or a threat. Is it possible my four new friends are actually responsible for these murders? Upset at not landing the new mining job that's attracted so much local attention? But I also have to wonder why the cops wouldn't have investigated this lead.

I decided my best course at this point would be to continue searching in the caves for clues the local force hadn't discovered or trampled over. Venturing deep within the cave, I drag along a flatbed hand truck loaded with enough generators, lights and wires to power the Rockefeller Christmas tree and the surrounding city blocks, but the most important things I brought are my guns. Stacy, a Glock 9mm, is safely tucked under my arm in a holster, while my unnamed Magnum rests comfortably in my hand. The leather grip has worn and contorted to my hand over the years making it second nature to wield, like a major league catcher and his glove, or an author and his favorite pen.

So comfortable is the gun in my hand that I can almost forget I'm holding it while searching these seemingly endless caves completely devoid of natural light and all life. I suppose not 'all life'. Something needs to be making these noises I'm hearing. After fifteen minutes of walking, these noises have become rhythmic, so it's easy to notice the break of monotony of a kicked rock. Unfortunately, the openness of the cave wreaks havoc on the acoustics, making it impossible to determine the direction of origin. I spin a full five hundred and twenty degrees before acknowledging the futility of it. "I'm armed and will not hesitate to fire, come out." Even though I will shoot, my threat was so unconvincing, even I doubt it.

However, it appears to work, "Easy there James, it's just us." Chuck says as he comes around a rock formation. Appearing from three different rocks, never can remember stalactite or stalagmite, are the twins and Gus, who has a rifle aimed at my head. "Easy, Gus, can't you see that it's our new friend Detective Peckman?"

"So it is. My vision gets blurry sometimes in these caves." I notice behind his slick smile that he never actually apologized for pointing a gun at me after trying to sneak up on me.

"What are you guys doing here? These caves are closed to civilians." The Magnum rests easily in my hand, but my finger never moves from the trigger.

Following a quick chuckle, Chuck answers "Haven't you been listening, Detective? This is a mining community; we belong in these caves more than most."

"Some would say miners have more power in these parts than the police." Gus quickly adds.

"And who is it that says that, the miners or the police?" I pause a moment before adding a nonthreatening chuckle. I don't like the situation, but I have to stay in control. "Either way it doesn't matter. I work alone and can't allow outside opinions to interfere with my investigation."

"Outside opinion? It doesn't get more…" Gus is cut off by a deep wailing that despite the bouncing echoes is clearly coming from deeper in the caves.

Mike nervously shouts the question on all our minds, "What the fuck was that?" His question is answered with a flint tipped spear striking the right side of his chest. I know that the spear is tipped with flint because another spear emerges from the shadows striking my Magnum-holding hand with a glancing blow. The gun skids across the floor away from me as I draw Stacy from her holster. I yell for the miners to retreat out of the cave as I reach for my dropped gun. Just as my fingers are about to caress the handle, a tomahawk flies out of the darkness, shattering the trigger and guard before bouncing off. Oddly, the tomahawk bounces perfectly back into the shadows from which it came.

The image of the disappearing weapon is replaced by a Native American in naught but a loincloth and red face paint, running at me at full speed. He must either have had another tomahawk on him, or he caught the one he threw off the bounce, which seems impossible. I don't have much time to ponder the details as he pulls back his arm to throw it again. Not giving him the chance, I fire Stacy three times, hitting him twice in the chest, dropping him on the cold stone ground.

Deciding to check on Michael before looking into the attacker, I find Chuck and Mike about to drive off in their truck with Michael in the backseat. Gus, who's outside the truck, is encouraging Michael, clearly not planning on going with them. The truck starts to pull off, when I shout for them to stop. "Gus, you should go with them. I killed the Indian, just going back to see what I can discover."

Shaking his head, Gus responds, "Uh-huh, there may be more than one of them, and that bastard attacked my friends and my family. Not something I can walk away from."

V.

Searching the area where the skirmish occurred, Gus questions if I'm sure I killed the attacker. Looking at the ground where the Native American fell I can't answer him. "Gus, I'm telling you, I shot that guy twice in the chest. He fell right there."

Following the line from my pointing finger, "There's no blood! How can there be no blood?" Pausing to catch his breath, "And you see how he hit Mike from the shadows? Had to be over thirty feet with a fuckin' spear." Turning his attention to the shadows, "Get out here you piece of shit. Show your face!"

With no response forthcoming, we set up additional lights, extending our area of view by nearly fifty yards. Fifty yards of the same monochrome gray that we've been surrounded by since entering the cave.

After the extra lighting was set up I reexamined the area where I was ambushed twice: first by my questionable new friends, and again by a fur-underwear-clad, red face-painted Indian who can apparently see in the dark, I notice that not only is there no blood, but both spears are missing. "Hey Gus, look at this," pointing to long drag trails moving outward from the general area where he fell. I say that Gus may be right about there being more than one, "Unless he literally dragged himself out of here with two shots in the chest."

Although I'm not familiar with cave mining I can tell that this area has been recently worked. The cart rails have no dust settlement on them, and there's more footprints than we would have created today alone. "Is this where the new work started? Where the miners were found dead?"

"That's about two hundred yards deeper, halfway down the path splits. We gotta head to the right." I ask what's to the left, and he explains the foremen haven't explored there: "That hasn't been reinforced yet." He finishes his sentence by knocking on one of the wooden support beams that can be found every twenty yards.

"How long before work begins are the caves reinforced?"

He tells me that it varies, but where the new ground was broken was a slow build.

"They had time between the location being chosen and the festival taking place. In fact, they finished the supports about two years ago. I remember because they had an accident also. There was a minor cave-in that took the lives of two of the workers. Inspectors couldn't determine the cause and after a little over a month, work resumed."

Seeing the curiosity on my face, he asks if I think the two incidents are connected. For an answer, I suggest we search the left path. Upon taking the path less traveled, I notice that the slight decline we've been traveling increased dramatically. "Yup, that's why the powers-that-be chose the other area, the ground is fairly level there." The angle of this path is making it difficult to continue setting up lights as we go. A fact that doesn't sit well with me.

The low light and steep decent bring our pace to a crawl, making me feel incredibly exposed. It also makes me wish I picked up night-vision goggles, but I had no idea where to get a pair in these parts. Interrupting my thoughts, a chant begins echoing off the walls, once again making it impossible to pinpoint its origin. Making matters worse, the single voice is joined by several more.

"It appears you were right, Gus, sounds like there's more than one." Not hearing a response, I realize that I hadn't heard from him for several minutes while lost in my own musings. "Gus, if you can hear me, make your way out of the cave. There's more than one of these guys and there's no way we could take them on ourselves."

Good job, James, I'm lost in a cave and sent my only assistance running because the two of us can't survive this. Now you've got to do this solo, in the dark. And all this is assuming that Gus and the others aren't actually responsible and playing me for a sap. Chances are just as good that Gus is dead as they are that he's hiding behind a stalagmite again. I sure as hell wish I had Thaddeus and Elizabeth here with me watching my back, but if they were around I wouldn't even be in this mess.

The chanting has continued uninterrupted, but now I see the dim flickering of fire coming from further down the decline. With the light increasing exponentially, I use it as my guide

52

through the cave, and while I'm positive that I'm approaching the source of the chanting, the volume remains the same, further supporting the theory of multiple assailants. Unfortunately, that also means I'm currently surrounded.

After less than a minute of careful decent, I find a break in the cave wall that appears to have been carved out ages ago. Cautiously approaching the portal into the lit room, I'm startled by the sudden realization that the chanting has stopped. Peeking into the room, I see a pair of torches ensconced in the frame of the opening.

Armed with my Glock 9mm, I slowly work my head around the wall to find two identical stone daises, one of which is occupied by Gus, who is nude and lying motionless. There's a limpness to his arm overhanging the dais that assures me he's dead before I can clearly see his face. The room is otherwise empty, meaning the red-painted attacker and his friends still need to be found.

I approach Gus' body to see what they did to him. The first thing I notice is that he's lost all the color in his face, much too soon for a recently deceased body. His chest has two bullet wounds, almost exactly where I shot the Indian, and nothing else seems out of place.

On the dais opposite Gus, which I thought was clear, are actually two spent bullets. Upon further investigation, the slugs are the same caliber and make that I use in Stacy and fired into the Red-Face. This reminds me of an African shaman that was able to transfer wounds and ailments from one body into another, or even to inanimate objects. If Red-Face and his friends are using a similar technique, it would explain how this tribe survived in these caves for so long.

Leaving Gus where he lay, I continue searching the caves. This gives me time to figure out how to stop a tribe of Native American warriors who're able to recover from two shots to the chest.

VI.

After what felt like a mile of walking but in reality was probably only five hundred feet made worse due to the uneven rocky decline, I reach a valley in the cave. There's a large flat clearing with some rock formations, low hanging pillars, a few small daises with some items I can't quite identify from here, and a path on the opposite side. The path looks like an artificially made tunnel on a steeper incline than the decent that brought me here, and is just big enough for someone to crouch in without having to crawl.

The room is lit with four torches built into the walls. Still no sign of Red-Face. I take the time to investigate the objects more closely. Nearest to me is a pile of flat perfectly round rocks, which I can't help but think would be great for skipping on water. There are about two dozen of the stones, and each of them has the same crude carving of a flame with some runes carved around it.

I walk over to the right of the room holding one of the stones, and take a look at a painted hide. While trying to decipher the meaning of the painting, I absentmindedly run my thumb over the carvings of the stones.

Suddenly my musing is disturbed by an intense heat emanating from the stone, but only from the engraved side. The shock of the heat causes me to drop the stone. Landing face down, the heat wave is so powerful that the stone is actually levitated off the ground, until it wobbles enough to flip over entirely. I can see the actual waves shooting upwards to the ceiling when all of a sudden the heat stops altogether. Cautiously checking the stone with a moistened finger, I find it miraculously cool to the touch, like a soldering gun.

Testing a theory, I rub the engraving with a part of my jacket, and nothing happens. Deciding it's safe to put the stone in my pocket without fear of being burned. Placing three more of the stones in my various pockets, I resume inspecting the painted hide.

Several skulls and crossbones are inside inverted 'V's that I assume are meant to represent mountains. I interpret this as a

54

warning of death to those who enter the mountains, but it doesn't really explain much as far as reasons go.

"You shouldn't be here."

Turning around, I see Red-Face standing at the mouth of the tunnel, holding that damned tomahawk that broke my gun. I hold up the hide and motion towards it with Stacy, "Yeah, I gathered that with all the skull and crossbones." I didn't imagine he'd speak English, and I tell him so.

"There's much you don't know."

"Like how you and your friends learned to speak English, but still paint on dead hides."

He questions the word 'friend', and expands his arms wide, pointing out the fact that we're alone. "While I do burn with the fires of my fallen brothers, I can assure you we're alone in here." He answers my question of hearing other voices by dismissing it as an acoustic trick of the caves.

I don't completely believe him, but I must admit the plausibility of his claims. Deciding it best to see both entrances in case he's lying, I position myself underneath one of the torches equidistant from each opening. This also gives me more options of escape if things go south.

Keeping pace with me the Indian circles around, always staying on the opposite end of where I stand. His new position gave him view of the now slightly diminished pile of heating stones, "Souvenirs?"

"Hey in my line of work these could prove useful."

"So this isn't just a one-time thing, you're a professional grave robber?"

After telling him I'm not here for any graves beyond the miners he killed, I explain, "I'm a detective and specialize in the paranormal and supernatural. A friend asked me to look into what happened here, suspecting there was something beyond what the police could handle."

Apparently sensing the truth in my words he lowers his tomahawk and spear. "I apologize, but I've been tasked by the elder chief to eternally protect my tribe's mountain burial crypt, and have done so for hundreds of years before your people came to this land."

Understanding the dedication someone could have to their duty, I think it's best to leave him alone in the caves. Besides, I wouldn't know what to report to the authorities. I tell him that I'll leave him to his sacred watch, and not attract any more attention to him, then turn to leave.

Instantly my view is obstructed by a spear embedded into the cave wall mere inches from my face. "I am the Red Soldier sworn to protect the secrets of my people. I cannot threaten my tribe's safety on your word alone. You are not permitted to live."

In between the realization that I'm in for another fight for my life, I wonder again where he learned to speak such proper English.

"Just one of those stones in your pockets at the entrance would set off a chain reaction creating a path to the entrance of our burial crypt." Still trying to avoid a confrontation, I tell him that I'll leave the stones I took, and will never return. "After experiencing your people's penchant for taking that which isn't theirs, I can't trust you."

With that, he whips his tomahawk right at my head. Ripping the spear from the wall, I use it to deflect the flying ax, splitting the handle of the spear in two. The tomahawk curves through the air and gently returns to Red Soldier's hand.

Using rocks growing from the ground for footing, the Red Soldier launches himself in the air before sending the ax once again towards my head. This time I take the torch from the wall above me and use the metal handle to protect myself, but before the ax could reach me it wavers and hits the ground by my feet. Red Soldier lets out a scream of pain that is echoed by a second voice seemingly coming from the flame as the fire dies out.

As the tomahawk magically returns to his hand from off the floor, Red Soldier commands from one knee, "Unhand that, you are not worthy to touch him."

Not letting the fact he said 'him' hinder me, I aim Stacy and shoot Red Soldier in his throwing arm. Little did I know this Indian happens to be ambidextrous. He takes the tomahawk in his left hand and once again throws it. Diving behind more rocks, I see the ax hover in the air still spinning, and then fly at an angle once again towards me. Without enough time to take aim and fire, I run towards Red Soldier, who is just now getting to his feet, and tackle him with all my weight. Positioning him on top of me my hopes of the tomahawk hitting him end when it simply returns to his grasp.

With inhuman speed he swings the ax at me, but I already had Stacy drawn at his midsection and unload the remaining five shots, stopping him mid-swing. Still alive but clearly in pain, I roll him off of me and make a mad dash towards the nearest torch.

Tearing it from its frame, I elicit two more screams of agony, while simultaneously diminishing the remaining light in the room. Like Gus had mentioned when we first reentered the cave, Red Soldier has superior vision, even in little to no light.

Taking the long way around to the next torch trying to avoid Red Soldier, I turn on three flashlights, pointing them in various areas of the room. Red Soldier grunts the same grunt from his previous two tomahawk throws. Either he sees me, or his magic ax can hit me regardless. I'm too far to reach either of the remaining torches, so instead I activate one of the heating stones from my pocket and aim it at the torch. In mere seconds a wave of heat blows the flame out and dislodges the torch. Immediately after, I hear the tomahawk clang to the ground by my feet.

Blindly searching for it before it can return to Red Soldier's hand, I grip the handle and feel it quickly tug against my hold before relenting and resting easy. Still not sure if he threw the ax at me because he saw me or because he could hit me either way, I opt to hold on to the tomahawk until I have an unobstructed view of the remaining torch.

Literally crawling on my hands and knees with Stacy in one hand and the tomahawk in the other, I crawl right into Red Soldier's legs. Before I can shoot or cut him, he delivers a swift knee to my cheek, flipping me over. I lose Stacy, but I make sure to keep the tomahawk in hand. Seeing the glow of the remaining torch behind a pillar, I throw with all the strength I can muster from my back, hoping whatever mojo that caused the ax to fly around like a bat was still active and worked for me. Before I can find out if the tomahawk still works, Red Soldier kicks me in the ribs hard enough to cause me to slide several feet. Coughing the remaining air in my lungs from my body, I know he cracked some ribs. Standing above me with a foot raised above my head, the tomahawk finally hits the torch, extinguishing the flame and dropping Red Soldier to the ground next to me unconscious. The tomahawk returns to my hand and cradles in my palm seamlessly. I raise the ax overhead, planning on striking Red Soldier in the head to ensure his death, but stop. I respect his mission too much, even if I don't understand, and can't muster the fortitude to kill him, especially with his own weapon.

VII.

Taking time to regain my breath, I collect Stacy, more of the heating stones, and the flashlights, the whole while Red Soldier lay lifeless where he fell. Respecting his mission and the sacrifice he made for his people, I decide to cave in each entrance of the room we fought in, and the top of the tunnel leading to the hidden stones. Not well versed with explosives, I'm not too sure how much it will take so I likely overdo it and draw a fuse to the entrance of the cave.

Hoping I did everything according to the directions, I flip the switch, and am left with thoughts of Red Soldier and the fact he sacrificed himself for what he believed in, and Gus who died in search of the truth of what happened to his friends. This all makes me wonder how I could ever question Elizabeth doing otherwise, even more so, how I could ever do any less.

As the explosion erupts and echoes out of the cave, I picture the eternal resting places for the two that fell today and remember the two torches by the dais with Gus. As I tip my hat to the two, I doubt the explosion was enough to put out the flames and maybe even hope the Red Soldier can finally rest.

VIII.

For the third time I stand on this stoop, and each time different emotions pulled at my heart. Victoria opens the door with tears staining her cheek, as though she hasn't stopped crying since the last time I saw her. Unsure of what words would be worthy in this situation, I instead present her with the two halves of the spear that Red Soldier had broken.

Silently, she takes them from my hands and reenters her home. However, this time instead of slamming the door in my face, or even cursing me off, she leaves the door ajar, and walks in.

Alex Azar is an author born and raised in New Jersey. After studying two years to become an electrical engineer, he realized he took every English course the college offered. Changing schools and majors, he is now a happily struggling author. This is his eleventh publication, his second with Mystery and Horror, LLC.

Night Walker

By D.J. Tyrer

The winter of 1528 was chill and The Mount was colored white by the recently-fallen snow. It was uncommon for snow to settle at this time of year, even this close to Christmas; more often the true winter would roar in on the north wind following the celebration of the birth of Christ. Still, even that which had fallen was a mere sprinkling when compared to the drifts that would surely follow. Yet, whilst it was still possible to leave the safety of their homes, none of the inhabitants of the houses on The Mount, whether those at its highest point in the shadow of the tumbledown ruins of the castle or those which clustered about the church on the saddle of the hill below, were willing to brave the night, not even to make the short stagger from The Star back to their homes after a few pints of ale or cider.

For the Hillfolk, winter itself held few horrors. Wolves had been purged from the land long before and the forests were a mere shadow of their ancient might, even in these parts. Mankind had tamed nature and with the end of the struggle for the throne decades before, mankind, too, had been largely tamed: there were still wandering beggars and brigands who were a menace, but the rule of law held firmer now than in times past and the Men of the Mount were capable of seeing off such threats. If anything, the Hillfolk were feared by others, rather than fearful. Yes, winter could be harsh, but they were used to it and would struggle through it as they did every year.

There were worse things than winter and brigands and the memory of wolves, though. Things that walked by night that ought not to walk at all. *Ganger Nos*, they called them, 'Night Walker', or *Laerav*, 'Revenant'. The dead who would not sleep soundly in the ground till Judgment Day, but which rose bodily from their graves to threaten the living.

Legend proclaimed that such 'Night Walkers' had haunted The Mount in ages past, but they had largely been relegated to a horror long since vanished or vanquished. That had all changed the previous year when, it was believed, such a horror had visited The Mount once again and slain the Lord, their protector. That, perhaps, was the greatest horror of the tale: tradition pictured the Lords of the Mount as great warriors and possessed of arcane powers that warded the hill and its inhabitants against their enemies, whether man or monster. For such evil to slay their Lord had left the Hillfolk even more horrified than such a fearful attack should. Suddenly, the old certainties no longer seemed so certain.

The previous winter had been bleak, but one of wind and rain and a terrible chill, not snow. The story had become known to them all, and even beyond The Mount, but only one could tell much of the tale.

It was a week till Christmas, and Simeon Mab Harley should have been in Towbouroy an hour ago, but his departure from his father's house in the shadow of the castle had been delayed by the sudden arrival of a storm that had forced him to assist in bringing the sheep in from the fold.

As he descended the slope of the hill, the wind howled through the trees like a demon fleeing the torments of Hell, accompanied by the staccato drumming of heavy raindrops against the sodden ground. The soil being no longer capable of absorbing the water, the rain collected and pooled, flowing freely in little streamlets that dislodged mud down shallow gulleys as they sought the easiest route to empty their content into the nearly-full ditches that ran either side of the lane. The low-lying lands that surrounded The Mount would be even more badly affected, not only receiving their own rain but that which ran down the sides of The Mount. The marshes would overflow and the fields flood. If it had not been for the necessity of the journey and his father's command, Simeon would not have left the safety of his home high above such threats.

Thunder crashed like the clash of heavenly swords and he knew that the storm would only get worse. There was a feeble flurry of snow; the pounding rain obliterated it from existence within moments of it settling. A spear of lightning struck one of the trees that blanketed the rear of the hill, splitting it in twain and momentarily sparking flames only for the rain to smother them as easily as it had the snow.

Trudging down the muddy lane, Simeon passed the church and the village beside it, passing over the crossroads beside which stood the tall sentinel form of the beacon which could be lit at times of danger or rejoicing. His thick coat was covered in a layer of fragile ice crystals and did little to keep out the bitter chill of the wind; it was already soaked through. This was the sort of night that the hellish huntsmen and their hounds might roam the dark skies above The Mount, led by Laren, whose saintliness had not saved him from such a fate; at least in local lore, if not in fact. At the thought of such horrors, he quickly crossed himself and offered up a silent plea to their saint for his protection.

Pulling his neck into his shoulders and digging his hands deeper into his pockets, Simeon marched resolutely down the lane towards the low-lying lands that the illumination provided by lightning flashes showed him were already beginning to flood; he had half a mind to turn back. But, teeth chattering, he kept on going, every step making a sucking sound as the mud of the lane held fast to his boots as if attempting to prevent him leaving the safety of the hill.

Where the lane ran past Towbouroy Common, it was even worse, his feet sinking deeper into the mud and the water threatening to overflow his boot tops. If it grew any worse, he was resolved to turn around and abandon his journey. He had business to conduct on his father's behalf in Towbouroy with Sir Thomas Muiretan, a knight of the shire, but no business was worth a greater risk than this.

Suddenly, ahead of him, Simeon became aware of someone walking along the flooded lane towards him. They had emerged like a ghost from the coal-black night. He had not expected to see anyone else out in this weather.

"Mayhaps I am not a solitary fool," he muttered to himself, then called out to the barely visible figure: "Ho! Friend! Thou art not from this region; pray may I be of assistance to thee?"

The indistinct figure approached silently along the flooded lane. It was his assumption that it was the noise of the wind and rain and the thunder of the storm that had masked the figure's approach, but later he would wonder at the point, stressing it in his retellings.

As the figure grew closer, Simeon could make some of his features out, although he was wrapped in a heavy black travelling cloak and wore a large wide-brimmed black hat that kept his face in shadow. The man – he could tell that much – was tall, over six foot, he thought, and lightly built. One feature that stuck in his mind, but which failed to strike him as unusual until later, was the fact that his boots were of a shiny black leather unmarred by the mud of the lane; his own boots were caked in muck.

"I thankest thee," the man replied in a voice that was barely audible above the relentless scream of the wind. "I am a lone traveler caught here by this cruel weather whilst travelling on important business." The story, identical to his own, caused him not to ask why he had not just sought sanctuary in Towbouroy. Like a fool, he didn't think to question the man, even after the request he then made: "I pray thee, couldst thou informest me of where I mayst find a lodging to see out this dreary night?"

"Yes," Simeon replied as loudly as he could. The English tongue remained a novelty in these parts and he hoped what he said made sense. "There is a house sited upon the very top of yonder hill, my father's house, the house of Harley, lord of this region. He will not turnest thou away. Travel swiftly now, lest the weather grow worst for our torment or the Devil and his imps ride abroad on their quest for men's souls. Travel swiftly – God's speed!"

64

The Hillfolk maintained the tradition of hospitality and Simeon knew that his father would not turn a traveler away, especially one that he had directed hence.

The stranger thanked him and wished him swift travel in turn as they parted company and Simeon proceeded on his way to Towbouroy. It was only a little later that he began to consider the peculiarities of that meeting, but he pushed such thoughts aside in favour of his business with Sir Thomas Muiretan until his return to his father's house the next day.

The conclusion of that night's horrific events was largely a matter of conjecture, although Hew Mago later stated that he had seen a tall, cloaked figure in a wide-brimmed hat at the door to the Lord's house. The main point upon which all agreed was that nobody could quite comprehend how it had happened.

The tale as told by Simeon, greatly embellished from the few available facts, went something as follows with his family clustering together for comfort from the chill of the night as wind and rain lashed against the great house.

Harley was a tall and powerfully-built man in his fifties with a thick mane of black hair. As ever, he was seated in the great black oaken chair that had been passed down from Lord to Lord through the generations. A fire blazed heartily in the hall of the house. His wife, Ana, was seated opposite him, wrapped in a woolen shawl and blanket and their eldest daughter, Miriam, was sat beside her, winding thread. Their younger daughter and twin sons were all abed, for it was late.

A sudden rap at the door, two firm knocks that carried over the wind that screamed around the house, pulled Harley out of his thoughts and he quickly rose and crossed to the door, doubtless pausing to pick up his heavy knobbed stick lest the unexpected visitor should prove a foe. Although brigandage was not the threat it had once been, it remained a danger to those in remote, provincial areas such as this. Surely, Miriam would have reached for the family longbow with which all of Harley's children had practiced.

Swinging the door open, his stave held easily in his hand, he would have seen the silhouette of a tall man in the doorway against the flash of lightning. The stranger would have greeted him cordially and explained that Simeon had bid him thence.

Harley, a kind man steeped in the traditions of his folk, would have invited him in, offering him a bed and food and drink. Had he suspected anything was amiss? Simeon doubted it, given his own obliviousness to the warning signs and the discovery he made next morning. The storm had been so terrible that nobody would have heard a sound, if a single noise had been made, which Simeon doubted.

Simeon returned to his father's house just after noon the next day, once the storm had ceased and the wan winter sun had begun to shine. The floodwaters had subsided only a little and his journey home had been just as hard as his to Towbouroy. He had concluded his father's business with Sir Thomas Muiretan and slept in his guest bed, it being impossible to travel home in the storm and darkness. It was early when he set out, but whilst the journey was not a long one, his progress had been slow for the road was a quagmire leavened with half-frozen patches. The region was always on the verge of becoming a marsh, more so now than ever. Tress had been toppled, further impeding his progress. Although the rain had ceased and the wind declined into a stiff breeze, dark clouds on the horizon held the promise of further stormy weather to come.

As he climbed the hill towards his father's house, he was surprised to see that there was no smoke rising from the chimney as one would have expected in such cold weather and, as he drew nearer still, he saw that the windows were all still shuttered. It was as if the building were abandoned. Trying the door, he was surprised to find it was unlocked. Something was very wrong.

Simeon stepped inside. There was a smell that he could not quite place. Neither his family nor the stranger he had sent their way were in the hall. Going into the bedrooms, he found his family but not the stranger. Not one of them would be rising this day; every one of his family was pale, as if drained of their life's blood. There was some blood splashed about, but far less than if their throats had just been slashed. He couldn't explain that, but the strangest aspect of the terrible scene was that not a one of them appeared to have put up a struggle; it was as if none had woken.

There were some dark whispers that asked whether Simeon might, somehow, have been responsible. After all, he admitted to having sent the stranger, the apparent murderer, to his father's house. Was it not possible that he might have arranged their deaths? Then, there was the fact that he stood to profit from his family's deaths: without brothers, he would inherit everything. The law of the Hillfolk said that, whilst he would receive the title of Lord, it was the youngest brother who would inherit the bulk of their father's estate as the carer for their parents.

But, such suspicions were in the minority; most believed his story and came to the conclusion it suggested, that a 'Night Walker' had visited The Mount to feast upon the living. Despite their fears, there were no more deaths in the aftermath of the killing of Harley. As winter wore on, the people began to feel that they were safe. Spring, Summer, and Autumn came each in turn without mysterious deaths and life returned almost to normal.

But, now, winter returned and the anniversary of Harley's death approached and the inhabitants of the hill began to worry, wondering if the evil that visited The Mount a year before would return. What horrors might the early snowfall herald? Mysterious footprints were spotted in the fields, walking out of the woods to skirt the boundaries of the villages. Whose were they? Did they belong to some vagabond who had come searching for food, only to find the villages shut up against them? Or, were they truly a sign that something dead walked when the night fell and hungered for the warm blood of the living to sustain their nocturnal peregrinations?

Simeon had abandoned the old house, refusing to live in the place where his kin had been slaughtered. He had moved down to the saddle of the hill below, closer to the village by the church and begun to construct a new house from which he could more adequately oversee the farmland that was now his.

Although he had stated the better situation of the house as his primary motivation for his move, all those who saw how he had staggered out from Harley's house in a state of terror and disgust knew his driving motivation. By the arrival of the first snows, his house was complete and sturdily barred against whatever threat the night might contain.

It may just have been a coincidence that Hew Mago died a year almost to the day after Harley, given his role in establishing the veracity of Simeon's version of events. He died in his bed, seemingly of some winter fever with no evidence of any stranger cause. Not that such reassurance prevented the spread of rumors as some said that, surely, he had died just as Harley had. Even if his death was natural, his corpse still presented a horrible sight, for he had frozen solid in the days before his neighbors broke down his door.

"It is a curse upon us," muttered Willeam Plaren in The Star as he supped a hot toddy.

"Foolishness," opined his cousin, Shon, the priest of The Mount. "Hew died of fever and the cold. No devil finished him off."

"Not true," stated Davyd Johns. Willeam gave his cousin an 'I told you so' look, as Davyd explained: "I saw Harley walking in the darkness two nights ago."

"Harley is in his tomb, laid below the sign of the cross. His soul is in paradise and his body is at rest."

"Not true," Davyd stated again. "I saw him with my own eyes, just as he was in life only with skin as pale as the snow and eyes like pits of darkness. I recognized him just as I would when he was alive. I have no doubt it is him."

"I have seen him, too," added another voice old but firm. It was Old Iewd. They all knew him to be strange, but none doubted the veracity of his words, save Shon; all could hear the certainty in his voice.

"That man is old and mad," Father Shon reported, his words carrying less weight to the drinking crowd than those of the old man.

"But, not blind," snapped Willeam.

"Yeah, I believe him," added Davyd.

"And, not just on winter nights," Old Iewd continued. "I saw him in the woods on a moonless spring night more than once and one time in the summer. Harley walks this hill and will continue to do so. It was his hill in life and remains so in death. The Mount is Harley's Mount. You know, in your hearts, that this is so."

"Nonsense." Father Shon would not be swayed.

"The Father is right," agreed Alan Dawson. "There are no horrors hiding in the night."

The debate continued back and forth with neither side willing to concede ground until the early approach of evening persuaded the patrons of the bar to head home before night arrived. The believers and those with no firm opinion but no desire to risk mortal body or immortal soul began to head home until only Shon and Alan remained within The Star with the barman and his wife.

"It is getting dark," observed the barman. "Will you be staying the night?" The barman had few doubts about 'Night Walkers'.

"I can easily make you up a bed," his wife added.

"No, no, thank you," said the Priest and Alan concurred. "The night holds no fears for me," he added, draining the last of his drink.

The barman warily drew back the bolts on the door and opened it for them and the pair stepped out into the snowy darkness.

The Priest's dwelling was the nearest and he went inside, leaving Alan with a blessing.

Alone in the snow, Alan stumbled tipsily along, swigging from an earthenware bottle he had brought with him from The Star.

"Just a little to keep myself warm," he muttered to himself. It was the last thing Father Shon heard the man say as he closed his door, shaking his head at the man's drunkenness.

Snow had begun to fall. The Priest said that was all that had befallen the drunkard: lost in a stupor, he had been killed by the cold. Certainly, his body was found frozen stiff a short distance from his own door covered in a blanket of snow. But, others claimed him as yet another of the nocturnal prowler's victims, some saying that Harley's killer had slain him and others that Harley was now the one doing the killing.

Old Iewd agreed with the latter, averring that he had seen the dead Lord wandering across the fields that night.

"He will never leave us," the old man stated. "The Mount is Harley's Mount and always will be."

In legend, at least, Harley continued to walk The Mount by night and the Hillfolk continued to bar their doors against him. Just in case.

DJ Tyrer is the person behind UK small press Atlantean Publishing and has been widely published in the British and American small presses, as well as being the driving force behind The Yellow Site, *the* King In Yellow *wiki. His fiction has most recently appeared in* Cthulhu Haiku & Other Mythos Madness *and* Sorcery & Sanctity: A Homage to Arthur Machen, *a novella,* The Yellow House, *the urban horror collection* Black & Red, *and two booklets of fiction parodies have also recently been released.*

DJ's website/blog can be found at http://djtyrer.blogspot.co.uk/

The Atlantean Publishing website can be found at http://atlanteanpublishing.blogspot.co.uk/

The Yellow Site can be found at http://kinginyellow.wikia.com/wiki/Have_You_Seen_The_Yellow_Sign%3F

A.L.A.N

By Jason Purdy

There was nothing more important in life to my older brother than his computer. I wish that were an overstatement. I really do wish that I was just trying to be dramatic, but in all honesty, the house could have burned to the ground around him and he would have sat there, his eyes glued to the screen, as the flames started licking under his bedroom door. If we were home alone and I fell in the shower and broke my back, then I'd have better chance of the cat calling an ambulance for me than I would of him doing it.

So yeah, my brother Alan cared most about his souped-up, over-clocked turbocharged gaming rig complete with cup holders and a vibrating chair that had suspiciously high power levels on it. I don't know why I thought that this would change when he died. I guess it was because everything else did.

Alan always said he rarely went outside because it was a dangerous world out there. He had reason enough to feel that way. He went out to get a pizza a few years ago, so that we could chow down on it while watching all the Evil Dead movies back to back. Alan had told me it was time for me to receive my education. At the time, he was nineteen, which meant to me that he was about the coolest thing since ice cubes. I was a lowly worm at the age of fifteen who knew nothing about movies, games, music, books, or anything, except for what Alan had taught me, and it was time for another lesson.

He came home without the pizza, his wallet or his phone, though he did have a nice knife wound on his side, soaking through his traditional outfit of obscure band t-shirt covered with chequered shirt. I remember that day it was a red and black shirt, one of his favorites.

For a moment I thought it was a joke. All I could do was ask him:

"Where's the pizza?"

"They took that, too," he replied, all pale-faced and with his curly hair matted with sweat and dirt. He'd been mugged. That was Alan's luck, right there. I'd have used that to sum him up at the eulogy but I had no words at that point, only tears.

He survived that. I called for an ambulance, and on the way there with him, I called my frantic mum and dad who cancelled their dinner and skipped their movie to meet us there. They told me I was so brave. I told them that there was nothing brave about picking up a phone, unless you had a phobia of them. Incidentally, that's actually a thing, it's called telephonophobia, which is enough of a mouthful to give you a fear of long words, which is another weird word, and not really relevant right now.

So then Alan became a recluse. I'll stop myself right here and tell you that the picture you're painting in your head of Alan is completely wrong. He rarely left the house, but he wasn't a slob, and he wasn't a waste of space. He managed to make money writing random articles and stuff all over the web, and he did some online courses. It seemed like he was constantly using Dad's printer to get diplomas and tape them up on his bedroom walls, alongside band posters, movie one sheets, and video games guides.

He got himself a treadmill and a set of weights—ordered online, of course—and he worked out for several hours every day. He was in better shape than I was, and I was hardly in the house. I was forever out: playing footie, chasing skirts, sneaking cigarettes and booze, all that normal stuff. Alan was the king of his own castle. He made money, he paid his dues in the rent and more, and he kept himself in shape. Half the time when I was at school and Mum and Dad were at work, he'd clean the house top to bottom. He was an inspiration, even if it was one with agoraphobia. That's the word for being afraid to go out, I remember him telling me that one, telling me that he had it. I asked him if it was self-diagnosed and he said one of his friends on one of his games was a practicing psychiatrist and he had paid him for several sessions on webcam. I made the obligatory joke about letting someone practice psychiatry on you. But I was surprised; you can find anything on that bloody Internet, can't you? Christ, I sound like my dad. Next thing you know, I'll be eating my cereal over the sink and wearing corduroy slippers.

All of this meant that the whole family lived pretty much in harmony, until the day that Alan got summoned for jury service. He tried everything he could, making endless phone calls and sending (metaphorical) stacks of emails, but when it came down to it, his particular condition didn't make him exempt, and if he didn't leave the house to hit up the court, he'd be leaving it to head away to jail for a tidy little stretch. He asked me to impersonate him, but I don't have curly hair, pale, milk white skin, and abs as solid as rock so there was no chance of that one working that well.

He made it through the case, and on the morning before he left for the final day of the trial, he told me that he felt better, that he was fighting his little problem. He'd almost had a panic attack the first time he left the house, but after that, day by day, he got better. Two weeks later and he was almost eager to face the world again. Two weeks later, as he walked home and picked up a pizza on the way there, he forgot to look both ways as he crossed the road and he ended up a crumpled pile of bones and blood lying in the middle of the road. The pizza didn't leave its box, and when I arrived at the scene with Mum and Dad, I saw it sitting there. I opened it in a daze as sirens whirled and screams punctuated the air around me. A miserable rain washed Alan's blood into the gutters and I opened the pizza and saw that he'd got ham and pineapple. I love ham and pineapple—but he can't stand it.

The thought of that still makes me tear up a bit. Every time I look at a pizza, I feel like rolling the slice up like a hanky and drying my eyes with it. We all tried to move on, but it was nigh on impossible. The house was messier than usual, and it was strange to not hear his muffled voice from behind his bedroom door, as he talked late into the night with strangers who were his only backup against endless hordes of soldiers, zombies, aliens, or whatever was the flavor of the month. But as humans, we're nothing if not adaptable. It was a gradual process, but there was a time where, as I crawled into bed late one night, after a hard day of job searching, tidying the house, and trying to dodge the blues, I realized that I hadn't thought about Alan once that whole day. I felt guilt. I drowned my pillow in miserable tears, but it got easier. The guilt never went away, but I learned to ignore it.

Then Dad's printer went on the fritz. It started printing weird stuff, reams of paper with words and symbols that made no sense, just gibberish. I went on my laptop and tried to research some of the stuff that came out, but there was no luck. The words looked like an ancient, primitive language, something scrawled when the first hairy cave man scratched his arse as he crawled out of the primordial soup. The pictures were worse, they were like ancient woodcarvings—dark, chilling tableaus of monsters that would have made Lovecraft shriek. We were freaked out, naturally. Dad called HP and got them to send a guy to fix it. The technician said there was nothing wrong with it, and for a while after that, it stopped.

I'd almost forgotten about the printer when I took a late night trip to the bathroom after staying up too late and getting drunk with some friends. We kept things cheap and cheerful, passing around a few bottles of god awful cider like it was going out of style. I knew I'd regret it in the morning, but my stomach was doing its best to let me know that the process of regret can be a long one. The hardest way to learn your limits when it comes to alcohol is to hug the toilet while your stomach tries to escape from whatever end of you it can manage.

On the trek back, with my gob freshly mouth washed and a glass of water in hand, I saw a blue light creeping from under Alan's door. For a moment, I was so out of it that it felt like back in the good old days where'd he sit up to all hours of the night, and you'd always have the slight sliver of light guiding you towards the stairs if you decided you needed a midnight snack or wanted to creep outside for a smoke.

Then I remembered that he was dead, and I felt my heart slither into my throat, along with a good portion of bile. I felt like

I was going to be sick again, but this time it was more with dread. I grabbed the door handle and pulled it open, to witness the splendor of his man cave, untouched since the day he died except for cursory cleaning. His computer was turned on, and it was running one of his favorite games. I never could remember the name of it. The whole thing was going on by its own volition, and I stood there, mesmerized.

A trickle of piddle crept down from my boxer shorts and soaked the carpet, and a distant part of my mind made a note to wipe that up in the morning, when the sun was up and the monsters weren't as strong. It was at that moment that the mouse shifted, and the keys clacked, touched by nothing but air. That was when I fled, slamming the door and running back to my room, a silent scream trapped behind my lips. I waited and listened for noise for the rest of the night, but I heard nothing. My parents didn't wake up, and as the sun started to creep into the sky and slip across my blinds, my fear started to fizzle out. I couldn't have seen what I saw; it was probably just exhaustion coupled with the dodgy cider. I never told anyone about the computer running itself: even to me, it sounded stupid. It was a bad ghost story, a cautionary tale from some Bible-bashing, computer-fearing technophobe. That's another mouthful, isn't it?

II.

I stopped getting out of bed to go to the bathroom, or go for a snack in the middle of the night, just in case the computer decided to play itself again. I fell back into my usual routine of job hunting by day, and casually drinking by night. By now, I've matched Alan at the merry old age of nineteen, and it feels like I might fall down the same pit that he did. I haven't had the same misfortune, but each time I step out of the house, I get this little pang of anxiety. There's nothing out there in the big bad world for me, and it's getting harder and harder to leave my laptop and the safety of my own bedroom. My world starts to shrink like a cheap jumper on a hot cycle.

I know my parents are worried about me. They were worried about Alan too, and somehow, that annoys me. It's as if

I'm destined to follow where he went, but forever in second place, right behind Alan, like an echo of him, his shadow. I mean seriously, who cares about the second man on the moon? Alan did it first; I'm just rehashing. I understand Alan on a level beyond what I did before, and maybe that's why I see the sun rise after many nights spent in the glare of my laptop screen.

On one of those lonely, zombie-like nights, I get an email. It's not spam about hot singles in my area, and it's not offering me the chance to upgrade my tackle by a few sizes, which is strange enough in itself. Stranger still is that it's from Alan. There's no heading to it, nothing in the email apart from these sparse words:

IT WORKED.

My hands start to tremble, and it's not just because of all the energy drinks I've been knocking back. I know there's no way it's Alan. I know that it's probably just someone playing a sick joke, or a spam bot or something, but that doesn't stop me frantically mashing a reply to him. A real essay of a message, asking him where he is, what is it like, what does he miss, and telling him that every day the world gets a little bit darker, and every day my sleep pattern slips slightly more towards the sort of model favored by owls and other nocturnal creatures.

He doesn't reply, of course. My plea for help goes unheard. Or at least I think it does. Weeks, and then months, pass as I sit at my desk and my stomach expands. My hair grows out, I don't bother to shave, and all my friends stop knocking. As winter rolls around, the house seems permanently icy cold no matter how long the heating is left on, and there's a misery in the air, a misery that we all share. My mum and dad give up on asking me about jobs or telling me to get out of the house. They give up, just like they did with Alan. But Alan was good, he was great, he made money, he kept fit, he cleaned. I'm just in the way, a waste of space. On Christmas Day, they go out for dinner and leave me at home. I don't mind; I feel that I actually would have been afraid to talk to them. Increasingly, the real world is an alien place to me. It's like I'm tied to a rock in the middle of the sea, and every human being I see is just a shape drifting in the fog, just out of my reach.

I become obsessed with the pictures and the words that the printer spewed out in what seems like a life I played on one of my video games, rather than one that I actually lived. I find the images buried in my drawer underneath my mobile phone— which has been dead for months. There's no point charging it to receive messages from no one. I scour the Internet endlessly for the carvings, the meaningless words, and I find myself gripped by a sort of madness, one where even inside my tiny house, I try to withdraw further into a shell of myself. Pulling away from my parents like I've done from the rest of the world.

I creep downstairs to get a snack, waiting as usual until there's no one in the kitchen so I don't have to face my family. I grab a handful of biscuits and I hear my mother in the living room. I creep towards the door, watching her as she tidies, humming a lifeless tune in a half-arsed sort of way. She has the feather duster, that rainbow colored, hairy monstrosity, and she's cleaning Alan's photo on the mantelpiece. I watch her dust it meticulously, getting right into the corners. I see my own photo on the other end of the mantel, between them, a football trophy of mine from eons ago, and Alan's proudest Internet certificate, a PHD in Archaeology. She picks up my photo, looking at my smiling face, and at the dust playing across the frame. She sets it down with a barely audible tut, and she leaves it as it is, dusty and wonky, balancing close enough to the edge to tip off and smash on the metal fire guard, which it does, a week later. I creep back upstairs like the shameful secret that I've become. Back to my little dungeon.

I don't know how I feel. I don't know what I am anymore. I begin to hate Alan, for being a better me, for dying as a victim and an inspiration, and leaving me to waste away to nothing. There are no jobs out there and I've long since stopped checking. Alan would have advice for me; he would have helped. But he's dead and I can't sleep, I see those monstrous carvings when I close my eyes, as if they're taped to my eyelids. Every night now, I hear his computer playing itself, the click and push of the mouse and the clack of the keys making a chorus that would drive you mad.

III.

It takes almost another year for me to snap. Things get worse day by day over that year, and by the time Christmas is mere weeks away, I'm about twice the size I was before. Leaving the house is the equivalent of climbing Everest for me. I hear that clacking of the phantom keys and the shuffling of the mouse, back and forward like a weary guard on patrol, and my brain snaps in two like a twig. I march right into his room, facing the computer running the game all by itself like it's not abhorrent, like this sort of thing happens all the time. I scramble into the shadows underneath the desk, expecting some toothed horror to jump out at me, and I grasp for the plug. When I see that it's not plugged in or switched on, suddenly the chill of the unused room and the winter air disappear. Everything feels hot, heavy and close, I feel static tingling in my hair, tickling my beard and making my unkempt hair stand up fuzzy and curly, just like Alan's did. I pull out from under the desk and stare into the screen, which is now black. Of course it wasn't plugged in; it's been unplugged since he died. I'm losing my grip on reality. Which was a tenuous thing at best anyway.

I reach out and touch the monitor, and I feel heat coming from it. Not like the searing heat of an overworked computer (not that his would overheat, his computer had more fans than The Beatles) but more like the heat of a human body. I stare into the blank screen, slightly lit orange by the street light by the window. I see my own face, hairy, greasy, chubby and spattered with spots. I've really let myself go. I look like the kind of kid that I used to beat up when I thought I was cool and Alan was still here to tell me what movies to like.

At that thought, the screen bursts into light, and I step back, tripping over his high backed, leather spinny chair, and falling flat on my arse on the carpet. One word appears on the screen, in black capital letters, a command that brokers no argument.

RUN.

I get to my feet, backing towards the door, my knees shaking like they're made of lime jelly. I feel my body screaming at me to leg it, but I'm frozen. I let out a little squeak.

"Please don't hurt me." I babble, and that is the start of a long stream of clichés, the kind of things that would make Alan turn to me when we're watching a movie, and roll his eyes, as if to say, can you believe this bull? The screen just keeps flashing that one word at me.

I scuttle backwards, towards the door. Before I can reach it, it slams shut behind me. I try to scream for Mum and Dad to help, but I've spent so many late nights recently screaming at someone over the Internet with my stupid little headset on, because they're not healing me properly or they were late for a raid, that I bet they'd ignore it. I start to sweat buckets. Well, not literally. A small face appears on the screen. It's built up of little dotted black pixels floating on a white screen. Like dead seaweed on the surface of a still ocean. It's two eyes, a mouth, and a tiny little nose, and somehow, from those little details, I know its Alan. It opens its mouth to speak.

"Run, Jake." It says clearly, its voice sounding half robotic, half Alan, giving the sensation that Alan is talking to me through a bad phone line and is standing on the surface of the moon.

Recognizing Alan in there somehow makes me more terrified. My back pressing up against the closed door, and my t-shirt clings to me, soaked with cold sweat.

"Please." I gurn, "What do you want from me?" The Alan on the screen rolls its eyes, in that typical gesture, the one thing everyone remembers best about him, even though the rest of the memories are grey and faded, worn around the edges like ancient photographs. A nostalgic smile hits my lips that is completely out of place set against my wide, wild eyes.

"I want you to run," he says clearly, and at that, the treadmill springs to life, beeping on his usual work out, 10k per second, 2.3 incline, something to really make you sweat. That was how he used to describe it.

I slowly get to my feet.

"Run?" I say.

"Yes, Christ," he says, and then he laughs, his voice more man than machine now, like Alan has pulled the veil back and is now more here than beyond. I walk towards the treadmill, laying a weak hand on it, staring at him. I know it's a screen, but I can see his face there, clear as the day that he left the house on that grey morning.

"I've missed you, Alan." I say quietly.

"I know buddy. But there's time for that later. You're a fat slob, hasn't anyone told you that?" he says, his voice teasing.

"Hasn't anyone told you that you're a bloody computer?" I say back, climbing onto the treadmill. I start to sweat almost immediately as it gets going, but it feels good.

"I'd been told that before anyway," he says, giving a quixotic smile. "Come on, run fat boy, run."

Of course Alan would never be able to leave his computer, not even little things like death or the laws of psychics could separate the two of them. I kept his secret, and over the next few weeks, the weight started to fall off me, and I felt better than I had in a long time. Better than I've ever felt since he died. We'd talk our usual rubbish about films, games, girls, whatever cropped up, while I pounded the treadmill. Any time I tried to ask him about what happened to him, how he was in the computer, and what dying was like, he'd refuse to answer me, but I bet I can make him crack—I was always able to make him cave in to my demands. It's one of the perks of being the little brother. By the time I went for my first jog in the melting late January snow, going outside was a non-issue again. I hadn't realized until I was out the door how easy it had been. I couldn't have done it without Alan.

I started to discover that there was one thing more important to Alan than his computer. One thing he stuck around for, and that happened to be me. Well of course, me, and the sequel to that one game he loved so much. He said he couldn't go before he'd beat that a thousand times over. From then on, everything was back on track. I got out of the house and started hunting for work, and Alan stayed in his room, doing whatever it is a haunted computer occupies itself with.

Everything was fine and dandy, until the BT technician showed up and told us he that our broadband speed had been cut for excessive downloading, most of which were probably illegal. I glanced at Alan as he told us this, because I hadn't been on my laptop in weeks. Because Alan is a computer now, it probably looked like I was just having a staring contest with my powered down PC. The technician gave me a look that implied I was loopy, but the joke was on him. As he tried to leave the house, every electrical appliance in the house attacked the poor guy, brutally murdering him and leaving a corpse covered in suction marks, ice burns, scalds, gashes and grilled flesh that the mortician couldn't make head or tails of. Nobody ever got in trouble for it, purely because the circumstances were impossible. The cause of death was marked as misadventure, and we all tried to move on.

I asked Alan how he managed it. He wouldn't give me a direct answer; he just told me that "Everything has the Internet in it, nowadays." I had to accept that at face value, because I didn't want to end up in a body bag either. Alan seems less human every day, but don't tell him I said that, for the love of God. Don't repeat it either, not in an email, not in a phone call, not even in front of a CCTV camera. He's everywhere lately, and he'll know.

Jason Purdy is 22 years old, and from Northern Ireland. He's been writing from a very young age, mostly silly little things, short stories, novels that never got finished, and occasionally scraping together an awful comic book consisting of stick men with impossible hair. He loves reading, listening to music, and playing video games.

When he can be bothered, he enjoys going to the gym or going for a jog. He isn't bothered all that often. He reads Media Studies and Production at university and is an avid film and television fan. He's an occasional film maker with his own gear that spends too much time gathering dust, and he has a fondness for screen writing as well as novel writing. He has a roughly a thousand screenplays all over the place, circulating, hopefully making some Hollywood executive shed tears of joy, but more likely probably just being used as door stops or mug coasters.

His debut novel, Cigarette *is out now. He completed it when he was 20 and spent the next two years on and off redrafting it between writing the two sequels and a myriad of other junk. He started writing* Cigarette *because he didn't want to be the kind of guy who has 'thinking of writing a book' written on his gravestone. So he started writing a book.*

His Goodreads page is at: https://www.goodreads.com/author/show/7055545.Jason_Purdy

Cold Dead Hands

By Jay Wilburn

Jill held her breath until her lungs burned and her hands shook by her side. She closed her eyes and pressed the back of her head against the icy, brick wall to try to hold out a little longer.

She opened her eyes seeing black spots against the colorless sky threatening another heavy snowfall from the thick clouds. Jill gave up and heaved out her breath in swirls of vapor around her head.

Blood throbbed inside her head and she blinked drawing in frigid air.

Through the white clouds of her breath, she saw the corpses turn their entire bodies to aim their stiff necks and heads in her direction by the wall.

She exhaled another blast of steamy breath before the first had completely dissipated. More of the bodies that meandered through snow-covered yards and street stopped with snow up to their battered shins. They slid their milky eyes in her direction. She doubted most of them could see well through their cataracted eyes, but they sensed her breath and trudged through the snow toward her from a dozen directions.

Jill looked back to the sky and sighed out another cloud. "During the summer, being quiet was enough. Now I can't even breathe without calling down trouble."

They opened their jaws and showed broken teeth as she looked for a path through them. They raised hands showing bone through broken skin on fingers. Their shoulders drew closer together as they covered the distance.

If this plague had never happened, I'd have started high school last fall. We would probably be out of school today after yesterday's blizzard and be sledding as snowplows tried to catch up. You all would be driving to work with chains on your cars and leaving me alone.

"You took everything from me and now I'm just cold."

The bodies approaching her listened in silence except for the crunch of their sneakers, wet socks, or bare feet.

Jill lifted her knees high to take bigger leaps out over the drift. With the bitter air and the resistance of the snow, her breath came in quick bursts. Each time, they adjusted their trajectory and clawed at her.

She ran close enough to them that she had to duck their reach to pass under their grasp.

One of them caught and lifted her stocking cap away from her head, pulling one long strand of her hair. The sharp cold struck her and robbed her of warmth down through her body with the shock. She glanced back and saw a dead man in a rotten tee shirt and swim trunks chewing on her toboggan with his yellow eyes rolled up in his skull.

"Is it the taste or the warmth?" she whispered.

Jill whipped around and pumped her legs without getting her answer. She felt her hair sliding back and forth on the smooth material of her coat. She imagined the next errant grab might get a handful of hair and they would have her.

I should have cut it a long time ago, she thought.

"My mother liked it long," Jill huffed for the hungry dead to hear.

They grabbed her by her hair and now she is gone. I'm still here. Stop talking to yourself and keep running, Jill.

As they whipped around to chase, she heard their joints crackle and saw their skin tear from the stress of the pivot. Through the new rips, she saw thick, ice crystals coated over and through the frozen muscles.

She remembered hoping that the winter might freeze them and allow her to roam free in the cold. She snorted and laughed out one harsh note at the thought.

Bodies farther up the street in both directions turned around and honed in on her last breath. Their dead flesh was only a shade or two different from the snow cover. No vapor escaped from their open mouths.

She heard the sharp clicks of teeth sound behind her. Jill shivered from the cold and the sound.

She thought, I actually miss hearing them moan. They were easier to avoid before they went silent.

"I can't wait for your lungs to thaw."

They clicked their teeth at her in response.

Jill left the snow covered street and charged up the hill. She rounded behind the houses and tried to put distance between her and the dead.

"You are too stupid to follow my tracks, but you moth right to my body heat."

I need more cold air between me and you.

At the fourth house over, she ran into the chain link fence with her gloved hands in front of her. The fence rattled shrill through the still air shedding snow and ice off the top.

Jill took a deep breath and hauled herself over the fence. The wire loops bit into her hands through the insulation of the gloves. A sharp end caught the side of her thick coat and tore it open to the cotton insulation. She stumbled to her knees in the backyard of the house splattering cold, wetness between her boots and her ski pants.

She regained her feet and slushed forward until the hand snagged her heel. Jill screamed and heard it echo back as she jerked her foot free. She looked back and saw the snow tumble off as the body lurched upward. She saw the face locked in a scream with an actual icicle hanging from one upper tooth. The nose pressed back into the skeletal face and the eyes remained still and empty. She couldn't tell if they were frozen in the sockets or if the corpse had nothing else he cared to look upon.

Jill turned and saw the snow billowing up from three other snowy graves in the fenced yard. She spotted one hand opening into a claw with a crack. Two fingers snapped loose and fell back into the snow.

Jill wasn't sure they could still bite, but she wasn't up for testing them.

She ran across the yard and hit the next fence at full bore. She flipped over and landed on her butt in the snow. Jill gritted her teeth feeling a harder layer of ice than she expected.

The creatures impacted the chain link behind her with four separate crashes pouring snow off on her hair and shoulders. She wasn't sure if it fell from the fence or their bodies.

She brushed the wet off her scalp and burning ears as she staggered up and forward. "I need a new hat."

Jill weaved by mounds of white over swing sets, collapsed sheds, and an above ground swimming pool. She fought the temptation to reach over and break the ice on the water in the pool.

The guy in the swim trunks eating my hat may have come from here. His girlfriend could still be under there in a bikini. I'm surprised the sides hadn't burst yet. They must have used really good materials.

She became hyperaware of bumps in the snow expecting each one to lunge out at her with frozen hands and broken fingers.

Jill rounded the curve of the street behind the houses and found a yard with a dry fountain tilted at a sharp angle near wooden railroad ties. The tie marked off lifeless flowerbeds. She felt her throat grow hot and scratchy looking on the outlines of familiar things.

Jill swallowed and flexed her numb fingers in her gloves as she turned to face the back of the house. The wood along the back splintered where the paint had been stripped and pressure washed, but the primer for the repaint had never been applied. An overhang above the sliding glass door buckled and warped under the downfall from the previous night. Icicles hung clear and dangerous through cracks in the stressed sheet metal. The concrete of the patio underneath was the only clear ground she had seen all day.

I promised never to come back here.

Jill approached the back of the house. "I'm out of options."

She stepped under the bulging metal and looked up at the sharp ice aiming at her head. The broken metal creaked and popped. She stomped her feet out of old habit to knock the accumulated snow loose from the tread of her boots.

Jill pulled the door at the latch, but it held locked. The weathered back of the house popped against its frame with her force. One of the icicles dropped loose and sliced another opening into the cotton of her coat behind her shoulder before she realized it had fallen. The ice shattered against the dry concrete behind her boot and she yelled. Her voice echoed and the metal above her groaned.

Jill heard none of the moans she had grown used to hearing during the warm months of the plague, but she heard snow crunching under exposed feet. She could not explain why, but a bare, bloodless foot in snow had a different sound than a boot. The creatures approached around both sides of the house and through the small pines behind the yards. The steps came slow, but steady.

Jill looked in both directions. She felt sure they had left one of the windows or doors unlocked, but she couldn't afford to run through the middle of the monsters checking each one.

She stepped to the edge of the concrete and ran her gloved hand through the snow along the side. He fingers bent back painfully on something solid and she cursed. Jill used both hands to sweep the snow away until a red concrete hat exposed itself through the white.

She grabbed it, wrenching the hat from side to side until the body broke loose from the ground. She hauled the lawn gnome up out of the snow with a grunt.

Jill gritted her teeth and spun in an unbalanced circle before she released it. The gnome punched through the glass sideways near the lock. Cracks laced up from the oblong hole to the edges, but did not shatter.

Jill frowned and approached the sliding glass door with her hand out to undo the lock. The glass fell in a wash from the frame and cascaded across the linoleum floor inside like water.

Jill drew back her hand, but stepped through crunching the glass under her feet.

The gnome wobbled on the floor near the stove.

She heard sharp cracks behind her and turned around.

The body stepping unto the concrete only wore shredded jeans. The brown flesh opened in wide sours and held the bone tightly from head to toe. Most of the dead man's hair was missing along with the scalp showing discolored skull bone. With each step, its right shoulder popped in and out of joint with exaggerated snaps forward and back.

Never enough time.

Jill looked from side to side in the kitchen for something blunt to open the exposed skull. She remembered a knife block on the counter, but the counter was bare except for the elephant cookie jar. She thought about whether the hollow ceramic elephant would get through to the monster's brain before it shattered in her hands.

Did we take the knives with us? I don't remember.

The snap and pop of the shoulder drew closer. The shriveled cadaver stepped a bare foot on the remainder of the icicle crunching it under his heel.

Jill stepped back until she bumped into the refrigerator knocking off the magnets. Her report card and her brother's letter offering a diving scholarship floated to the floor.

Run, stupid girl.

Jill whispered seeing her breath in the darkness of her family's kitchen. "I'm cold and tired."

Snow fell around the bare skull from above as he popped toward the shattered door. Crystals packed around the base of his sunken eyes, but the man did not blink nor did he look away from Jill at the refrigerator.

The sheet metal folded down and smacked him in the bony forehead staggering the decrepit body. A mass of snow and ice avalanched down on top of him covering the concrete and making him seem to vanish from sight.

Jill smiled as she looked to see if he would pull himself off his face from the blanket of snow. Before he did, the overhang snapped from its bolts and folded down over the door with a loud clap plunging her into darkness.

Jill jolted and covered her mouth. She dropped her hands and looked back and forth in the dark kitchen.

Will that actually hold?

She heard hands crack and bang against the other side of the misshapen metal. The breaks opened back showing light and clawing hands on the other side. The metal shook, but stayed over the shattered door.

Jill turned and walked out of the kitchen up the hall. She saw motion through the other windows in the rooms on both sides, but did not stop to watch.

Then, she passed her brother's room and her parents' room without turning her head. She walked into her own room at the end of the hall and cleared her throat.

She shivered and sniffed realizing the inside was just as cold as the outside without the wind.

Jill shook her head and began digging through her things. She scattered figurines off the top of her dresser and flung clothes off her bed onto the floor.

She approached her closet and gripped the handle. Jill took two deep breaths and prepared to pull the door open on a hungry corpse.

She paused and got down on her hands and knees on the carpet. Jill took another deep breath and blew the vapor out under the edge of the door. She waited hearing the hands pounding metal from the other side of the house, but nothing from her closet. She stood and pulled the door open.

Jill yanked out her neon yellow backpack. She unzipped the main pocket and dumped out notebooks and packs of paper. The covers had pen drawings of angels with feathered wings and hearts with knives through them.

She stared at her drawings from the eighth grade school year she never got to finish. "You have to stab them through the head. Not the heart, stupid girl."

Jill raked her hand through the pack dumping piles of photographs out of the backpack. She opened the other pockets and shook out mechanical pencils, highlighter markers, loose rubber bands, paper clips, and more.

She ran her fingers through the clutter on the floor and uncovered the pads in bright, green plastic. She shoved them back into the pack.

I'll need more. Why are hygiene products harder to find than food?

She paused over the pictures and flipped a few over on the carpet.

Jill squinted. "Why did I have all these in my backpack?"
Was I making another collage?

She flipped them back over and read messages scrawled on the back that told her to stay alive, don't get bitten, and we'll make it together. Jill shook her head and blinked.

She remembered being in the middle school as an emergency shelter when things had gotten bad very quickly. The adults were scared and confused. The kids had phones and watched videos uploaded from around the world. They had seen movies and knew what was going on. The adults were still whispering about Ebola and rabies. It was the day school pictures were distributed. Kids cut them, wrote messages, and passed them around. They swore to look out for each other as they sat along the wall waiting for further instructions.

"Why did I forget this?"

Jill remembered that some parents arrived pounding on the locked doors to the office. The campus safety officer had refused to let anyone inside. Some of the kids ran past and opened the doors. One of the men tried to take the gun and the officer had opened fire. The dead came to the pounding, gunshots, and open doors. Jill had run. She did not even remember who left with her or how she got home, but she was alone when she arrived at the house. It was warm that day and she could hear the moans and growls of the ones that had followed her.

She ran her fingers over the photographs on the cold, bedroom floor considering whether to take them with her.

She stood up straight. "If I want to see dead people, I'll just walk outside."

Jill ran her hands through her closet screeching the hangers. She pulled clothes off the wire and crammed them into the bag.

She ran her hand over the top shelf knocking down board games. Cards and tokens rained down on the closet floor.

She knelt by her bed and swept her gloved hand through the dust underneath. She paused as she touched the side of the guitar case. She licked her chapped lips. Instead of pulling the case out, she stood and walked to her dresser, holding the open backpack.

Jill jerked open the drawers. They resisted as the wood stuck from seasons of heat and cold, but she pulled them free. She shoved a couple of thicker pairs of socks and fresh underwear into the pack.

She held up mittens with no finger separations in them. Jill considered them, but decided to drop them back in the drawer.

She pawed through each drawer twice looking for another stocking cap, but she didn't find one.

"I know I had one."

Jill stepped back to the doorway and paused. She turned and scanned the room in the harsh light off the snow outside her window. She eyed the posters and snorted.

"I don't remember who this girl is. All these actors are probably dead and walking around."

Their lungs are too frozen to growl.

Jill tilted her head. "Maybe it is warmer where they are."

A shadow crossed her wall from the window that faced the street from her bedroom.

She backed into the hallway and listened. The pounding and scraping still came from the kitchen. None of them were at her window yet.

They are following the sound of the monsters banging on the metal.

Until they sense my body heat in here.

Jill turned.

Maybe there is a stocking cap in my brother's room.

She stopped in the hall and turned her back on her brother's doorway. "I bet my father had one."

Her throat became thick and she rubbed the back of her gloves against the wet heat building around her eyes.

She tried to push the thought out, but all she could ever see of her father was the last moment. Her brother had pulled her backward out of the passenger's side of the backseat of the car. Her father had crawled out from behind the exploded airbag. He put himself in the seat between her and the creatures tearing through the driver's side of the car. He screamed and held his leg above a broken bone that stuck out of his leg and the material of his pants. Jill fought, but her brother still pulled her out of the car from behind. Her father grabbed the seat on both sides and held on as the dead chewed on his back. They pushed him, but he would not let them through as her brother pulled Jill backward down the alley away from the wrecked car and their screaming father.

Jill could not rewind her memory to anything earlier about her father without getting stuck on him holding the monsters away from her with his body. She hated the fact except that it spared her from remembering the details of the dead hands tearing her mother's beautiful hair off her head before she could get into the car.

"I have to find a hat."

Jill realized she was staring at the picture on the wall next to her parents' door. The reflection off the glass was bright, but she could see herself at age two and her brother Jack a few years older sitting on a hill with an old-fashioned, wooden pail sitting between them.

"My parents think they are so funny."

Thought ... my parents thought they were so funny naming their kids Jack and Jill probably just for this picture.

A crash sounded from the kitchen that never seemed to finish. Jill cursed.

I need to get food from the pantry. Why am I just standing here?

Jill ran toward the sound in the kitchen. She stopped where the carpet met the linoleum under a row of brass strip and tacks.

The slim corpse with the bald spot that went all the way to the bone staggered through the torn metal and the collapsed frame. Other crackling bodies shoved through behind him.

Jill looked at the pantry door across the kitchen and back at the crumbling body covered in frost. He caught the sharp edge of a shard of glass under his bare foot and punched it clean through the top. She saw solid, black sludge suspended inside the open wound around the protruding glass.

"You are going to stink when you thaw out."

Glass shattered behind Jill. She turned and saw a wall of bodies slicing themselves as they forced their way through the picture window in the den.

Jill zipped the backpack and charged to her room. She heard them bounding back and forth between the walls in the narrow hall. Pictures lifted off their hooks and fell to the floor to be stomped by frozen feet.

She slammed her door without looking and pressed the lock button.

Jill shook her head. "That will hold them off for zero seconds."

She went to her window and looked outside. A scattering of corpses crossed the yards and street diagonally toward the far corner of her house.

Be fast, stupid girl.

"Thank God we live in a one story house."

Lived... we lived in a one story house.

She turned the lock on her window with a pop. A few bodies turned from side to side, but none of them focused in on her yet. She pulled up sliding the window with a sharp crack. One corpse actually spun around twice trying to locate the sound echoing through the neighborhood.

Jill dropped the backpack behind the brown hedges first. She swung her leg out and sat on the windowsill.

This is the first time I ever snuck out of the house. I was a good girl.

"Am ... I am a good girl."

Jill heard the door bounce in its frame as the dead reached her bedroom. She looked back in at the posters.

"Will you brave men hold them off while I escape?"

Jill remembered her father holding the seats and feeding them his back. She coughed and slid out the window landing behind the hedges. She reached up to close the window, but could not stretch far enough to pull it closed.

She heard the door splinter in her room and dropped down to her knees.

Jill pulled her arms through the straps of the pack. The thick coat made it a bit of a struggle.

Socks, underwear, and a few maxipads...

"This was not worth it."

She stared through the hedges at the street. She had excellent cover.

Jill exhaled and saw all the bodies in the yard turn to face the bushes.

"I used to love winter."

Jill shoved through the hedges scattering brown leaves on the snow. She ran between them ducking her head and trying to hold her hair.

"I should have gotten a headband or even one of the rubber bands I dumped out of the backpack. Stupid, stupid, girl."

Jill crunched over the street and stumbled on the next curb falling to her knees in the drift. She struggled up as the creatures closed in around her. She saw the icy hands poking out of the snow palms up and she jumped away.

Jill saw the can of beans clutched in the left hand. The right hand held a revolver in a tight grip. The trigger finger of the right hand had broken off below the second knuckle leaving a sliver of bone jutting out.

They've started setting traps with bait.

She dropped down and pulled at the can, but watched the gun. The label tore away as she pulled the can free from the hard skin. Both hands bobbed with the force, but then stilled. She watched, but neither hand moved again and the snow didn't break.

You were still one of us just trying to escape with your dinner, I guess. Did you run out of bullets or run out of time?

"If you'd left the gun, you could have carried two cans."

A dull shadow crossed over her from behind and she bolted.

Jill ran between the houses with the unmarked can in her grasp. She entered the trees behind the neighborhood and weaved between the trunks. She saw shadows stumbling through to her left and right, but she kept running.

Jill saw the banks of the creek with an icy layer in the middle. She picked up her pace and leapt across. Jill spilled onto her stomach on the opposite side. The can rolled loose from her grip. She dug it back out of the snow and took a moment to put it in one of the side pockets of her old, school pack.

Jill reshouldered the bag and continued her run through the trees. She heard loud cracks behind her from bodies crashing through the ice in the shallow creek.

She emerged from the narrow strip of forest out on the main road. A few businesses lined the opposite side of the road in strip malls and office parks. Roofs had collapsed in a few spots from the ice and lack of maintenance.

Jill scanned the street to try to gain her bearings. She felt like she was looking through a filter that washed out the color and sharp edges in the world. Everything looked familiar, but not as she remembered from warmer days uncovered.

She whispered, "I wish Jack were here."

They would just be twice as attracted to our combined body heat. When will winter be over?

She saw them crossing in the open near a gas station with shattered windows and snow drifts billowed back into the store blocking the shelves.

Jill shook her head, still not believing it could be true even after seeing it all winter.

The naked women passed behind the building as the fatter men lumbered after them. Their bare butts and pot bellies jiggled as they ran. Jill looked them up and down for frostbite, but their feet pumped in and out of the snow too quickly for her to tell.

The polar bear club? How can they stand it?

As the last man crossed behind the station, Jill whispered, "Shrinkage."

The women emerged from the other side of the building wearing nothing except for duffle bags. The bags hung heavy from their shoulders as their breasts bounced from side to side with their motion.

"You'd think they'd at least wear a sports bra."

The dead staggered along the road as the polar bear club jogged by them unnoticed.

"I guess it works."

Her breath swirled around her head and the dead bodies in the street turned toward Jill. The naked men ran out from behind the gas station. They heaved for air sending clouds of steam into the air, but the dead continued to hone in on Jill like she were the only warm blood in the area.

She shook her head. "Still not worth running naked in the snow."

Jill ran across the highway and down the slope behind the strip mall.

She hooked around onto the access road. She darted her eyes back and forth between the trees and the slope leading up to the larger Interstate. Jill didn't realize how compact the space was until she traversed it in the cold silence of the snowfall. Her footsteps seemed too loud in her ears.

Jill crossed behind the fire station and an elementary school. The stone walls still stood, but most of the rest of the structures were gone and buried below the snowfall. She could still see the blackened scorch marks from the fires.

She stopped shy of the utility shed in the narrow field below the high tension power lines. Jill shielded her eyes and looked up at ice hanging down like spears. She imagined them snapping and crushing the shed. Jill pictured the ice falling around here like deadly rain.

"I'll need to move soon."

Jill waited a moment longer, but saw no movement.

She crossed the field and pulled the snow back with the door and slid through the opening. Jill closed the door and allowed her eyes to adjust to the light coming from the vents high around the walls. Jill dropped her backpack off her shoulders onto the floor.

She shook her head. "I'm tired of being cold."

Her voice rang back at her.

Jill decided to risk it.

She took a few books down from a shelf without looking at the covers. Jill tore out pages and placed them on a broad grill sitting on top of a generator casing. Jill felt around the shelves and found the cardboard box. Only a few matches still rattled inside. She tried to strike them off the side, but the cardboard folded and the sandpaper had worn away. Jill struck it off the vent of the generator and dropped it on the pages in the grill.

She searched for a can of lighter fluid, but found none. Jill sighed and tore more pages out onto the fire. She picked up a chair in the corner and slammed it against the floor a dozen times until the wooden legs broke loose. Jill tossed them in the grill and fed more pages on top.

She took her gloves off and shoved them in the pockets of her coat. Jill turned her hands over above the flames. Her eyes rolled up in her head. She thought about lowering her hands into the grill to cook and actually felt tempted.

Jill stepped away and knelt by her pack. She pulled the can out of the pocket and retrieved a can opener from the shelf.

She couldn't figure out which was the top without the label. She locked the opener on one end and turned the handle until she heard a boom at the door.

More cracks and scratches sounded around the metal walls.

Jill set the can down without looking, the opener still attached to it. She watched the door pitch in its frame. If the creatures turned the knob and pulled, she would be trapped.

She climbed up the shelf and leaned out to peer through the vent. The dead lined the walls around the shed three rows deep and more were emerging from the woods.

Jill jumped down. She stared at the door and watched the knob shake.

"I'm already trapped."

Something popped and hissed behind her. Jill spun expecting to see them folding back one of the walls. She looked back and forth in the empty shed.

I'm losing my mind.

She saw fluid spray into the air. Jill spotted the can of beans sitting in the fire of the grill. She cursed and ran forward. Jill grabbed up the can and screamed. She dropped it and it bounced off the floor.

She clutched her wrist and saw blisters forming on her fingers as she watched.

The can exploded and blasted lima beans up one wall all the way to the ceiling.

Jill screamed and backed away.

She sighed, "I didn't like lima beans anyway."

Did I really set the can down in the fire?

Jill pulled her gloves back on and groaned as she irritated the burns on one of her hands.

Jill lifted the grill by the handles and carried it to the door. She set it down and took two breaths. She turned the knob and pushed, but the press of bodies outside kept the door closed.

"I'm going to die in here."

She turned the knob and threw her shoulder into the door. She shook and her face turned red with the effort.

Come on. Help me feed myself to you, monsters.

Jill broke the door open to pale daylight. She continued to push until grey fingers closed around the open edge and began to pull. She reached down and lifted the grill.

As the door opened, Jill threw the grill out to the side. Flame blasted up over the front of two of the dead. One ignited and staggered backward. The others turned to face him. A few grabbed hold and even bit down on the burning flesh, igniting themselves.

Jill charged and pushed through the crowd in the field.

More piled onto the fire, but others turned and followed Jill below the power lines.

She ran and jumped over a wire fence. More emerged from the trees on both sides. She approached the road, but saw more of the monsters following the roadway in a herd.

Jill turned to look for another way to go. She glanced down and saw long, brown singe marks over her coat. Jill swallowed and bowed her head.

"Jill, come on," the voice echoed up from below.

She turned and looked toward the road. She saw him pulling a sled loaded with boxes ahead of the dead following along the road.

She waved him off. "Jack, no, just go. I'll be fine."

"Shut up and come on, girl."

Jill groaned and ran toward her brother. She grabbed the rope to the sled beside him and they pulled it down the road ahead of their pursuers.

Jack's legs were longer and slimmer and Jill had to work hard to keep pace with him. They left the road and made their way through a park she did not recognize.

Jack stopped them at a set of stairs leading down to a cellar door below the snow under a building.

Jill reached down to lift a box, but Jack grabbed her shoulder.

"Hold up, Jill. Let's get out of sight while they are still too far to find us."

She looked up from the supplies. "You just want to leave all this stuff out here?"

Jack looked back and forth. "It's not like the rotten snowmen are going to eat it. Let's go."

Jill followed him down the stairs. Her boots slipped out from under her on the icy stairs. Jill grabbed the railing and twisted around. Jack held under her arm and helped her the rest of the way down.

He pushed her through to the cellar of the park office and closed the door behind them. Jack slid a board into hooks over the door she suspected he had added himself.

Jill sat down on the floor against a metal support pillar in the storage area. She crossed her arms and shivered.

"I'm tired of being cold, Jack."

He lifted a blanket off the cot. "Looks like you tried to catch yourself on fire."

"I had to use a grill to distract them," she said, "I burned one of my hands."

He wrapped the blanket around her and pulled her up from the floor. "You'll lose heat on the floor. Sit on the cot."

She let her brother lead her to the cot and they sat down beside each other.

Jill looked around. "I thought we had a no basement rule. People got trapped hiding in basements. We saw it happen, Jack."

Jack shrugged. "There are three ways in and out of here. It is also a few degrees warmer down here. I think it masks my body heat a little. Speaking of rules, you started a fire?"

Jill turned away. "I should go. Two of us in the same place will attract them worse. We are just putting each other in danger until it warms up. We saw it happen, right?"

"We'll be okay for a while," Jack said, "It's not like when there were five of us. Maybe we should rethink this plan though, Jill. I don't like you being out there alone. You burned yourself and I can't protect you, if we are separated."

Jill wiggled her toes and felt wetness in her socks as the numbness left her feet. She frowned.

I left the socks in the backpack at the shed. I can't do anything right. I'll get him killed just like when Mom and Dad tried to keep us alive instead of taking care of themselves.

She said, "I'm taking care of myself just fine. I can't do that if you're drawing them to us like a big, tall furnace."

Jack shook his head. "If you are taking care of yourself just fine, why did you go back to the house? We had a rule."

Jill cut her eyes at her brother. "How would you know that unless you went to the house too? Or are you following me?"

Jack smiled and looked away. "A little of both, I guess. The place is a mess now."

Jill bowed her head and blinked. "It's not like we were ever moving back in, Jack."

"What did you go back for?" he put his hand on his shoulder.

I'm no good at finding food.

"I lost my hat," Jill said.

Jack took his stocking cap off and pulled it down onto her head. He started tucking her hair underneath the knitting. Jill pushed his hand away and finished tucking her hair herself.

Jack put his hands together between his knees and rubbed his palms together. "You have to keep your hair covered. You saw what happened to Mom."

Jill let go of the cap and pulled the blanket tight around her. "I was with Dad getting in on the other side of the car. I missed most of it, thank God. Between you and Dad, I'm not sure my feet touched the ground most of that day."

Jack sighed out a cloud of vapor. "I can't stop seeing it. It was awful. I had her hands and they had her hair. I tried to pull her away, but she let go and pushed me. I was a couple inches taller than her and she shoved me like a linebacker. I slammed into the side of the car backward."

"That's when I looked." Jill said.

Jack cleared his throat. "Any memory I try to pull up of her starts with her hair being pulled out. I hate it."

"I'm the same way with Dad," Jill said.

Jack nodded. "Yeah, I missed most of that. I had blood in my eyes after the crash. Between the two of us, we have quite a tragic set of memories. I used to look at pictures of them at the house sometimes. I didn't take any of them, but I kept going back for some reason."

Jill sniffed. "I'm sorry I messed that up for you."

Jack put his arm around her shoulder and squeezed. "It's just a house. The part that still matters is right here. Mom and Dad would agree."

Jill felt warmth from his arm through the blanket and coat. "I need to go. Being here isn't safe. I'll make better choices, Jack. I promise."

Jack held her and pulled her back down on the cot. "Wait. Why don't we stick together, Jill? We could keep moving. We could move south until the cold isn't a factor and winter passes. We considered it before. This has to be better plan with what we've seen. I would feel better about our odds, if we found a way to stick together."

I would feel better about your odds, if you didn't have to look out for me. Maybe I will go south and you can take care of yourself.

Jill shook her head. "If we run up the snowy hill together, you'll fall and break your crown."

And I'll come tumbling after.

Jack leaned back and dropped his arm. She felt cold with the absence.

He said, "Mom and Dad thought they were so clever, didn't they?"

Thought...

Jill said, "I need to go. Being here is a bad idea. We're going to get hurt."

Jack allowed her to stand up. "Jill, take the blanket and some of the supplies. You can have the sled. I'll find something else and help you find new a place."

She dropped the blanket back on the cot. "I'll be fine."

Fists beat on the outside of one of the doors on the far side of the cellar.

Jill clinched her fists inside her gloves. "This is my fault."

"Don't be stupid, Jill. That's just our cue. Come on."

I am stupid and it will get us both killed.

Jack lifted the bar away from the door they had entered and opened it. He led her out and helped her up the frozen steps. They looked over the edge across the snow and saw a wave of bodies filtering through the trees toward the building from all across the park.

"We shouldn't have been here together, Jack."

Jack patted her on top of the cap he gave her. "I got this, girl. Take what you want from the sled and find shelter. Remember, more than one exit and no fires. I'll check in on you in a few days."

"What do you mean, you got this?"

Jack winked and stepped out into the snow. She reached for him, but he was gone. Steam rose off his scalp from the missing cap. He lifted a lighter and flicked it as he ran. He dodged past the sled and the dead followed him. The park cleared as the corpses weaved back into the trees.

Jill sighed.

One of the monsters rounded the corner and grabbed the cap off of Jill's head. She stepped away and slipped. Jill yelled as she tumbled down to the bottom. The creature took a step and tumbled down after her.

Jill pushed through the door and slammed it closed. She set the bar and limped to the center of the room holding her back. The fists pounded on two doors.

She started crying.

"I'm tired of being cold. I'm tired of being scared. I'm tired of being alone."

I'm tired of being alive.

She went to Jack's shelf and took down a can of lighter fluid. The can crinkled as she sprayed the top of a table. She dropped the can and searched the shelf for matches. She found another lighter instead. She flicked it open and locked it. Jill dropped it on the table and watched it go up.

She pulled off her gloves to warm her hands and saw the fingers of the gloves had caught. She tossed them into the fire and cried more.

Jill held her hands out and felt pain in the blisters.

She gritted her teeth. "I will be warm at least."

After several minutes, the bar splintered on the door behind her. The door burst open and all the dead that fell down the stairs stumbled into the cellar. She did not turn, but heard them regain her feet and crackle as they approached her and the fire.

I'll let them have my hair and my warmth and I'll be with my parents again.

She stared into the fire as the frigid hand closed on the shoulder of her coat. One finger slid past the collar and brushed her neck.

Jill pulled away and knocked over the table. A few of the bodies fell into the flame as she pulled away from the cold hand.

Jill ran for the third door and cast aside the bar. She barged out into the cold and held the rails to get back up to ground level.

As she ran through the snow between bodies without her gloves and without her brother's cap, she cried.

He is going to be pissed when he gets back and finds out I burned down his shelter. Stupid, stupid, girl.

Jill topped the next hill and saw the dead approaching from every direction.

"Time to tumble down."

She dropped to her knees and clawed at the snow on the hillside. Her hands burned with cold and the blisters split on her palms.

I'll have frostbite by morning.

Jill laid down on her back and pulled the snow over her. She packed the snow around her face leaving her mouth and eyes uncovered. She burrowed her arms under the blanket of ice and waited.

A grey-skinned woman in a sundress stepped up beside her and turned from side to side. Jill held her breath. Something down the hill caught the dead woman's attention and she went back the way she came.

Another creature passed from the other direction and walked out of sight.

Three more walked over her. A big man stepped on the edge of her arm. Jill showed her teeth, but he stepped off and kept walking.

Jill held her breath until her lungs burned. She breathed out a puff of steam and sucked in cold air again.

One of the corpses paused over the top of her in the dissipating vapor and turned in a circle. She held her breath until the creature walked away. Others followed passing Jill in the snow on both sides all going down the hill.

She lost feeling in her hands and feet, but she waited.

Another walked over her and knelt down in the snow.

Well, it was a good idea while it worked.

Jill closed her eyes.

The hands lifted her out of the snow. "Jill, burning down the house and burying yourself in the snow was not the plan."

She sighed and her teeth chattered, "I'm sorry, Jack."

He pulled her to her feet and she opened her eyes seeing smoke rising into the sky. "They are all going for the fire now, Jill. I'm thinking the answer is more heat instead of less. You may have figured it out."

She shivered. "I'm a genius."

Jack put his arm around her and led her through a break in the distracted corpses. "We're staying together, girl. I can't do this alone anymore."

"Okay," she said, "I'll carry your weight for a while, I guess."

Jack said, "Did you lose the hat again?"

She brushed the snow out of her hair with her throbbing hands. "Don't start."

Jay Wilburn lives in the swamps of coastal South Carolina with his wife and two sons in the Southern United States. He left teaching after sixteen years to care for the health needs of his younger son and pursue full-time writing. He has published a number of zombie stories including Loose Ends: A Zombie Novel and a zombie short story in Best Horror of the Year volume 5. His latest novel is Time Eaters. Follow his dark thoughts at JayWilburn.com and @AmongTheZombies on Twitter.

Sheltered

By R.T. Tandy

Eva had never felt cold like this. She'd been cold many times before, of course, but this was different. The cold she was feeling was more a physical force than a temperature; a cloying mist that seemed to permeate every part of her body. She felt she would instantly freeze if she stopped moving for even a second and be found like an ice sculpture, liable to shatter at even the faintest touch.

But she also knew that the cold was not the only thing in the forest she had to worry about. She powered over the snow-covered landscape, her long, boyish legs covering the rocky terrain as quickly as she dared move. Beneath the forest floor's white coating lay a myriad of holes and fallen tree branches, and she knew a misstep could mean a broken ankle or worse.

As she ran, she risked occasional glances over her shoulder, her ears strained for the sound of approaching voices over the rush of the wind. She knew she'd been no more than two hundred yards away from the men when they realized she had disappeared, but even with her head start and knowledge of the terrain she could not outrun a pack of trained soldiers for very long.

After a few more minutes, Eva felt her reserves of stamina begin to drain and her pace slowed. She wound down from a sprint to a gentle jog, her eyes scanning the area for a place to rest a moment. A little way off to the left there was a particularly large tree, its trunk three times thicker than that of its nearest neighbor. At the base of the tree was a small opening between its thick roots, and Eva ran gratefully towards it.

She dropped to her knees and peered inside, relieved to discover an area large enough to shelter in. She lay down on the freezing ground and pulled herself into the gap, turning on her side as she entered and tucking her legs underneath her. Inside the small opening it stank of decaying wood, but the snow had not managed to enter here and the thick roots provided shelter from the wind outside.

Eva lay silently for a while, her eyes and ears alert to the first hint of movement. After a few minutes of silence she began to relax, shifting her position to get more comfortable. The thin woolen coat she had managed to grab as she was forced from her home was scant protection when paired with her long white nightdress, its hem now muddied and damp. Such had been the panic and confusion she had not even had time to put on her boots, and the coarse socks she wore to sleep in were now soaking wet and rubbing terribly against her feet.

Of course, she'd known that they would come eventually. For weeks she had begged her father to flee the village and escape to Siberia, where many other Jews had managed to avoid the death squads and concentration camps of the Nazis. But her father, a tall, thin man with a mass of black, curly hair, had refused, feeling they were safe in the far flung corner of Poland where he and his whole family had lived for generations. As a fifteen year old girl, she knew that any counter argument she might make would not be taken seriously.

But her father's optimism had proven to be misguided, and they had come earlier that night under the cover of darkness, kicking in the doors of the small collection of houses one by one and pulling the occupants screaming from their beds. Eva had been sound asleep when the soldiers had entered her house, and she had barely enough time to register the sound of the door smashing open before she was being grasped painfully around the arm and yanked from her slumber.

The soldier who had dragged her out of the house was young, no more than eighteen or nineteen by the look of his smooth, unlined face. He stank of leather and sweat. Eva had tried to fight back, but the boy had been too strong. Once outside, she was thrown into a cowering crowd of people, the faces of those she had known her whole life mirroring the terror and revulsion she was feeling. As the rest of the houses were cleared other soldiers stood watch, their machine guns unslung and pointed directly at the group. Eva could still see the looks of contempt etched upon the faces of the young men who stood in front of them, ready to execute at the first sign of resistance. Even with the dark grey uniforms and shaven heads, it was the hatred in their eyes that had intimidated her most.

When the houses were cleared the soldiers began to sort the group, diverting the men into one truck and the women and children into another. As they worked their way through the mass of bodies her father pulled her close to him, as if he could somehow bind the two of them together and prevent their parting. Eva squeezed her father with just as much vigor, although she knew there was nothing either of them could do to stop the inevitable.

But as the same soldier that had dragged Eva from the house reached them and placed his hand on her shoulder, her father had suddenly leapt towards him, his speed catching the younger man by surprise. He struck the soldier hard and knocked him backwards, using the momentum to crash down upon him and pin him to the floor. As they struggled her father had turned to her and told her to run, his words feral and harsh.

She took off before her mind had fully processed what was going on, and was halfway towards the tree line before she heard the first shots. As she entered the forest her ears were filled with the sounds of gunfire, and she was showered with wood chippings as the bullets tore into the trees on either side of her. She kept her pace as she entered the forest, daring not to look back and risk seeing the death that was surely pursing her, and was enveloped by the darkness of the canopy.

Back in the shelter of the old tree Eva felt hot tears spring to life in the corners of her eyes. If her father had managed to avoid being shot as he wrestled with the young soldier, it was unlikely the Nazi soldiers would be merciful once they subdued him. He had sacrificed himself to save her, and she could not even to kiss him good bye. She curled herself into a tighter ball beneath the old tree and wept, her wracking sobs mercifully drowned out by the howling wind.

It was thirty or so minutes before Eva stopped crying. As a little of her grief began to subside, she became aware of how cold she was; the heat she had generated while moving had long since dissipated and her wet clothes hugged her thin frame uncomfortably. She knew that she had to move soon or she would continue to get colder, eventually succumbing to a wintery sleep that she would not wake from.

She forced herself to shift position, her stiff limbs protesting every motion, and made her way to the opening. Cautiously she moved her head out of the gap and looked around, eyes peeled for any sign of movement. Once convinced that the area was clear she eased her way slowly out from beneath the tree and into the cold air. The temperature had dropped even further since she had entered the shelter, and she hugged her arms close to her chest for warmth. She had been in these woods a thousand times before and knew the layout well, and it only took her a moment to get her bearings before she set off in the direction she had been running previously.

But it only took a few minutes of walking for Eva to see the folly of her plan; the nearest village was twenty or so miles away and a day's walk in good conditions. With no shoes and the temperature dropping every second, she knew that she was unlikely to make it before she succumb to the cold. Wrapping her arms around more tightly around her chest she let out an involuntary snort of laughter; how ironic it would be that she escaped death at the hands of the Nazis only to perish in her attempts to flee. But even with this knowledge she pressed on, the flame of defiance that burned in her chest forcing her forward. She would rather die out here a free soul than in some terrible camp, imprisoned on all sides by ignorance and fear.

Eva had been walking for an hour before she paused again to get her bearings. She was sure that she had strayed from the snow covered path some time ago, and while she knew the general direction of the village she did not know exactly where in the vast forest she was.

Although there was still two or three hours before sunrise the moon was hanging full and high above her, and its rays were reflecting off the fallen snow, illuminating the forest as if it were sunset. As she stared ahead, Eva was struck by the complete silence around her; the cold had driven all the animals into shelter, and the carpet of snow beneath her feet was serving to muffle any and all sound. Her breath hung in front of her in semi-transparent clouds, and even in her present condition she could not help but marvel at the beauty around her.

But even the perfect view could not take her mind off her peril for long, and soon she had set off again in the direction she knew salvation potentially led. This time she had been walking only a few minutes before she stopped again, although this time it was not through exhaustion or appreciation but superstitious dread as she realized where in the forest she was.

In front of her stood another huge yew tree, even bigger than the one she had taken shelter beneath. It was over seventy feet tall, its thick trunk disappearing into the sky above her. Curiously the tree had only two branches, each one placed around fifty feet up and stretching out nearly twenty feet on either side. This strange configuration gave the tree the appearance of a crucifix, an impression that was further enhanced in winters such as this when the elements had shorn the tree of all foliage.

Shivering in a way that had nothing to do with the cold, Eva took a tentative step towards the tree. In her village the men had spoken about this tree in hushed tones, calling it the *bies*, or devil, tree. They said that the area in which the tree grew was a place where powerful darkness lived, and that anyone who dared venture into the shadow of the *bies* tree would never return to tell the tale.

These stories had terrified Eva as a child, and there was a time when she wouldn't set foot within thirty yards of the forest. Back then, her father had calmed her by explaining that as long as she stayed on the path when she walked she would be fine, as the tree lay in the deepest, darkest part of the woods. She felt fresh tears welling up in the corners of her eyes as she though back to this, a terrible longing to hear her father's voice piercing at her chest.

As she reached up to wipe her face, Eva became aware of a shift in the atmosphere around her. The hairs on the back of her neck stood on end, and she felt as if she was being watched. She cautiously glanced around the silent forest until a movement off in the distance caught her eye.

There appeared to be a figure stood watching her from behind a distant tree. She was too far way to make out the details of the face, and for one awful moment she thought that the Nazis had finally found her, but as she stared she realized that the watcher's clothing was much lighter than the grey uniforms the soldiers had worn. The figure did not move or make a sound but simply stood immobile, watching her silently.

Eva began to walk backwards slowly, her eyes fixed on the distant silhouette; although she was too far away to make out any details she felt a deep, supernatural dread. But as she retreated the figure suddenly moved behind the tree and out of her line of sight. Eva stopped again and stared, waiting for the figure to re-emerge. As the seconds ticked by and the figure didn't come back into sight Eva started to relax, willing her heartbeat to slow back down to a normal rhythm. Finally convinced that she was alone she turned and began to walk away from the tree, only to be stopped in her tracks by a sharp cry that rang out through the forest.

Eva spun in the direction of the noise, fearful that the figure had somehow gotten behind her, only to see not one person but a small group of soldiers. There appeared to be four of them, pointing towards her and trudging through the snow as fast as their bulky uniforms would allow. At the front of the group was a particularly fat man, his face red with the unfamiliar exertion, who appeared already tired of the chase. He took only a few steps more before raising his machine gun and opening fire at the spot where she stood.

The first rounds passed Eva close enough that she could feel the disturbances in the air, and she was once again showered in wood and debris as she dropped to her stomach. Scrambling on the floor like an animal in distress, she managed to turn herself in the opposite direction and took off, stumbling clumsily to her feet. Even as she ran she thought that this was the end of her race; she was exhausted and frozen to her core, and the soldiers were sure to catch her even with her slim head start. But still she ran, knowing that if she was caught her father's sacrifice would have been for nothing.

She leaned her head back and pumped her arms, caution thrown to the wind as she attempted to put distance between herself and her pursuers. But this speed came at the expense of awareness, and she was suddenly thrown through the air when her leading foot caught a fallen tree branch half-covered by the snow. Eva hit the ground hard, her momentum dragging her across the floor and covering her hands and face in cuts.

She tried desperately to get up but could not, her lungs fighting as she tried to replace the air that had been forced out of her chest. She heard approaching footsteps and a muffled cry before she felt herself being pulled to her feet. She lifted her head and looked up at her attacker, the same young soldier that had pulled her from her bed hours before. He was again gripping her on the upper arm, his strong hands squeezing hard enough to make contact with the bone. She began to struggle but he struck her hard across the face, causing a thin stream of blood to fall from her mouth. Confident she was subdued, the soldier turned his attention back towards the way he had come, waiting for his less athletic compatriots to catch up.

Although dazed from the fall and blow to her face Eva knew that she had only a few seconds before the rest of the soldiers arrived. She squirmed in the soldier's grasp and turned, pulling his arm up towards her face. She bit down on the hand that was holding her as hard as she could while swinging a leg in the man's general direction, and was rewarded for this effort as her foot hit the soldier between his legs. She felt the soldier's grip slacken on her arm as a hiss of pain escaped from his clenched teeth and seized her moment, wrenching herself free.

But this time she only made it a few feet before she heard the crack of the gun shot, and felt the terrible, burning agony in her shoulder. The force of the bullet pitched her forward but she managed to stay on her feet. Driven by agony and fear she tried keep going, but before she knew what was happening she felt herself falling again. She tumbled over the incline and hit the frozen ground hard, falling end over end to the bottom of the hill. She took the impact on her wounded shoulder, and had to exert all of her will to not cry out in pain.

Lifting her head, she saw a small cave entrance ahead, almost entirely obscured between a tree and a large rock outcrop. Knowing that this was her only option, Eva climbed unsteadily to her feet and began to limp towards the shelter, trying to stem the flow of blood as she moved so as to prevent the soldiers from tracking her. But despite her best efforts the wound could not be staunched, and dotted the pure white snow underfoot with specks of pure crimson as she ran.

As she made it to the cave's entrance she heard another shout from the soldiers, further away than the last. She was dimly aware that inside the cave might lurk hibernating bears unhappy that their slumbers had been disturbed, but in her present state of exhaustion and blood loss she was less inclined to worry about such trivial matters.

She walked into the semi-darkness, her senses alert to potential dangers both in front and behind. As her eyes adjusted to the gloom she could see that the cave ceiling was twice as tall as she was, but the smooth walls were very close on either side. Limping as best she could, she continued forward, hoping that there would be some smaller alcove ahead she could tuck into and avoid detection. As she moved deeper into the cave the darkness enveloped her, and once or twice she heard what sounded like scurrying noises ahead. She silently prayed that there was nothing larger than a rat accompanying her inside the pitch black cavern.

After two minutes of walking Eva became aware of a dim light source ahead of her, and she could feel a light breeze playing across her face. Quickening her pace she moved towards the light, noticing the passage widening slightly as she approached. Finally the light became strong enough for her to make out the details of the way ahead, and she was amazed to see snow lining the floor as she exited the passageway.

She found herself standing in what appeared to be a large sinkhole, the top of which was fifteen feet above her. The area was littered with small groups of rocks, and the whole area was covered in a thick layer of undisturbed snow. Feeling slightly lightheaded Eva smiled to herself, thinking that it looked like something from a story book. But as she gazed around she heard a movement to her left and turned, her eyes widening with terror as she realized she was not alone.

The figure that emerged from the shadows was almost human in appearance. It was dressed in a simple woolen shirt and trousers that had faded and dirtied with age, and the clothing hung from its painfully thin body. He (for Eva felt certain that the figure was a he) was not wearing shoes, and his feet and toenails were muddied and torn. But it was his face that terrified Eva most: the eyes, sunk deep into the sockets of his drawn face, were entirely black and magnified by the chalk-white pallor of his skin. His ears were slightly pointed at the top, and the cheekbones stood out prominently on his face, completing his half-starved bearing.

The creature stared at Eva as he approached, black gaze fixed upon her. Despite his emaciated appearance the creature moved lithely, as though poised to strike at any moment. Eva took another faltering step backwards and found herself pressed against the wall of the cave, sure that this was the same figure that had been watching her in the forest. She dropped her hand from her wounded shoulder and, eyes still fixed on the terrible creature, desperately searched the cave floor for something that she could use as a weapon.

The creature continued to approach her until he was only a few feet away. He cocked his head to one side like an inquisitive bird, and Eva felt as if the only thing that had stopped the creature from tearing her apart was his surprise that she had walked so willingly to her own death. For a long moment the two considered one another, hunter and prey, but as she stared Eva felt another wave of light-headedness, and she her legs gave way as she sank onto the cold floor. The creature flinched, as if intent to move towards her and finish her, but was interrupted by a shout from the forest above them. The creature looked in the direction of the noise and took a step backwards, snarling. From a standing start he leapt, clearing the top of the sinkhole and vanishing from sight.

Eva looked up at the spot where the creature had vanished, her brow furrowed with confusion. She tried to stand but could not, her legs no longer willing to support her. She weakly lifted her hand and placed it again on her wounded shoulder, more out of comfort than any medical benefit. Her shoulder was on fire, but despite the pain she felt dull-witted and sleepy. Above her she heard voices, two men talking. As she leaned her head back against the wall she heard a scream that was abruptly cut off, followed by a burst of gunfire.

Suddenly alert, she tilted her head to one side and tried to pinpoint the direction of the noise, but her confusion and the acoustics of the cave made it impossible. From somewhere above she heard more shouts, confused and frightened bursts of German she could not make out. There was another scream, this one slightly deeper in tone, and then a wet snapping sound that reminded her of the butcher's shop in the village.

She raised her head and tried to focus her blurring vision on the top of the sinkhole. But before she could bring the scene into focus, a large object fell from above and landed in front of her with a sickening thud. Eva pulled her legs towards her and huddled her back further into the wall, staring at the sudden intruder. The shock seemed to jolt some life back into her confused brain, and she let out a gasp as the object swam into focus.

Lying in front of her was the young soldier who had pulled her from her bed and shot her in the back. His right leg was jutting out at a strange angle, the bone clearly visible though the grey material of his uniform, and his neck and face were covered in deep, irregular scratches. He had landed on his front, and upon realizing that he was not alone reached out towards her. Eva shuddered as she realized that the hand that he stretched out was missing two of its fingers.

Eva remained pinned against the wall, a mixture of revulsion and fear keeping her motionless. The soldier was mumbling to her as he reached, and despite her situation she could not help but feel sympathy. The clear blue eyes that had once held such hatred were now filled with terror and confusion, and she knew that his thoughts were a mirror of her own, a crushing sorrow at the prospect of death far away from the ones they loved. Eva heard another thump to her left and turned to see the creature before her once more. She tried to speak, to make some contact, but he did not turn his head; his attention was focused on the broken soldier that lay in front of her.

Following her gaze the soldier turned, his mumbling turning to plaintive cries for mercy as the creature began to close in on him. The soldier managed to turn on his back as the creature approached, desperately clawing at the ground in a doomed attempt to drag himself away. The creature watched for a moment, impassive, and then, without warning, leapt at the soldier, landing hard on his chest. Grabbing a handful of hair the creature pulled the boy's head to one side and bit down on the soft flesh of his neck.

Eva watched in horror as the creature seemingly latched onto the soldier like a leech, his throat working as he drained the body of blood. At one point the creature paused and lifted his head towards her, exposing its gore soaked face and open mouth, each one of the dozens of irregular, razor sharp teeth stained claret.

As the creature continued to feed, his focus seemed to shift entirely to the corpse of the soldier. Knowing that this might be her only chance to escape, Eva pushed herself to her feet, her back squared against the wall for leverage. She only managed two steps before her legs gave way again, this time pitching her head first onto the ground.

Her wounded shoulder took much of the impact, and she let out a scream of pain that echoed around the cave. She rolled onto her side and stared back at the creature, who had thrown the drained body to one side and risen to his feet, watching her closely. As she tried to lift her head her vision began to blur, and she felt a feeling of lethargy overtake her once again.

The sensation of warmth running down her back and chest told her the impact had reopened the wound, but she could no longer raise the energy to stem the flow of blood. Eva's head dropped down to the floor as she watched the creature walk towards her, and she felt an unexpected feeling of warmth begin to spread through her body. As her eyelids fluttered shut and the darkness enclosed her, her last feeling was one of flying through the air, and she smiled at the prospect of seeing her father again.

When Eva awoke briefly two days later, she was shocked to find that she was not in heaven, but a large truck surrounded by people she had never met before. The wound on her shoulder had been attended to and dressed, and there was not a Nazi uniform or monster amongst the people she was travelling with. Content that she was in no immediate danger, she immediately fell asleep again.

When she awoke again a few hours later, she was quickly plied with food and water. As the days stretched by Eva began to regain her strength. She was able to sit and converse with the other occupants of the truck, soon coming to recognize many of their faces from the trips she had made to the next village with her father. Once they were satisfied her wound was healing, the villagers wasted no time in recounting the tale of how she had come to be in their midst.

When news had come that the Nazis had been spotted in the area, they decided they could not stay any longer. The one truck in the village, owned by a local coal merchant, had been loaded with provisions, and the villagers prepared to leave the next day. But when they came to the truck the next morning they were shocked to find Eva neatly laid out in the back, half frozen and covered in blood but still clinging to life. Assuming that she had somehow escaped the Nazi cull they had taken her with them, patching her up and keeping her warm as they made their escape through the mountains in the rickety vehicle.

Eva had listened to all of this with an open mouth, for she could not recall anything after she slipped into unconsciousness in the cave. For days she fervently questioned every one of the villagers, desperate for some answer as to how she had gotten there, but none of them had seen any trace of the mysterious figure she described. Although many of them confessed to having heard the stories of the *bies* tree none could imagine a scenario where the monster she described would have done anything other than tear her apart, and dismissed her claims as fever dreams brought about by the extreme cold and loss of blood.

And yet, as she rode out the rest of the journey in reflective silence, Eva knew that the villagers were wrong. The creature was real, and for reasons unknown had not only spared her life but saved it, carrying her to safety. She did not know his motives but at that moment, wounded and starved but still mercifully alive, she was just grateful that he had chosen to act as he did.

Eva saw out the remainder of the war in Serbia, eventually returning to her old village a few years later. She had the option to remain amongst the people she had come to count as family, but she knew in her heart that the village was where she belonged. The others who had survived and returned welcomed her warmly, praising her hero of a father who had given his life so that she and others who had taken advantage of the confusion he caused could escape.

And there she remained, living out the rest of her life in the contented isolation that such a place could bring, making herself a part of the community and never speaking of her experiences. Every year, on the anniversary of her father's death, she would bake a loaf of his favorite bread and leave it on the spot where he had died, a silent offering to the sacrifice he had made.

There was also a second, less understandable tradition that Eva observed each year on that day. After leaving the loaf of bread, she would lead a small goat or sheep into the woods, straying from the path into the darkness, and not returning until many hours later. When she did eventually emerge, remarkably unscathed, the animal was not with her and no trace of it was ever seen again. Her fellow villagers would often remark darkly about this, muttering about the *bies* tree and the evil that lurked around it, but Eva ignored them; she felt that whatever the creature was, the fact that it had saved her life was proof that it was not the monster people though it would be. Besides which, she knew that whatever demons might lurk in those woods, true evil did not have fangs or talons: just hatred in its eyes.

Ryan Tandy is a writer working in both traditional fiction and graphic novels, and his short stories have previously appeared in Another 100 Horrors, Ugly Babies: The Anthology and E4's Frightfest *magazine. He currently lives in Cardiff, Wales with his fiancée Sarah and their slightly demonic cat Kaylee. Follow him on Twitter @TheTandyMan*

Coffin Dirt

By Tom Wescott

Dearl Strongfellow stood at the open door of his cabin, trying to think of a better way to die and coming up empty. His eyes had grown numb to the whiteness, indifferent to the pain. If the snow didn't get him he had every confidence he could think up something that would. He certainly wasn't lacking in motivation.

But Death in all its forms would have to be patient with Dearl if only for a little while longer. He still had a job to do.

Tyson is his son.

-was-

Tyson was his son and he had only been dead a week. The freeze had come in quick and heavy, the snow not helping matters much. In all his years - fifty-four of them at last count - Dearl had never seen anything like it, though he'd heard stories from his grandfather of what mountaineers of his day called a "bullet freeze": a freeze so isolated and sudden that a man could feel his own blood turn to ice, could hear his skin crack and break open at the joints, and could die without even falling down. And according to Grandpa Jonesy, that's just what happened to poor ol' Harley Jessup, out tracking deer and just never you mind when the frostbite sunk its pearly whites into him. The freeze lasted only a few short hours but that was time enough to make a charity-case widow out of Mrs. Jessup.

Jonesy (he hated it when Dearl called him Grandpa) and the other boys from the peak had to wait two days for the snowfall to clear before they could posse out. When they found

Jessup, "as stiff as a dime-totin' sailor with a ten-penny whore", they'd at first mistaken him for a snowman. A human-shaped mound of white standing tall in the middle of a field. *Slap a coupla pieces of coal over his eyes and a good fat button for a nose, and youda had yourself one jolly happy soul. And that woulda been a first for Harley Jessup, damn fool that he was.*

Harley had been affectionately named "Rubber Lip" by some of the men for his penchant to stuff his face with enough long cut tobacco to give an elephant trunk cancer. It was a habit that - much like the man - died hard, and from the looks of him once they'd managed to chisel enough ice and snow crust off his head (along with an earlobe, courtesy of Charlie "The Hammer" Conley, a carpenter who'd retired early from his trade for all the wrong reasons), ol' Harley had been in mid-spit, his lips puckered over a brown-speckled yellow icicle. But it were his eyes that seemed to stay with Jonesy the longest and pinch the hardest. He would mention that moment to Dearl sometimes when the gloom came over him. It wasn't often, but often enough.

A man sees a lot of death in his time, Dearly, and it ain't never a happy thing, even lying down. But when it stands up and looks you in the eye... I'm telling ya...something in ya just gives a little, and there ain't no puttin it right once it does.

Dearl stepped back from the threshold and closed the door. He hadn't conjured that memory in over 30 years until this week. And why should he have? They don't have bullet freezes in Butler, Missouri, where his father had taken him to live when they moved from the peak. He was eight then, four years younger than Tyson.

Tyson.

The chill from the open air had left him now and gone along with it was the good part of him. The safe part that lived in a world where Jonesy still rocked in his hand-whittled chair and spat crusty nuggets of random wisdom; a place where people like Rubber Lip Jessup and Hammer Conley still paused to tip their hats and say Hello and distract his mind from whatever it was that made it seek distraction. People he called family and people

122

he never knew. People long dead. And that's what made the world of his distant past and Jonesy's far more colorful life – relayed to him on the air of stale beer and plastic teeth – so inviting.

So safe.

Dead people can't hurt you. They've left the big world and now reside only in the little world of your mind, where you're God and you can pull their strings and make them come to life if you want, or set them in a corner until the next time you need that little something they bring. You can edit out the bad stuff and keep just those shining moments. It doesn't always work that way and sometimes a piece of the bad will pop up and stick a needle in your brain. But that's okay, because sometimes you need that.

And besides, they can't hurt you. Not these people. People dead long years.

That's the world Dearl left behind when he shut the cabin door. The world he now faced was his here and now and it was all too mortal. Tyson had only been dead a week. Not long enough by near to grow strings.

Dearl reached into the rickety closet that had once housed Grandpa Jonesy's hunting arsenal and pulled out an old pair of snow shoes that he and Tyson had found their first week in the cabin. He remembered how Tyson laughed and called them "clown shoes" and that one hurt more than a little. But he dropped them in front of the couch and sat down. He still had a job to do.

As he bent to strap on the snow shoes his eyes glided along the old worn wooden floor, past the discarded whiskey bottles that had been his diet for the past week and up to the door he'd just been standing at and where he had last caught sight of Tyson a week ago this day. He blamed himself. How could he not? It was his idea to bring Tyson to the cabin. He wanted to share a piece of his childhood and the generations of family that came before on Ratchett Peak.

Tyson had been eight when his parents divorced. Or more to the point, when Dearl's wife Rachelle had taken Tyson in the middle of a work day and fled to an already furnished apartment across town. Their marriage had been dead for some time but she made it perfectly clear to Dearl that it was his drinking that forced her to leave. She couldn't have Tyson around that.

It was the wake-up call that Dearl needed and it saved his life. He hadn't touched a drop since. Not until last week when the cabin fever hit him. But that hadn't stopped Rachelle from moving Tyson 300 miles away last year to live with her ailing mother. He understood Rachelle's obligation to her mother and her desire to take care of her in her final days, and he understood her unwillingness to let him keep his son. But he knew it wasn't a good environment for the boy. He was too young to watch someone he loved die. He could hear it in his voice when they spoke, read it in his words when he wrote. Something in the boy was changing.

He had planned on a week in the cabin with Tyson but the weather had made other plans and the harsh snowfall on the peak made it impossible for them to leave. There was no Internet, no telephone, no neighbors, only vast fields of white dust and iced trees and all the time in the world to grow either closer to or further away from his only child. Something inside Dearl chose the latter when he discovered the bottles of whiskey he'd left at the cabin on his last visit many years before.

There had been a bullet freeze on the last night of Tyson's life. Tyson had tried to talk to him about something but he was two bottles in and three sheets to the wind and passed out without hearing a word. He woke to the sensation of his nose freezing and realized the cabin door was open. Standing there in his blue cotton-knit sweater but with no other protection from the cold was his son, droplets of snow collecting at his feet.

Dearl's eyes met Tyson's. At least they looked like Tyson's, but there was something extra there. Or maybe there was something missing. He couldn't tell which and it no longer mattered when Tyson shut the door behind him and ran from the cabin. Ran from his father and into Death. Dearl couldn't understand how it was possible to run in such hard snow, but there was no sign of the boy when he stumbled to the door to look out.

In only the moment it took for his eyes to scan the moonlighted landscape Dearl felt his moist, blood-engorged eyes begin to freeze. He knew he wouldn't make it more than five feet from the cabin before he'd end up like ol' Harley Jessup, damn fool that he was. He wanted to run out and find Tyson with every fiber of his worthless being, to bring him back inside before it was too late. But somewhere deep he knew it was already too late, and deeper than that, at his primal core, there was even a part of him that did not want to die along with his son. Dearl was surprised to feel the pulse of his survival instinct, to realize he even still had one. But he obeyed it and closed the door.

That was a week ago now and all that remains are the pain and the dreams. Pain really isn't the right word but it will have to do since no word has ever been invented that could explain the feelings of a man who continued to breathe air when his son no longer had that right. It's a kind of disembodying anguish that works to erase everything around you, leaving you only your two eyes, and even those don't see like they used to. Instead, they turn around and stare inward, into the space that was behind them but is now all around them. It's the place where horror goes for Winter and it's the only thing you've got left when you let your own kid kill himself. It's a kind of numbness, and anyone who tells you numbness can't hurt, can't kill, is just pissing in the wind.

And then there are the dreams.

The pain was excruciating – a hell in his own mind – but Dearl could understand it. Could make real sense of it. But the dreams were not so mercifully disjointed. They were like a film, only with texture. They were a kind of reality, but couldn't be real, because in his dreams Tyson was alive. He was standing beyond the trees many yards from the cabin, staring back. Just standing and waiting (for what?).

Dearl couldn't make out his son's face in the dreams and that was no small mercy because a week out in this weather changes you something terrible, and to see his son before he was ready

(somethin in ya just gives a little)

might be all it would take to cave his mind in

125

(and there ain't no puttin it right once it does)

and then he'd never get the job done. The job of bringing his son home.

Dearl knew this moment would come. The moment when there'd be nothing else to distract him, not even himself. He put on every sweater within reach, most in varying degrees of stain – blood and tears, mostly, and only a little food. Even after almost a month in the cabin food was not a problem. There'd be enough to last all Winter if necessary, but Dearl had little use for it. It just didn't seem right, is all. His son was dead.

He now stood at the open door of his cabin. It was no longer cold enough to freeze his face on sight and the last snowflake had hit ground zero at the same moment Dearl had drained the last drop of liquid lightning two nights before. The sky was clear and the moon high, allowing him to see almost to the tree line. As calm as everything appeared on the peak, he knew it was waiting out there for him. The snow, that is. That and maybe something else.

Something more?

Tyson? No, that's impossible.

He stepped out onto the porch and from there he placed his foot where he was pretty sure the porch ended and the earth - buried untold feet under the snow - began. He found the uppermost layer of snow, though not fully crusted, supporting enough, and he thought of how tragically suitable it was that all should come to an end here, where his family had lived for generations. His father had been the first to move from Ratchett Peak and seek a life less white in the city, although he never cut his ties and sold the cabin, just as Dearl could not bring himself to do. Tyson would have been the first.

His father, an educated man who often found joy in speaking over the heads of others, referred to snow as "the Great Equalizer", a saying he'd probably culled from some great book (like most self-proclaimed intellectuals, Henry Strongfellow was utterly unimaginative). It was years before it finally clicked in Dearl's brain what his father had been saying. It was the same as what Jonesy had told him, only harder to comprehend. His father was telling him that all things died an equal death in the snow.

And that was Nature's intention. It's not a Winter Wonderland as the song goes. It's Great White Death.

Nature with teeth.

Dearl would marvel at the people he worked with in Kansas City, celebrating the coming of Winter with festive sweaters and faux snowmen in their yard. At first snowfall their eyes would light up and their mouths would flex with endless "Ooohs" and "Aaaahs" as they watched everything around them lose its color. They would turn to each other and remark on the beauty of it all. When they'd look to Dearl, he'd turn away, as people who know both the truth and that they're in the minority for recognizing it are wont to do.

It's not that he didn't have the heart to tell them that God created snow for the sole purpose of killing off His own Creation, We-the-People included. That much was common knowledge - disturbing and often ignored knowledge, yes, but on the books nonetheless – and pointing it out would only have made him look like a Scrooge. No, the real reason he kept quiet was that he didn't want to kill that gleam in their eyes. He didn't detest their naiveté. He envied it.

Dearl knew he was only distracting himself from the task at hand by letting his mind wander. But the trees were still some distance away and somehow he knew that's where he'd find Tyson (*waiting?*), so he saw no harm in letting himself step into another world in the few moments he had left to himself. And in his head he pulled the strings of one Christine Markland, a young woman who'd come to work at his office following his divorce from Rachelle. She had astounded Dearl with her enthusiasm over what had always looked to him like so many dehydrated potato flakes.

She told him, in a girlish tone that was far louder than necessary (but fine just the same because talking so loud made her cheeks blossom rose red under a set of eyes so blue you could only call them peculiar and you stood an inch taller than your driver's license said you could every time they picked you out to look at) that she'd come from California during the summer and had never seen a white Christmas. Dearl wanted to kiss her but more than that he wanted to tell her that where he came from a

127

white Christmas was the stuff of nightmares, not dreams, and that a man could die spittin' or shittin' and still be doing the same when his buddies found him two days later. But he didn't tell her that. Standing there, her cheeks flushed cherry over peaches and cream skin, she looked just like the first girl he'd ever loved. The only one that hadn't broken him in some way.

Wanda, Dearl thought to himself. *Why...I hadn't thought of her in years until Christine. And then not since. Wanda... Wanda Bailey.* The trees were bigger now, or at least that's how they had appeared to Dearl. He was getting closer.

Wanda was the daughter of Patrick Bailey, a man Dearl's father bought seed from when they had the farm outside Butler. Dearl had only been nine at the time and he would have stuck his tongue out and yelled "Blah!" if you'd accused him of being smitten with little Wanda. But he would've blushed, too, because it was the truth.

He'd occasionally ride along with his father on weekend errand runs, but it was an unspoken agreement between them that he'd always ride along when the seed was low and he knew Miss Wanda would be chasing shadows from her porch swing, smiling that smile, and all the while giving Dearl that strange feeling he couldn't quite understand, where he felt both self-conscious and take-on-the-world confident at the same time.

Wanda had been eight during those months and would have been nine in January. But they'd had a very white Christmas that year. And a very wet one as well. One day her father left a shovel leaning up against the porch while he went inside to get a cup of coffee and say a few words to the Missus. Wanda's first intention had probably been just to move the shovel to get to her swing, but a spirit got into her then and instead of setting the shovel aside she lifted it over her head and aimed it toward the long, jagged spikes of ice (Nature) that hung down from the awning, making the porch look like a giant, gaping mouth (With Teeth) waiting to swallow her whole.

She aimed it and she swung. She swung and swung and swung. And then it happened. And that must've been when she dropped the shovel because it was the noise of it hitting the porch floor that brought Mr. Bailey running. He told the investigating

128

officer that when he stepped out onto the porch he saw his little girl standing as if at attention, staring at him, her lips pouted in shame and a giant icicle darting out from where her left eye should have been. She told him that she'd hurt her eye as if she expected to be punished for it.

He took hold of her by the shoulders, careful not to jiggle her too much lest the ice dagger shift inside her head and do God knows what. He eased her onto the edge of the porch swing, all the while having her hold the icicle in place, and called for her mother who went into tornado-siren hysterics the moment she caught sight of her well-mannered daughter, sitting there all prim and proper, with eight inches of hard water sprouting from her eye socket.

Mrs. Bailey went to pull the ice out but the Mister would have none of it. He'd heard that pulling a knife out of a man's gut when he's stabbed is akin to pulling the proverbial cork from a dam and he thought it best not to be too hasty.

There was no 911 in those days and Patrick Bailey (who would've been the right man on the scene if his daughter had managed to lodge a knife in her gut instead of ice in her eye) wouldn't hear of putting his little girl into the rusted old truck for the bumpy run across town to the hospital, not when Doc McGurdle could be there in fifteen minutes. Only Doc McGurdle wasn't there in fifteen minutes, and by the time he'd arrived on the scene - toupee crooked and shoes unshined - almost a good half an hour later, the only thing left for him to do was witness Wanda's final, convulsive moment, record the time of death, and spend the next six months trying to get a good night's sleep without being haunted by Mrs. Bailey's howls of anguish. Noises he didn't think possible from a human being, but had been possible, and were now recorded for posterity somewhere in the darker recesses of his mind where it seemed something had its finger waiting (*always waiting*) on the PLAY button whenever he turned out the lights.

And then there was the look on Mr. Bailey's face when Doc told him – *had* to tell him – that it was his own actions that had killed his daughter. That the icicle had not hit any nerves going in, which was why the girl felt so little pain. That if he had removed the icicle immediately the blood would have been minimal and easily controlled. That what killed little Wanda was his leaving the ice in her head to be melted by her own blood and body heat and that it was this water which seeped into the wrong hole and drowned the poor little girl's brain.

Doc McGurdle took a well-deserved holiday following the funeral only to be called back to work when Patrick Bailey's body was wheeled into the mortuary. He'd taken his rusted old pick-up truck out to the middle of his pasture and ate a bullet. The shovel that had been Wanda's last toy was found on the seat beside him. Dearl's father had to drive an extra fifteen minutes outside of town after that to get seed anywhere near the quality of Bailey's, but Dearl couldn't tell you where he got it from because he no longer went along.

Wanda wouldn't grow strings and come alive inside of Dearl's brain for a good forty years, not until he met Christine Markland. Like Wanda, she'd dreamt of a white Christmas; like Wanda, she got it; and like Wanda, she wouldn't live to see it again.

When Dearl heard the news he wished he'd told Christine what he knew about Winter. What he knew it could do to people who loved it. Maybe then she would have taken her time crossing that bridge, would have seen the black ice in time, and would have had a holly jolly Christmas and not a closed-casket funeral. And perhaps, at some point much later on, Dearl would have asked her out and maybe said something funny and she would have laughed. Perhaps. Maybe. If only he'd met her in the summertime.

Dearl traipsed across the endless field of snow, hoping to see some sign of his dead son and dreading the moment when he would. He thought of Tyson, buried under a blanket of Winter, and all of a sudden there was Jonesy again, sitting by the fire in his hand-made chair, smoking a hand-rolled cigarette and filling little Dearl's head with the kind of treasures you just can't buy, not even on eBay.

Jonesy was not what you'd call a TV grandpa – always ready with a smile, a pat on the head, and a bowl of Werther's Originals – he's that other kind of grandpa. The kind who just didn't seem to have a smile left in him, who didn't look you in the eye except to tell you what a pain in the ass you are and the kind you couldn't really appreciate until he was long dead and you could no longer pass for thirty. When Jonesy spoke of "respect" what he meant was "fear". And time and time again he'd tell Dearl how the Strongfellow men always made their life in the snow and gotten along well in it…because they *respected* it.

Dearl could only now see what his grandfather was saying all those years ago. It wasn't respect, because that's mutual. It was Fear, raw and ancient. And it occurred to Dearl that maybe that's why Jonesy spent so much time by the fire – because he thought that what he feared couldn't reach him there.

Jonesy had a special word for the snow, a word Dearl couldn't recall just then as he continued in a straight line from the cabin that shrank in the whiteness a little more each time he looked back. Only a hundred more yards to the tree line, but then what? Then he'd find Tyson and maybe he'd learn the answer to the question that's been tearing him apart this last week – *Why'd you do it, son? Why'd you run out on me like that? Why'd you go and kill yourself?*

He'd looked for the answer all week in the cabin; looked through Tyson's things, looked for drugs, a note, an anything that could shed any light at all on why a normal, happy boy would want to freeze to death. But there was nothing to be found except the lingering scent of laundry detergent and the designer cologne that Dearl had given the boy on his twelfth and final birthday.

All he knew for sure was that something in Tyson had changed. Something more than growing pangs, more than puberty, and more than Dearl might be willing to comprehend. He'd seen it in his eyes that last morning, but he knew it before. He wanted to blame himself for it all, on how he nosedived off the wagon and into a bottle of whiskey that final night. But as much as he wanted to take the blame on himself, he knew that whatever had changed in Tyson had done so before that.

So he blamed himself for bringing Tyson up to the cabin in the middle of Winter. After all, they don't have bullet freezes in the city. But many fathers take their sons on such outings.

After all, Winter is for children (*I'm sorry to have to tell you this, Mr. Bailey...*), and he only wanted to share a piece of family history with his son. He tried so hard to blame himself, if only to gain understanding, but none of it was coming together.

Dearl heard a loud crack underfoot and was startled. It was the first noise he'd heard in what seemed like ages. He looked down to find he'd stepped on a frozen branch and only then realized he was at the tree line. The snow was beginning to fall again, not heavy but steady, and he realized his luck (*now there's a pisser!*) wouldn't hold out much longer. But he wasn't worried because he knew that he was nearing the end of his journey; that he would find what he was looking for and that it wouldn't be quite what he expected; that when he found it, something inside him would just give a little and there'd be no putting it right once it did.

He stepped under the first patch of trees and it suddenly grew dark, the moon not daring to enter with him. He knew that when he entered those woods, like his grandfather almost a century before him, he'd find a man, a *boy*, standing in the snow. He knew that what he was about to see would bear only a superficial resemblance to the boy whose happiness had been his only prayer. He knew that Tyson would be there, waiting.

He stepped beyond the first trees that stood like gate posts to a dead forest and he allowed the thought to enter his mind that in six months' time the woods would be alive again and he'd be dead. Funny how Nature chooses her company, abandoning the weak for the strong on a whim. A fair weather friend to the end.

And that's when he saw Tyson. It happened all at once after that. It couldn't have happened any other way, not really.

Dearl was about four yards from the tree that Tyson was hiding behind. He saw only a sliver of blue from the boy's sweater, but amongst the backdrop of white fluff and silvery-brown bark, it was a throbbing thumb. He approached the tree with caution, with dread, bracing himself for the sight of something less than Tyson. He expected his boy to look like Harley Jessup when Jonesy and the other men found him: skin a pale green, mouth frozen open to reveal the purple tongue and gums inside, glazed eyes that fixed on you and took a little something away. Everything except the tobacco spit. Of course.

When Dearl rounded the side of the large oak he found his son standing there, just as he knew he would be: waiting. He found him with his arms to his sides and his legs together, gently leaning against the tree. But he wasn't the horrible sight Dearl had prepared himself for. Not the gruesome image conjured up by Jonesy's tales. He was pretty. Impossibly pretty.

And then the dead boy blinked.

"Ty...son." Dearl said. But it wasn't his voice. The sound was hollow, echoing. You can't quite say which part of him it came from, but it wasn't his voice box, of that you can be sure.

"I'm okay, Dad." Tyson said in his normal tone. It was too normal, Dearl thought. It wasn't the voice of a boy who'd spent a week in a freezing blizzard that would've claimed a healthy man in a matter of hours, or even minutes if you count the bullet freeze. Those kinds of boys don't have voices.

"It ain't...it just ain't possible!" Dearl's voice was broken and raw, but now his own. "Aren't ya...cold?" he asked, knowing right away it was a crazy question, and not caring a speck, because under the circumstances there could be no other kind.

"It's not so bad out here, Dad. You just never saw that before. But I'm glad you're here."

He sounded so mature, so alive.

"I...I can't..." Dearl choked, unable to find the words or the air to make them real if he did.

"I love you, Dad. I love you to cinders."

"Oh Jesus...my...oh my God...*my boy, my boy*." Dearl was weeping now, hard and tearless, the chill air having parched his eyes. He faltered, grabbing a tree branch to steady himself. He still hadn't touched his son.

"Aren't you going to say it back?" Tyson asked, once more the innocent boy.

"I...love you too...son. Love you to cinders." Dearl replied, meaning it now more than anything he'd ever said in his life and weeping harder when he saw it had made Tyson smile. It was a little saying they'd shared for as long as he could remember.

"I'm sorry I ran out, Dad. I'm sorry if I made you sad." It was the understatement of the year and it came from a dead kid.

"But…why?"

"I had to go. If I didn't go then, I never would've, and then I would grow up. I couldn't grow up, Dad. Not in this place."

Dearl wasn't sure what his boy was talking about – didn't have a clue, in fact – but he knew that by "this place" Tyson did not mean the cabin, or even Ratchett Peak. He meant the world. Somehow he knew *that*.

"I'm sorry I drank. I didn't know…"

"It's all right. You didn't do this, Daddy. It was something in me that hurt, and it's been in me a long time. It hurt so bad I had to stop it and it had to be soon before I…went bad. I just couldn't let myself…"

"Grow up." Dearl said, finishing the boy's sentence so he wouldn't have to hear him say it. "But why, Tyson? Aren't you happy? Why don't you want to…grow up?"

"I am happy. I mean, I love Mom and I love Gramma. But Gramma's dying, only she's doing it real slow and Mom'll go into her room, and I'll hear 'em talking. Mom'll say something funny and I'll hear Gramma laugh. It hurts her to laugh, I can tell it does, but she does it anyway. And when Mom comes out she's always crying, like it hurts her too. And it shouldn't be a sad thing, making somebody you love laugh."

Dearl couldn't quite grasp what he was hearing, couldn't quite get his ears around it. He was hearing his son's soul. "Your mother loves your grandma, son. That's why she had to go down there. She wanted to be with her and do what she could for her. When you love someone like that it's always gonna make you sad to see them hurt. When you really love someone (*clownshoes, I'm wearing clownshoes*) even the good things can hurt."

Tyson nodded but he didn't speak. He already knew all this.

Dearl saw he knew it, but continued anyway. "Your mother's not cryin' cause she made your grandmother laugh, son.

134

She's cryin cause the day's comin' when it won't be there to hear."

Tyson nodded again. "And Gramma laughs even though it hurts because she knows Mom's gonna miss her. I know. And I don't want that...I think it would kill me, slow, like Gramma."

"But you don't know that, boy. Dammit, you're only twelve! There's a lot in life that ain't sad, I promise you that. And the sad things...well...you can get used to them over time." Dearl felt a pang then. He knew his words weren't completely truthful, but that wasn't what bothered him. What bothered him was that he knew there was some truth in them. Life is like a shirt you wear and there are some stains time just can't wash out, so you either learn to live with them or you decide to throw the shirt out with the trash. Dearl kept his shirt, Tyson threw his out. It was that simple.

"Too many people go bad, Dad, and they don't even know it. They get used to being sad and can't tell it from happy. That's when they go bad."

"It's not going bad, it's growing up. There's a difference." That was a lie. "I don't want ya dead, son. I'm not gonna live without ya." That was a truth.

Tyson looked away from his father and wrinkled his lips in a pouty pucker. It was a mannerism Dearl remembered from when the boy was eight and he'd managed to render the neighbor's cat unconscious doing his best Nolan Ryan during a particularly intense game of catch with the boy next door. The boy, whose cat played such a lousy outfield, thought it was hilarious, but Tyson had been devastated. He knew even then when something he had done was hurting someone else.

Tyson kicked at the snow and spoke the last words his father would ever hear him say. "I guess I love too much."

When he heard these words, something in Dearl just gave a little. Something that should have given a long time ago.

"You're the only thing I ever did right. Please know that." Dearl said, realizing that he no longer felt cold. He was in the presence of someone amazing, someone he loved. He knew that whatever this was, it wasn't an illusion. What he saw and what he heard was real. And it would be their last moment together. He didn't want to waste it thinking human thoughts. Instead, he gazed upon his son – *beheld him* – and spent those last few seconds truly appreciating him. Not as a memory, or a mind-muddled perception of Tyson. Just him, as he was. There was such poetry there. It was a moment Dearl would have called pure joy if he'd had a basis for comparison.

Tyson looked up then, his brown eyes no longer heavy, lips no longer pouty. He knew that his father, on some level, had come to understand what he did. Might even approve of it. He saw his face, possibly for the first time. There was no longer any sadness there, no regret. Tyson smiled. He smiled because he'd been able to give something back. That's why he had waited. He wanted to share what he knew and see his father's eyes when they weren't somewhere else, but right there. Right there in the moment he was living, seeing it for what it was and loving it. He'd taken away his father's stains and that made him happy. And he smiled beautiful.

The wind came fast then, icy and hard, and Dearl had to close his eyes against it. But before he did he caught a glimpse of the trees swaying, dropping their heavy white loads, and of the snow dust rising from the ground, kicking up dancing ghosts. And amidst this landscape of Winter come to life, he saw Tyson. He noticed that not a hair on his head had moved in the wind, and although Dearl had to once again depend on that well-placed branch for his balance, Tyson stood like a rock. Their moment, perhaps the only one that ever mattered, had passed. Standing next to the giant oak was his son as the earth knew him, and as the wind blew out and Dearl's eyes adjusted to this new image, he heard a voice. It was Jonesy again, lighting a little candle in his brain:

I can't tell you the number of men, Dearly, so don't ask. But there was too damn many. And it was me and the other men on the peak who had to dig them fools out of the ground come the end of frost. We'd be out there with our shovels from dawn until damn near dusk, plowin' away. It musta been quite a sight, the lot of us. But we did it cause we'da wanted the same done for us. And we did it because we knew em, and up here that means somethin'. We were all fools, you see, it's just we with the shovels, we'ze the lucky fools. It wun't the snow that was the headache; that went by easy like loose soil…it was the ice that was the pisser, cause that's where the bodies'd be, and then we'd have to bring in the pickaxe. You ain't never seen nothin so wrong-sighted, not in yer life. We was like gravediggers out there in a big graveyard that didn't make no sense. And we were diggin' through coffins to get to our buddies. That's what the ice was, a big coffin. And the snow? We called it –

Dearl remembered now. He remembered the special word Grandpa Jonesy had for snow, and all at once his mind lit up like Jonesy's fire and everything he'd ever felt, ever experienced, ever thought he knew but didn't, suddenly fit together and shined. He knew now what his son had been telling him, what he had given him, and he weakened under the burden of his new strength. But it was a nice weakening, one he could be proud of. Because he'd just seen love, and it wasn't a rose.

That God-forsaken rose.

Dearl thought of how we are trained from birth to see love as something tender, pretty, and fragrant: A Rose.

But what of the Thorn? If the rose is to be Love, it can't be taken in part, but must remain the *sum* of its parts. And that's what scares people so. The petals are a pleasant distraction, but they are simply a prelude. It isn't until you bleed that you know you've been there and that comes only after the wilting. And it's not until your eyes turn inward to that hollow place inside and ache at its very passing that you know you've loved. When a good thing ends, that's when the love, if it was ever there at all, truly begins. It was something his Grandfather had known, had feared, and it was what he was talking about when he told Dearl of the men he dug up on the peak.

"Coffin dirt." Dearl said. He thought it only right that it should be spoken aloud. Jonesy called the snow coffin dirt, and he was right, not because it's something morbid or unwholesome, but because it means love. It's God's way of taking you back and letting you know that you'll be safe with Him, in the same way that it's always the person who loved you most who throws the first handful of earth onto your casket when they put you in the ground. They're telling you that you'll be safe, that you were loved.

The snow *is* God's way of killing His own Creation, but only so it might come back stronger.

Dearl worked at the crusted snow that reached up to his son's waist, encasing him. This poor, sweet body would never grow another inch, but that no longer made Dearl sad. It was only his petals that had wilted.

When he'd burrowed down deep enough to see shoelaces he stood and wrapped his arms around his only child, pulling him close, breaking him free from the frozen ground. He kissed him then, just a peck on the cheek, and a piece of ice came loose and melted in his mouth. He didn't mind. And if the wind hadn't robbed his lips of their moisture he might have stuck to him, and that would've been okay, too.

Tyson weighed a ton as Dearl laid him down in the fresh snow. And when he crawled in beside him, wrapping one arm protectively around him and gripping a shoulder so unbelievably cold and solid, Dearl marveled at what he had learned. He saw the random moments of his life weaved into a patchwork quilt and handed to him by something so big he couldn't see it. He held that quilt up before his mind's eye and looked at each moment for what it was and wondered how he ever could have seen them as anything less than that. He wondered if someone he'd met during his life had taken something good from having known him and would let him come back to visit on those days when the shirt they're wearing seems almost too dirty to keep.

He wondered, when the men found them after the thaw, two corpses entwined, thawed and ripened, cinders in the snow, would they see the love in it? He doubted they could, as he couldn't before, but he hoped. Because there was so much here to see –

Love, for one. Dearl had seen love. An inheritance from his son. And it wasn't a rose.

Love is a shovel in the snow for someone you called a damn fool but loved just the same. Love is letting an icicle melt in your brain because the man who was your world said it had to. Love is watching your mother die and finding new ways to make

138

her laugh even though it kills you a little each time. And it is knowing when to let go because you love too much.

(and maybe, just maybe, it's the word for what people feel who keep on breathing even when their child no longer has that right)

Love is not just sitting by the fire because it keeps you safe, it's what comes at you when the fire has gone out. It's trying to think of a better way to die and coming up empty. It's when a good thing hurts. And if you know nothing else, know this: Love is not a Rose, it's a Thorn. It is nature with teeth, sharp and pointy, and it's not beautiful. It can't be. It is something more.

Love is the people in your head who won't stay dead because of that little something they bring you. It's the time that comes after Goodbye, when you're alone in your room and you learn how small you are, but you grow because you can't believe how much you feel. It is Fear, raw and ancient. It is the Other Side of Beauty, but can never be only beautiful.

Because it is something more.

Because it is so much more.

love is coffin dirt

Tom Wescott is an American criminologist specializing in the Jack the Ripper mystery. He has authored numerous original research pieces for journals such as Ripperologist, Ripper Notes, The Whitechapel Society Journal, Casebook Examiner, *and* The New Independent Review. *In 2014 he will publish two full-length investigative works related to the Ripper case:* The Bank Holiday Murders *and* The Berner Street Mystery. *He lives and works in Oklahoma.*

Fear of the Future

By Gareth Barsby

There was the graveyard and nothing else. There were no trees, no land beyond the iron fence and gates, only more of that slippery, thick fog oozing about. Though Mr. Mumford was more than old enough to know that cemeteries were supposed to be places of reflection and honor, he felt like a kid again, afraid such places were home of zombies and the bogeyman. Each of the gravestones was a blot against the white fog, complementing the monochrome area perfectly.

There. There it is, standing at the end there, black robe and all.

The Ghost of Christmas Yet to Come.

This was it; this was the final moment of his journey. This was how the story always ended. Though Mumford briefly wondered if he should feel glad about that, everything else that he had witnessed – his past, present and future – pounded in his brain. As he approached the Ghost, he saw his ex flash before his eyes. Her angry words as they broke up echoed through his ears. There was no one in the graveyard besides him and the final Ghost, and yet he felt the presence of the other two spirits, as if they had joined their friend. He found himself staring at two other graves, as he was certain the children of Ignorance and Want would be behind them. He heard the words of his ex again, but this time, he swore he could hear her laughter.

The Ghost stood perfectly still, except for the shaking of its skeletal hand.

It was pointing at a gravestone.

Mumford already knew what was on it.

He didn't need to look at the gravestone, yet the Ghost wanted him to anyway. It ceased pointing so it could grab by the shirt and force his face against the cold stone. There it was, there was his own name.

Of course it was there. He knew it was there and so did the Ghost. Yet he read his name thrice, he ran his finger over the letters, and scraped the ground with his foot to remind himself that he wasn't dreaming. It was real, it was all real.

A hand burst out of the grave.

And then another.

A whole array of hands – pale and rotting and skeletal and dead and all sorts of things – came out, and the fog cleared, as if making room for them. The hands rose, and their arms seemed to elongate, and one of them grabbed him by the ankle and then another grabbed him by the other ankle and then another wrapped around his neck.

Of course, he deserved it, didn't he? He deserved to be haunted. None of his employees got haunted, and that was because they worked hard and cared about each other. Not him though. Not Mr. Mumford. He was important and miserable enough that he required demons and ghosts from beyond to make him change his ways.

Another arm rose. Another long and skeletal arm that leapt up and grabbed him in the face, pushing harder and harder. Its fingertips were like matches, they burned his face, they burned his entire body.

Then the cemetery disappeared…no, it didn't disappear, it melted. It melted away into the void. The dark and empty and ever-growing void.

There we go. I show Mr. Mumford his unmourned grave, Paul got to help out with his "creeping hands" trick and I got the guy back to bed safe and sound. All in all, it's been a good night. Him breaking down into sobs when he first met me was the icing on the cake.

Paul turns back into his regular form – a nice little floating bedsheet – and I pay him for his services. You should

142

have seen the show he put on last year; he's a right Ray Harryhausen. Giant bleeding skulls, booming voices, whatever you can name, he can pull it off. The bigger the better, that's what it's all about these days.

I sometimes wonder if Charles Dickens writing about me and my kind was the best or the worst thing that could have happened to us. His book made people more aware of us, yeah, but it's been so exposed over the years – over the century – that it's hard to keep the whole thing feeling fresh. People have found ways to prepare for us – I had to deal with one bloke who kept going on about how "I've seen this all before". This means I've had to use more spectacle in my hauntings; more horror, more fear of God.

Not that I'm complaining; I love a bit of the kooky-spooky stuff, me. I'm the Ghost of Christmas Yet to Come, after all. Call me Diane.

So, with the Christmas Eve hauntings over and done with, I receive my payment and then return to the Spirit World and back to my house. Oh, everyone thinks that I live in a mansion and that I'm rich – "Don't you get royalties from all the Christmas Carol movies they make?" I like my nice little house though, wouldn't swap it for anything. It's got a lovely garden outside.

As soon as I enter, I lie on my bed, still wearing that tatty old robe I go to work in. Even though I don't need to sleep, I still have a bed; I use it when I want to think. When you do a job and you do it well, it's worth thinking about, isn't it?

So, what do I think about then? I just think about the good I've done. Old Mr. Mumford will treat his employees better, and he'll generally be a more popular person. Yes, he is going to change this time. I know humans. The way he spoke to me meant what I showed him really did have an effect on him. It's the first time in ages I can say that. Too many people have recently just dismissed me and Past and Present as a dream. Too many people have ignored what we said. I've been told to show these people the error of their ways and they don't see it.

It's a problem on their part, I think. One thing you learn in your old age – I'm older than I look? Thank you – is that some people never change. They're happy being mean. They're happy being evil. But then, why was I asked to haunt them then? I have been specifically told not to haunt certain people because they're unable to change, haven't I?

So is it me then? Someday, will they fire me and have some younger, more "with it" ghost in my place? No, they wouldn't. I know what's going on in the world; I've changed my techniques a bit over the years. Just like Santa, really. He's still around. He hasn't been fired. He's had new elves and new reindeer over the years, and he makes new toys too.

I take another look at my robe. Santa wears his red suit every time he goes out; the classics never die. My robe is a classic too, but I wonder if maybe I should try something different. Paul suggested that if I appeared as a horned, flaming demon, people would reform much faster. I can occasionally take on different forms, but only at Christmas Eve, when my abilities are at their strongest. I once took on human form one Eve just because there was a pub that looked nice.

Maybe I'll try it right now. I turn into a dog. My powers have weakened now that Christmas Eve is over so that's the best I can do. I shrink down into a little mutt and my robe shrinks down with it. That was fun. Back to my regular form. Back to being a human skeleton with eyeballs. That's how I was born, after all. I was never dead; I just formed as a skeleton because my intended role was to do with death.

That's the way spirits are. Despite my job title, I'm not a ghost, I'm a spirit. Different things.

With my thinking for the moment done, I take off my robe and into my casual wear. With my evening's work done, time to crack open my little Christmas gift to myself; a DVD set of *Breaking Bad* and a twelve pack of Carling. I don't need to eat to survive; I eat and drink for the fun of it. Likewise, I don't need to reproduce, but, oh, you get the idea.

There's a letter on the floor.

It isn't until I've watched one episode and had two Carlings that I notice the letter by my door. It smells like…at first I thought it smelled like dust, then I thought it smelled like cinnamon, then I thought it smelled a little like both. With a smell like that, I supposed that the letter was important enough to pause the DVD for a while.

I find myself picking up the letter slowly, as if I'm worried picking it up will trigger a trap of some kind. I almost feel like I need tongs. Digging my finger into the envelope, I pull out a letter.

An invitation to Santa's Christmas Day party.

One of those. I've been around for centuries and yet I've never been to one of those. Those parties are just for Santa and his happy little elves and his happy little reindeer and his happy little wife. It says "Diane" on the invitation, though, and it's addressed to me. Is it a trick? Those bloody elves invited me over so they could have a go at me. Bastards.

I've heard them. When I'm taking a break from my hauntings, sometimes one of them will come up and slap me or throw candy canes at me (I don't even like candy canes). "Go home," they say. "We don't want you out tonight." Because Christmas is supposed to be a time for joy and cheer, they say, there's no room for skeletons and graveyards. "We're going to give little Johnny a puppy," a reindeer said to me once, "That's going to give him Christmas spirit, and it'll teach him to be nicer more than sending someone into a grave would. You really think Christmas is the time for that sort of stuff?"

I've never seen or spoken to Santa though. I've lived – somewhat – for centuries and I've never spoken to Santa. I've had elves leer at me and reindeer give me the evil eye, but I've never spoken to Santa nor do I know what he thinks of me.

So what do I think of Santa then? I can't really complain about him or what he does. He has a nifty job, all things considered, or maybe I just like the idea of giving toys to kids for free every year. Yes, I said giving. I like giving. I give lessons, don't I? I'm not sure kids would want a skeleton in their house, but at least they'd get stuff out of it.

I take another look at the invitation. It has Santa's signature on it and Santa's official seal. I know a fake when I see one, and this one is genuine. It wasn't the elves or the reindeer that invited me; it's Old Saint Nick himself. He wants me, the scary skeleton, in his house, celebrating with his helpers. Or maybe he wants to tar and feather me. He's had enough of me perverting his beloved Christmas, and now he wants to punish me once and for all. I've haunted my last miser; coal shall be the only punishment from here on end.

Wait, am I implying that I'm afraid?

I'm not going to the party because I'm scared of the reason I was invited?

The elves accuse me of giving fear instead of joy, and they're half-right. I do give fear, but it's good fear. It's like the fear of not passing school or the fear of God; it's the type of fear joy stems from. But I digress: I am the Ghost of Christmas Yet to Come. I don't get scared, I make people afraid.

Christmas Eve is gone and the 2013th Ghost of Christmas Present is dead, and thus my powers have weakened. Had I received the invitation earlier in the evening, I could have shown myself what could have happened if I had received the invitation and what could have happened if I had refused. Now I can't, so there you go.

I'm going to go to the party.

Then I'll find out why I had been invited for the first time ever.

Then I'll show them I'm not afraid.

Then if they do have a plan to punish or kill me, I'll foil it. Maybe I'll even expose Santa and his elves to the masses and they'll reject him and then maybe they'll make me the new Santa.

I really don't like how my mind works at times.

So anyway, I spend a lot of the following Christmas Day doing what I usually do on December 25th. I open presents from my friends – oh, Paul got me another bracelet, how nice of him – but then in the afternoon, I tell myself I am going to the party, and I am going to Santa's workshop. The invitation said that someone would come along to pick me up – I only have teleportation abilities on Christmas Eve – and I would let them.

I can't make myself look more "normal", so I'm going to the party as a skeleton. I'm a skeleton and proud of it – I'm going to wear my favorite dress, one that shows off my bony legs. I'm putting eye shadow near the eyeballs that bulge out of my sockets, and lipstick above my yellow teeth. Dresses, needless to say, fit me better than trousers do.

I take a look in the mirror. This is what's coming over to the North Pole. I'm not going to give two shits what the reindeer or elves think of me; I'm going to do what I do at all parties I attend. I'm going to drink myself silly, even if the drinks are going to be non-alcoholic. I'm going to dance like an idiot to the music. If I had hair, I'd swing it about.

I even have a little beer to compensate for how sober the party likely will be. With me in my black dress and black high heels and my pearl necklace and make-up, I have some more Carling and watch a little more *Breaking Bad*. If any of the characters in the show were real, I wonder if I'd be called to visit them.

Ding-dong. There he is. The guy who's taking me to the North Pole. I'll welcome him with open arms, the same way…well, the same way Fred welcomed Uncle Scrooge.

"Diane!" A reindeer with a giant grin on his face.

"OK, cut the crap" I say to him…yes, I can actually talk. I just do the silent act…oh, never mind. "What is this all about?"

The reindeer began wringing his hooves as he looked at me. "I suppose I should have expected that. Look, you've been invited because Santa wants you there. He doesn't want to hurt you, he just thinks he hasn't been giving you or your people much attention over the years, and he just wants a chat…oh, wait…" He scratches his head before he continues, "I actually suggested it to him, you know. My name's Randall, and I'm a big fan of your story."

Maybe it's the beer, but I laughed.

"So…" He's got a copy of the Dickens book right in his hooves. He's holding it out in my face. "Would you sign my copy?"

Part of me wants to check the book for any traps, but a greater part of me just makes me go to my bedroom and get out a pen. I write, "For Randall, Merry Christmas, Love Diane" and it doesn't snap shut or anything. He's smiling.

Outside is a miniature sleigh, and there, sitting right there, is my work colleague, Mark. The Ghost of Christmas Past. "Diane!" he calls out. His appearance changes every year – this time he's wearing a tuxedo and looks like Anthony Perkins – but I always recognize him.

"Mark!" I cry as I approach the sleigh, "How are you?"

"Can't complain," he said, "So, how about that Mumford guy? He had a messed-up childhood, didn't he? No wonder his girlfriend left him!"

"You should see what I had to show him," I reply as I get in the sleigh. "Paul really outdid himself, you know."

"Well, he's changed now," said Mark, "I thought he never would."

"Oh, you two," said Randall as he readied to pull the sleigh. "You're lucky. This year was a real photo finish for us." He sighed. "Another supervillain."

Oh yes. Every other year a supervillain invades Santa's workshop and tries to sabotage the operation, but then some hero bursts in and saves the day or Santa fights the villain himself.

"Dr. Detestable," said Randall as we began our ascent, "The old 'never got any presents so he doesn't want anyone else to get any'."

"Oh," said Mark, "If I had a quid for every time I've seen one of those."

"He sent in an army of robots all dressed like toy soldiers which all put us in nets, and just as he was about to pilfer the presents, old Captain Mighty himself popped in and beat him up. Managed to escape though, but I wouldn't worry about him. He was an idiot."

Dr. Detestable. I've heard about him and his plans for world domination. His many, many failed plans. Maybe people would take him more seriously if he changed his name, but when one of your plans involves trying to eradicate all the bunnies in the world, I doubt it.

We arrived in the North Pole in seconds, the time you'd expect given what Santa does, and looming before me is a mansion covered in icing sugar, fairy lights and giant gumdrops. The windows flash all sorts of colors, but I know the music and the activities in the house are all U-rated. They're playing "Jingle Bell Rock" though, and I always liked that song. I even dance a bit in the snow.

"Diane." Mark covers his face with his hand. "You can't go anywhere…"

"They want jolly people, don't they?" I reply.

"Come on," said Randall, smiling a weird smile. "Y-you two are guests of honor, d-don't argue…"

He leads us into the building, and sure enough, there's elves and reindeer dancing everywhere, soda instead of beer, and when I enter, all the party guests turn to me in silence, narrowing their eyes.

"Presenting," says Randall in a pseudo-authoritative tone, "Marcus and Diane, the Ghosts of Christmas Past and Future." I wave and grin. Yes, I can grin without lips. I can make my teeth go up and down to suit my mood.

"Who invited her?" "Doesn't she have a graveyard to be at?" "This is Christmas, not Halloween."

"Guys!" cried Randall, waving his hooves about, "These two help people who hate Christmas, like Christmas! You may not think they're jolly, but they…they have some jolly movies! You lot like Mr. Magoo, don't you? Mickey Mouse?"

One of the elves put up their hand. "If they're so great, why didn't they go haunt Dr. Detestable then, so he wouldn't set those robots on us?" The others all go "Yeah!" but who cares about them? At least their surprise meant that I wasn't invited here just to be persecuted.

"And a "Howdy-doo" to you too," is all I say, and I just go for the drinks. Coca-Cola and not a Carling or a Foster's or a Guinness to be found. What makes cola more morally acceptable than beer anyway? Cola rots your stomach…but then again, I don't have to worry about that, do I?

"OK then," says Randall, tugging at his antlers, "well, what about our movies then? Don't you remember The Lonely Yeti? There was a yeti who wanted friends to spend Christmas with him, but no-one did because he was ugly….and..." The elves seemed to leer the more at him, with Mark looking for the exit. "Then Santa gave him some friends and everyone learned that

Christmas is about accepting other people, as…as well as making friends, love, following your heart, being yourself…the birth of Jesus Christ…"

"At least the Yeti never sent anyone to Hell!" Oh, them. Always with the Hell. I've never sent anyone to Hell. They send themselves to Hell, don't they know that? And oh look, Mark just left. Don't blame him. Still, it's Randall the elves are attacking now, so they're ignoring me, at least. More cola for me.

"Stop this right now!" A voice shakes the entire house, the music is silenced and the elves stop their bickering. Randall won't stop fidgeting though. There stands Santa Claus, donning the classic crimson, his eyes blazing. "Diane and Mark are our guests."

"Mark just left."

"Oh," said Santa, scratching his neck. "Well, anyway, Diane, I would like to see you in my office." He eyes the plastic glass I'm holding. "I have liquor."

Out of curiosity more than anything, I follow Santa. Away from the main party room and down the halls lined with paintings of famous reindeer, miniature Christmas trees and poinsettia-patterned wallpaper. All bright, all colorful, yet I try to prepare myself for the worst. If something bad happens, I'll be prepared. If something good happens, I'll be pleasantly surprised. Then again, maybe I should be slightly optimistic since he mentioned liquor…

Oh, never mind. He pressed a button on his wrist and teleported us to a dark room. At least I prepared myself.

Turning around, I see another Santa, tied to a chair, gagged. Classic. There is no sound in the room except a small humming, and nothing else except for me and the two Santas. Though I know that I'm unable to feel cold, I get a very small chill. Those are rare.

"Ah," comes a voice. "I think my Robo-Santa is back now, and he's brought me my guest of honor!" The voice sounds like it has a lot of phlegm buildup. It makes the tied-up Santa – the real Santa – shake and mumble furiously.

A door slides open, and in walks…

150

"Dr. Detestable." A short man, looking about seventy or older, with frazzled hair erupting from the sides of his face. Coke bottle glasses rested above a red bauble-like nose, both of which accentuated the dark circles under his eyes.

I couldn't help but laugh. I laugh every time I see him on the news, I laugh every time I see his face on the Internet, and I laugh when I see him in person, even when he has me in his clutches.

"Stop laughing," he snorted, spraying saliva everywhere. "It's no longer Christmas Eve, so your powers have weakened. You can't show me the error of my ways now, so you have no choice but to stay here with me!" And then he burst into the good old fit of maniacal laughter.

I may not have much in terms of powers, but I'm still a skeleton, so I just detach my arm to get out of the Robo-Santa's clutches. "Nuh-uh," says Detestable as he pulls a remote control out of his pocket. The Robo-Santa lets go of my arm, as his own arm turns into a giant bazooka, aiming at the real Santa Claus. "Try anything funny, and Santa gets it!"

That's when the chill returns, even stronger than before. There are ways spirits can be made to die, and with all the times mad scientists and curmudgeons have invaded Santa's workshop, Santa has almost died in the past. A lot of his opposition have been idiots, but sometimes I find myself surprised that Santa hasn't died already. And to think, if he were to die because of me...

I sigh, and let Detestable escort me out of the room. "That's the spirit, no pun intended. You see that Robo-Santa? That was my little failsafe. Since my army of toy soldiers failed, I built him and had him invite you to Santa's party."

"And what do you want with me?"

"I'm glad you asked. You see, every Christmas Eve you go about making people think the way you think they should think. Well, next year," he said, leaping about in excitement, "You're going to be working for me, and you'll be making people think the way I think they should think!"

I must admit that's a new one. "So, are you going to brainwash me, then..."

151

"Don't be silly!" barked the Doctor, leaping up and down again. "If I had a brainwashing machine, I wouldn't need you." He then sighed, and I could sense some genuine disappointment. "Don't you know much I wanted to use the Robo-Santa to deliver mind-control devices to the kids? But no, I can't build one!"

"I'm sorry," I say, more or less by instinct.

"Enough!" yells Detestable, "You will haunt people and tell them to make me their king unless they want to suffer the consequences! If you don't, I'll have Robo-Santa kill the real Santa, and it'll be all your fault."

I am scared. I am actually scared of the short and stupidly-named Dr. Detestable. I'm actually scared of the elves and reindeer who slandered and accused me; what would they think if I indirectly led Santa to his doom? What would happen to me if I couldn't find a way to…I can't believe I'm about to say this…save Christmas?

There are much more powerful forces than I out there, and they are the ones who tell me who to haunt, they pay me for my services, and they punish me if I do anything wrong. Yes, I did things wrong when I was younger, and they punished me. I'd rather not talk about that, though. I'd prefer to think about it.

Then maybe I'd think of something that could help me.

"That's a good ghost," said Detestable as he escorted me to a cage. "Now sit there and don't come out until I say so. Don't worry; I'll have your two little friends in there soon enough."

"The Ghost of Christmas Present is born and dies on Christmas Eve," I tell him. Another instinctive thing; I always have to tell people that when they just see me and Mark together.

"Oh, all right then," grumbled Detestable. "I thought you'd be a little more impressed, actually."

"Why is that?"

"Because I'm not afraid of you."

I know a fake when I see one. "Oh really? Then why did you abduct me when I was at my weakest?"

"Well, to make things easier, you idiot."

"You've known about me for a long time, haven't you? You've always been worried that I'll pay you a visit and show what your future holds. You fear ending up like Scrooge, you fear no one loving you, and yet you don't want to better yourself. Or maybe you're just too stupid to fully comprehend my existence."

He doesn't even think of pushing the button on his remote. "What are you talking about?"

"Just think, if I exist, other ghosts must exist too. If they exist, then there must be an afterlife. What do you think will happen to you in the afterlife? You'll turn into an angel?"

He shudders a little. "Don't talk like that to me! I'm going to kill Santa right now!" He pulls out his remote. "Just keep your cake-hole shut and I may reconsider…"

"Don't…" I find myself grunting, "dare…"

This isn't Christmas Eve. That's when my powers are at my peak. When it isn't Christmas Eve, I cannot teleport, see the future or turn into anything more complicated than a dog. Yet right now I feel my form inflating into that of the blazing demon I became a couple of years ago for a particularly difficult case. Crimson-colored flesh covers my bones, horns protrude from my head, my teeth sharpen, wings even sprout out from my back.

Dr. Detestable pretty much pisses himself, then faints.

In a second, I turn back into a skeleton. I thought of detaching my arm again to get the key, but the guy left the cage unlocked. With him unconscious, I walk over to him and nick his remote, removing the batteries after I have it. Then I smash it under my foot, and drag Detestable into his own cage. Regular James Bond, I am.

Off I go to save Santa then. The Robo-Santa stands lifeless so it's just a matter of undoing his ropes and removing the gag. "I knew you would find the true spirit of Christmas!"

"Um, I did, I guess?"

"The fact that you were worried about me ignited your power!"

So that's what that was? Seen stranger things.

"You learned that love is more powerful than fear!"

"Actually, I knocked him out by turning into a giant demon."

"Really?"

"You didn't see that? If you can see children misbehaving…"

"Demons don't have anything to do with Christmas…"

"You go on about how bad fear is," I say as I help him up, "and yet you scare kids into behaving. They're good because they fear not getting presents. If they don't get presents, their reputation will drop among their friends and their parents will be disappointed. They fear that. What if they unintentionally misbehaved? They fear being known as a bad boy their whole life. The elves and reindeer work for you because they fear disappointing children and you, and they fear dying without accomplishing something."

As we try to escape, I find myself talking to Santa about my philosophies more and more, until a window crashes open, and none other than Randall comes in. "I heard a sound, saw a flash, saw you gone with a big black mark where you were, I put two-and-two together and here I am."

"Randall!" barks Santa, making the reindeer instantly jump to his hind legs and salute. "Do you fear me?"

"I think he just answered your question right there," I tell him. "He came here because he feared for your and my safety…"

"OK, OK!" said Santa, "I get the point! Now Randall, get us home!"

"Thank you," I say, "Now, Santa, I think you can do better to the bad kids by giving them coal. I know a guy named Paul…"

Gareth Barsby studied Creative Writing and Journalism at the University of Chester, but has written stories for most of his life. He has submitted short stories to various publications and has self-published a novelette called The Werewolf Asylum.

The Woodshed

By Lance Zarimba

When the Northern winds blow off the lake, any moisture in the air turns instantly to snow. The delicate flakes float through the air, as light as wisps of cotton, swirling into patterns as they collect on the ground. The texture of the earth's surface sculpts the snow into a crystalline form which slowly smooths and evolves into an amorphous shape.

Cam looked out the kitchen window and watched the flurries collect against the woodshed. Even on the hottest days of summer, the woodshed seemed to absorb all the light that struck it and never let it go. On such a gloomy, cold day like today, it sucked all warmth from anything next to it.

Cam shivered as he felt the cold descend deep inside his twelve-year-old body. He always felt the woodshed was watching him, even as a little kid. He never wanted to explore the inside; it always scared him. As he helped his Grandpa fill it with wood all summer and fall, he felt the cold darkness from inside.

The floor was dirt. The woodshed smelled of wet, rotting earth. The dampness chilled him even when the thermometer read in the nineties. The small window barely let in any light, and there was never a fresh breeze that blew through the door.

Rows and rows of split and cut wood lined the space, floor to ceiling. Dry and ready to be burned on the cold winter's days.

"You glad the snow is coming?" his Grandma asked, startling him from his thoughts.

He let the curtain fall back into place and turned to greet her. "Good morning, Grandma."

"Are you hungry? Are you ready for breakfast?" She opened a cupboard and pulled out an old black frying pan. Her small arthritic hand shook as she placed it on the stove. She turned the burner on and a small blue flame burst to life. She opened the refrigerator and pulled out eggs, bacon and milk. She placed a few slices of bacon in the pan and the meat started to sizzle. She scrambled the eggs with the milk as the bacon sizzled.

Even with the maple cured smell in the kitchen, Cam could still smell the wet earth of the woodshed. He could feel a prickling on his neck even with the curtains closed and the woodshed behind him. He stepped away from the window and sat down at the table.

Grandma put some bread in the toaster and poured him a big glass of orange juice. "Grandpa wants the wood bins filled today. Could you do that after breakfast?" She set the glass down next to him. "I'd hate for him to slip in the snow."

"Sure," Cam said, before he bit on his lower lip. If he did it soon, before more snow fell, he could make it in three or four trips, but if the snow got any deeper, he'd have to carry less and make a few more runs. "I can do it now." He stood, but Grandma pushed him back down.

"It can wait. I just don't want him traipsing through the snow." Grandma turned back to the frying pan as the toast popped up. She set everything on a plate and handed it to Cam.

Cam just finished his last bite as Grandpa shuffled into the kitchen. "Morning, Gramps."

"Morning," he said with pain in his voice. "Old Arthur is sure banging on my bones today." He rubbed his hands together as he sat down at the table.

Grandma set a steaming mug of coffee down in front of him. "Your plate will be ready in a jiff."

Cam picked up his empty plate and set it in the sink. He walked to the back door and pulled on his coat.

"Where are you off to?" Grandpa asked.

"I thought I'd fill the wood bins up before the storm got any stronger." He slipped on his cap and gloves.

"I was gonna..."

"No worries, Gramps." Cam nodded as he opened the door and stepped out into the snow.

A rabbit bounced across the yard and headed to its hole under the woodshed. A small tuft of grass poked up through the snow by the door, but the rabbit jumped to the side as Cam approached.

Cam loved all the wildlife around his grandparents' place. After his parents were killed in a car accident, Grandma and Grandpa took him in. The only thing he hated was the old woodshed. He spun the piece of wood nailed into the door frame that held the door closed. He pushed it open and took a deep breath. The damp, rotting smell hung in the air. He rushed in and grabbed an armload of wood, as much as he could carry. He kicked through the swirling snow and started to reach for the door, when it swung open.

Grandma had seen him and opened the door for him.

"Thanks Gran." He kicked off as much snow as he could and walked into the living room. He carefully stacked the wood in the old copper boiler. One more load would fill that up and then the kitchen bin. He saw the snow he tracked into the room and bent to pick it up.

"It's clean snow, and it'll melt," Grandma said standing in the doorway.

Cam still felt guilty. He hurried to get the next load. As he opened the back door and stepped out, he saw the rabbit jump to the tuft of grass. Its nose wiggled as it sniffed it. Cam wondered if he should let it eat or just get the next load.

Grandpa said, "Cam, come here for a second."

Cam watched the rabbit move closer, but he saw a gray thing at the edge of the door. It moved slowly and stopped, holding perfectly still. Cam came back into the house, and peeked out the door's window, but saw no more.

"Can you make sure you bring the wood from the west wall first?" Grandpa asked. "It's older and drier."

A scream echoed through the backyard. It sounded like a child's cry of pain.

"What was that?" Grandma asked.

Had the woodshed door swung shut in the wind and caught the rabbit? Cam hurried to check it out. He rushed out the door and across the yard. A spray of blood shot across the snow by the door and a drag mark inside slowed Cam's run. He paused at the door and followed the trail of blood and snow across the dirt floor and to the pile of wood.

A sudden whoosh by the corner and a flash of white disappeared between the stacked wood. The chunks were tightly piled, so Cam doubted a rabbit would be able to fit between the pieces of wood.

He neared the spot and a noticed a few drops of blood on the ground and a few white hairs stuck to the ends of a few pieces of wood.

The ground smelled sweeter inside. Could the blood have made the difference? He quickly grabbed another arm load of wood and peered from the corner of his eye at the spot where the rabbit had disappeared.

Nothing.

He hurried into the house and filled the living room boiler.

"What was that scream?" Grandma asked.

"I think a rabbit got caught by something."

"Poor dear. I know they are pests, but they are so cute." Grandma wiped her hands as she finished scrubbing the frying pan. "Remember how you kept dropping rocks on Mrs. Briers' trap in her garden? I don't know how many rabbits you saved last summer."

"Too bad Cam didn't get it first. He could've started on a winter coat for you." Grandpa brought his mug to his mouth and drank.

Grandma shivered. "I don't care how warm a rabbit coat is, I couldn't wear one."

"PETA would be proud of you, Grandma," Cam said.

"Peter who, dear?"

"I'll explain after I get the wood in." Cam hurried out the door and headed back to the woodshed. He stopped at the doorway and looked in. The snowflakes were larger and falling harder and faster. He blew a clump away that landed on his lips.

A smooth gray thing moved back into the wood between the chunks.

Cam grabbed as much wood as he could carry and raced out of the shed. He closed the door and twisted the lock. As he headed back to the house, he wondered if he should have left the door open for whatever was inside to get out. As he neared the back door, a bad thought hit him. Maybe it was already home.

The snow fell all day. Grandma baked bread and cinnamon rolls, and made the house warm with smells of baked treats and brown sugar.

A fire burned in the living room fireplace and kept the house so warm Grandpa napped all day in front of the television watching old westerns.

Cam tried to read his new mystery, but he wasn't able to concentrate on the words. The gray thing in the woodshed kept returning to his mind. He felt a cold presence each time he passed a window that framed the woodshed. What could that thing have been?

He watched the small window on the woodshed for any sign of motion inside, but the day's gloom and storm made the shed even darker than usual. Cam could feel something inside. He knew it. As he walked through the living to get a hot cinnamon roll, he noticed the wood in the living room bin was getting low. Grandpa had been having fun feeding the fire. As dusk was descending, he figured he'd better get more wood for the night.

"I'm going to refill the wood bins," Cam said as he put on his jacket.

Grandma looked up from her dish washing. "Thank you so much. I don't want Grandpa out there at night."

What did Grandma mean by that? Had she seen the gray thing? Did she feel that presence too? Or did she just mean the snow and darkness? Cam wanted to get the wood in fast, so he would ask her later.

He stepped out into the storm. The air felt heavy on him, pushing down as he forged through the foot and a half of snow. Blizzards like this made him claustrophobic with all the white heavy snow and the feeling it would never stop. Cam kicked the door so the snow would fall off and warn the thing inside he was coming in.

He turned the piece of wood that locked the shed and pulled the door open against the snow. The door plowed a small arc of open space. Suddenly he was struck from behind and knocked down to his knees in the snow. Cam twisted around as fast as he could and saw Mrs. Briars' German shepherd, Fritz, bouncing away.

"Fritz! Bad dog." Cam stood and brushed the snow from his clothes.

Fritz ran around him and barked.

Cam waved his arm at him, and Fritz ran away. "Go home." Cam entered the woodshed and grabbed an armload of wood. He exited without checking the spot where the rabbit disappeared. He rushed into the house and deposited his load. He headed back outside for one more load. Just as he locked the shed, Fritz returned. He came to the door and scratched on it. He whined and whimpered at the shed.

"There's nothing inside for you. Go home," Cam tried to chase him home, as he made his way back to the house.

Fritz ran around in circles and then jumped at the door again.

Cam stood at the back door and watched Fritz. "Home," he shouted through the storm.

Fritz jumped against the door again and hit the lock. It rotated and unlocked the door. He bounced again and the door opened. Fritz stuck his nose in the opening and barked and barked.

"Home!" Cam yelled again.

Fritz jumped back and growled. His lips pulled back and exposed his yellow teeth and low guttural noise came from deep inside him. He hunched his body and readied to pounce.

Cam's hand touched the back door knob and watched. Fritz growled again and held his ground.

A gust of wind blew and snow rushed into Cam's face. He closed his eyes and when he opened them, there was a flash of movement. A gray limb reached forward and grabbed Fritz. There was a high pitched yelp, Fritz's whole body tensed, and then all four legs ran in place as fast as they could, but he could not pull away. There was a splash of red against the snow and then Fritz's body was pulled into the shed.

The door swung shut, but Cam didn't wait to see it. He ran into the house and dropped the logs into the wood bin.

Grandma saw his panicked expression. "Are you okay? What happened?"

Cam looked over his shoulder, his breathing came in short bursts.

Grandma rushed over to him and felt his face. "Are you okay?" Worry filled her voice.

"I … I … almost slipped is all." He closed his eyes trying to push away the image that was burned into his mind.

"Are you sure?" Grandma held his face and waited for his eyes to open. She knew he was lying, but didn't know why.

Cam finally opened his eyes and looked at his Grandma. He forced a smile. "I'm fine."

Grandma released his face and backed up. "Okay, if you say so. Supper will ready in ten minutes."

Cam hung up his coat. "I want to wash my hands, I'll be right down." He raced up the stairs to his room. He peeked out his window and strained to see the woodshed. The snow and the dark blocked his view. He pulled the curtains closed and headed to the bathroom.

The phone rang just as they were finishing their meal. Grandma rose to answer it. "Hello."

Grandma nodded as she listened. "No Mrs. Briars, I haven't seen Fritz today." Grandma turned to Cam as she covered the phone with her hand. "Cam, did you see Fritz today? Mrs. Briars can't find him."

Cam swallowed hard, hoping his delicious supper didn't come up. "No, I haven't seen him all day."

Grandma returned to the phone. "He hasn't seen him either. Okay, I hope you find him. Good night." Grandma hung up the phone and turned back to Cam. "If you see Fritz call Mrs. Briars, okay?"

"Sure," he said.

"That damn dog is always on the loose. If she would chain him up, she wouldn't be calling over here all the time looking for him," Grandpa said.

Grandma smiled at her husband. "I think she is lonely and needs to hear a voice more than she is looking for her dog."

"Well don't invite her over here. She talks non-stop."

"Does she cut into your nap time?" Grandma teased.

"I was resting my eyes."

Grandma came back to the table. "Anyone want any more?"

"May I be excused?" Cam asked.

"Your plate is clean so you may go." Grandma smiled. "Did you want dessert?"

"No, I'm fine." And he went up to his room. He lay on his bed, but didn't pick up his book. Should he tell his Grandparents about what happened, what he saw? Maybe he should call the police? Would they even believe him?

The storm had picked up at dusk, and now the wind howled and rattled the windows. His bedroom was a lot cooler now that the fireplace was going in the living room. It kept the thermostat warm, and the rest of the house cooled way down.

Cam knew he would need an extra blanket on his bed tonight. He shivered, but it was more from what had happened to Fritz than feeling cold.

Cam didn't sleep that night. Each time he closed his eyes, a shadow danced across the window or the curtains rustled as if the monster from the woodshed was coming for him. He finally fell into a fitful sleep at five in the morning.

"You slept in this morning. I didn't have the heart to wake you up." Grandma set a plate of hash browns, scrambled eggs, bacon and biscuits in front of Cam.

Cam rubbed his eyes and ran his hand through his hair. "I couldn't sleep last night."

Grandma poured a big glass of orange juice and placed it next to the plate. "It must have been the storm."

Cam looked around the kitchen and stared at the empty space on the wall. "Where's Gramps' coat?"

"Oh, Grandpa couldn't wait to get the wood today, so he went out to bring some in. Come to think of it, he's been gone a long time."

Cam's heart stopped.

"I told him not to shovel, but you know how stubborn he can be." Grandma walked to the back door to peek out the window. "The snow stopped, the woodshed's door is wide open and there is no sign of the old fool." She scanned the snow banks for his body. Grandpa wasn't lying face down in the snow.

Cam rose to his feet and rushed to his coat.

"Sit back down; your breakfast will get cold."

Cam stepped into his boots, still in his flannel PJs. He pulled the door open and rushed down the stairs and across the yard. As he entered the woodshed, all he saw was his grandfather's hand sticking out of the wood pile and inch by inch being pulled deeper and deeper in. Blood oozed between the pieces of split wood, as a low groan was heard from deep inside the shed.

Cam dove for his Grandpa's hand and grabbed it. The hand clasped around his as if to shake, Cam pulled with as much might as he could, but he couldn't move his grandpa. He felt his whole body being pulled closer to the wood pile.

Grandpa's grasp weakened and slowly his fingers opened.

Cam braced his feet against the wood and pulled. For a moment he thought he was winning, but there was a slow release and Grandpa's hand came off and landed on top of him. The end was bloody and torn. Cam scrambled away from the hand that lay on the floor. His back hit the wall, and he screamed. He rolled over onto his hands and knees and crawled out of the woodshed as if the monster was grabbing for his legs. He finally found his feet and ran into the house.

"It's about time…" and Grandma stopped. "What's wrong?"

"It got him." Cam burst into tears. "The monster got Gramps and pulled him into the wood pile. I couldn't get him out."

Grandma rushed to her grandson and held his sobbing body on the kitchen floor. "There, there."

"We have to call the police. We have to save him. His hand pulled off in my hand." Tears and snot poured out of him and onto Grandma's hand.

She didn't flinch. She caressed his head lovingly and rocked him back and forth. "I'm sure he's fine. I'm sure he's fine."

Cam jumped up from the floor and ripped the phone off the hook. He dialed 911 and shouted into the phone. "Send the cops, it got my grandfather. I couldn't stop it. It ripped off his hand. Send them immediately." He gasped and his head started to spin as the room became warmer and warmer and spun faster and faster and then the world went black.

Cam awoke in his bed. His Grandma sat next to him in a chair. She leaned over to him with a glass of water. "The paramedics feel you had a panic attack."

"Where's Grandpa?"

"The police are looking for him."

"He's in the woodshed. Something got him."

"No, they found footprints wandering away from the house. You know how he's been getting forgetful. I know I shouldn't have let him go out there alone, but I wanted to let you sleep in."

"He didn't wander off. A—a monster got him in the woodshed. It pulled him into the wood pile. I pulled his hand off. It was lying on the floor."

"Honey, the police didn't find anything in the shed. Grandpa just wandered off."

"It's all my fault. It's all my fault."

Grandma let go of Cam and reached into her pocket. "Here, dear, take this. The paramedic gave it to me for you."

"I don't want any pill, I want Grandpa," Cam cried.

Grandma handed him the pill and gave him the water glass again.

Cam took it and drank the glass empty. "There. I took it. Now, will you listen to me? I went into the woodshed and …." A big yawn came out of his mouth. "… and I …" and he yawned again. His eyes became very heavy, and he felt as if his tongue had swelled up in his mouth. Why was he having such a hard time focusing? He had to tell his …. And he was out.

Cam awoke to a cold house. He shivered as he pulled the down comforter around him. The lights were off, the house was dark and Grandma was nowhere in sight.

His bladder was full and he had to pee. He slipped a foot out from under the covers and touched the cold wooden floor in his room. He wanted to jump back under the covers, but he needed to go to the bathroom too bad. He grabbed the fluffy robe from his chair and put it on. He padded barefoot to the toilet and used it.

"Grandma?" he called.

No answer.

Cam stood at the top of the stairs and felt a cold rush of air coming up the steps.

"Grandma?" he called louder.

Nothing.

He slowly descended the stairs and walked through the living room, passed his Grandpa's empty chair. The fire had died in the fireplace. He neared the kitchen and saw the back door was wide open.

"Grandma?" came out as a croak.

He stood in the open door and stared out into the night. The moon was out and shown bright over the white snow. The woodshed cast a dark shadow across the back yard. The woodshed's door stood ajar and one of Grandma's slippers lay in the snow bank by the door.

Cam slammed the door closed and locked it. He reached for the phone and there was no dial tone. He dropped the phone and ran upstairs to his bed. He jumped in and pulled the covers over his head. His breathing came in sobbing gasps. They were both gone. Now what could he do?

Cam tried to slow his breathing and think.

Think. Think. Think.

Then he heard it.

There was a creaking floorboard from the hallway.

He stopped breathing.

Cam held perfectly still.

He knew he had locked the back door. He was sure of it.

But then the thought flooded his mind. What if it was inside before he locked the door?

He heard a scratching and a scrape, a scratching and a scrape across the hard wood floor. He felt the down comforter pull down slightly to the foot of the bed.

What was going on?

He curled his fingers around the comforter and held it as tight as his fingers could hold. He didn't want it pulled off of him as he lay exposed on the bed.

Scratch, scratch, scratch sounded across the hard wood floor and underneath his bed.

Something had slipped under the comforter and was crawling onto the mattress at the foot of the bed.

Cam felt a cool draft blow over his feet as the comforter rose up, just before a cold gray hand grasped his ankle and pulled, dragging him toward the woodshed .

Cam felt a cool draft blow over his feet as the comforter rose up, just before a cold gray hand grasped his ankle and pulled. Cam fell back on the bed, hit the head board with his head, and saw stars. Dazed, he wasn't able to pull free from the tangled comforter. Another tug and he felt his body slip off the bed and land on the floor. The hard wood floor was smooth, and he slid easily down the hallway to the stairs.

His numb mind tried to make his hands reach out for the door frame or the railing as he passed, but he wasn't able to get his arms to work. The comforter caught on something and pulled off of him.

Thump, thump, thump, he bounced down the stairway. As his body hit the living room floor, he felt his direction turn toward the kitchen.

Was the back door locked? He struggled to remember if he locked it when he closed the door. After seeing his Grandma's slipper in the snow bank, he prayed he had locked the back door.

The pressure on his ankle released and something dragged around him and opened the back door. The crisp night air flooded the kitchen. The moon was full and shone down on the new sparkling white snow.

Cam turned his head and saw the drooling face of a zombie. But this walking corpse looked familiar, he looked like his dead father, and Cam knew where they were heading.

Cam reached out one more time. His nails scratched over the wood and missed their hold on the back door's frame. Inch by inch, he felt his body being dragged over the snow and into the woodshed.

Lance Zarimba lives in a haunted house that the man who invented Old Dutch potato chips built. He is an occupational therapist living in Minneapolis, MN. He has a mystery, Vacation Therapy*, and three children's books:* Oh No, Our Best Friend is a Zombie, Oh No, Our Best Friend is a Vampire, *and* Oh No, My Brother is Frankenstein's Monster. *He has over 100 short stories in print and can be found in* Mayhem in the Midlands*, Pat Dennis'* Who Died in Here? 25 mystery stories of crimes and bathrooms*, Jay Hartman's* The Killer Wore Cranberry*, Anne Frasier's* Deadly Treats*, Jenni Rector's* Shadow Masters*, and Sarah E. Glenn's* All Hallows' Evil.

Mit Den Augen Der Toten

By James C. Simpson

This story was related to me some years ago from a man who claimed to have served in the Wehrmacht during the Second World War. He had served in most of the major campaigns, from Poland through Barbarossa. This man was decorated and had fought valiantly throughout the war, ending his life as a soldier, shortly after the Bulge, where he surrendered to Allied forces.

For the better part of 50 years, he has kept this story a secret. I expected some tale of horror and atrocity some to light, but instead found something unexpected and eerie. Whatever its validity may be to the reader, it is my earnest belief that what has been related to me bears the burden of truth, however fantastic or incredulous.

Below I have translated the account as best I could from notes and memory.

I do not hope to do justice to those words, especially as they were told to me in that quiet German voice beside the fireplace of my Pennsylvanian home more than a decade ago. Those reflections still haunt me as I am sure they will stay with many of you who read the following account of one who served under the Third Reich and discovered something far beyond our world.

I will not attempt any sort of rational explanation, for that would be fruitless. I'll let the text speak for itself.

It was dreadfully cold that winter. You could feel the wind chill you to the bone, no matter how many layers you had on. The Russian winds were as fierce as their soldiers and as deadly. They constantly reminded us of death and its inevitability as we remained isolated and exhausted. This was in nineteen hundred and forty three, two years after Barbarossa had been unleashed. We were triumphant in the beginning and had every right to feel so victorious. The world was at our feet and at home; the Fuhrer would remind us that we were indeed, the master race.

I had never swallowed such notions, though I knew a great many who did. As young as I was, I felt too old for illusion. The reality of war was and is a terrible thing to endure. Even when we were winning the battles, there was little joy in my heart, witnessing the wreckage that we had wrought and the peoples whose lives we had destroyed. I still cannot rid my thoughts of those staring, mournful expressions. My dreams are haunted not by figures, but parts, mainly the eyes, which follow me and plead with me, just like they did as we marched through so long ago.

I became numb to the blood and gore that permeates warfare, as soldier wont to survive should. We become conditioned in our minds to desensitize and ignore, though I confess it was always an arduous task. Before the war, I had been a novice painter and poet and I did not integrate well with the Hitler Youth, as many of my comrades had. Politics did not bother me, nor did I spare them any thought. I was interested in living, that was all.

Thoughts of my childhood sprang to mind when I was on the front. Sometimes when you imagined a warm summer day, an idyllic one, sunny and cheerful, it could make you feel warmer, even in such bitter cold.

The men in my company had grown desperate. We were not used to this kind of warfare and I saw many hardened men, brave soldiers, break down. I think the cold drove some to a state of madness, making them strange and frightening things. Some of the men would try to run to stay warm, but they were much too weak and often would collapse from exhaustion.

We were hungry, too, as supplies became less plentiful. The Russians cut off our supply lines and we had to make do with what we could find. At first, we would devour pieces of bark and frozen vegetation we dug out of the ground with trench shovels. Then we would resort to roasting leather and feasting on truly terrible, inedible things.

My company had been whittled down since our last offensive and we were not much of a fighting force. Our weapons were as inadequate as our clothing for the Russian winter. The bolts on our rifles were prone to jamming and the automatic weapons could barely function, which left many defenseless. My father had been a mechanic and he would have been surprised had I told him that petrol can freeze. I saw the petrol in our trucks turn to gelatin in the cold. I've never witnessed such a thing before.

Things had gotten increasingly desperate among the ranks and these frozen, starving, frightened men began to partake in maddening acts of desperation.

We came across an abandoned farm, one of the few not razed by the Soviets in their retreat. It was an eerie sight to see in the winter; all the livestock were outside in the field, a vast, frozen waste. There were cows and horses, all standing upright and still. The wind howled with much ferocity, but they did not move an inch, even as we neared them in our trucks.

One of the men took aim with his rifle and brought one of the cows down, and several of the soldiers jumped from the back of the transport truck and raced towards the fallen animal. When they got there, they stopped and stood around it, looking as if they were in a stupor. I approached them and discovered that the cow was frozen solid, as were all the animals, who had perished in the uncompromising winter of that year. They had all died where they stood, the field nothing but a graveyard for these poor animals.

The men were so desperately hungry, though, that they tried to harvest some meat from them. However, the flesh was so tough, that no knife could slice through it. I saw men hack and beat the carcasses with trench shovels and axes; some even shot them in frustration. Finally, the men began to pour kerosene on the dead and frozen animals, in an effort to "soften" the meat. Our officers forbade it, but it did no good for these mad and hungry men. A great many of them were poisoned as a result.

171

To make matters worse, the shelling began. This was open country and save for the petty ruins of an old farmhouse, there was very little cover. We could not dig in, save for the snow and more were killed from exposure, nowhere to hide. Those frozen animals that were standing were blown to smithereens by the shells and I saw fragments of their frozen carcasses act as shrapnel, killing a number of the men. It was yet another grotesque irony in that bloody and awful war.

We were told by the surviving officers to take a position on a ridge overlooking a summit. I was sent up there with a forward platoon and we observed a great valley below us. In the distance, we could see the approaching Russians and their guns. They had these great artillery pieces with them, which they dragged not by horse, for surely, they must have needed the meat as badly as us.

No, they carried these massive guns by sheer *manpower*. I had never seen anything quite like it. They were not human, I think. Our propaganda had dehumanized many of our enemies, but I witnessed this first hand. I remember being told to fire at one that was at the front of one of these guns, carrying it by way of a rope. I shot him with my rifle from many yards and he fell in the snow. Somehow, this did not slow them down and they kept on advancing. By the pace they were making, we knew they would be upon us by morning. It was nightfall, a clear night with a full moon, but it still seemed as if in the twilight. This was the time when we were most anxious and most frightened. We fired upon them several times, but realized we did not have the ammunition to withstand such an assault.

Desertion was becoming more prevalent within the ranks, even though if one was caught, it would surely mean death. We had to choose between which death we preferred and our own kind won out. The Soviets were approaching like creeping death over the hills, ants about to swarm over a hive. We were not just inadequately equipped, but many of us did not know *where* we were. This was all so alien to us; this land beyond was so different from our Fatherland. Where I had remembered all those dark, beautiful forests of my home and the scenic roads and the beautiful rural villages, this place was like a nightmare. There was no color and no beauty over the hundreds of miles we had marched. It was very much like a cold place in Hell.

As the dawn grew nearer, the men grew anxious and they started to make their way to the forests and across the plains. Our officers shot at them, but none would listen, even if some of the bullets met their targets. This is what true fear does to one's soul. It gives you flight and power beyond comprehension.

I had been a loyal soldier of the Wehrmacht for four years, but my fear consumed me and as the shelling began anew, I turned and ran along with most of the others.

The voice of my Commanding officer is still in my head, even now. I can hear him screaming such obscenities at us as we turned and ran like frightened schoolboys. You should never look back, when you leave something for a final time, which I recall my Father telling me. I wished I had remembered it than, for as I glanced over my shoulder, I saw that the Russians had arrived and in the distance, as I made it to the forest, I could see that the remaining men that we left behind were nothing but a bloody jumble. The shadows of our foes were all that were left standing on the farm.

I ran for what seemed like hours, despite the cold, despite my hunger and exhaustion. My men were nowhere in sight and I was too out of breath and too frightened to call for them in the dark.

There are many things that one experiences in war that cannot be rightfully explained. Such strange and haunting phenomena occurred that I cannot account for. Whether it be the standing corpses of frozen beasts or the melted mockery of humanity found after a bombing, none cannot be readily explained to one who has not experienced such terrors for themselves.

It was still the night and I was alone in a destroyed and frozen forest. I could see the moon shine above me, almost a comfort in my loneliness. There is nothing quite worse than finding yourself alone in combat. It feels like you are the only one left in the world. In such an environment, I guess you could say it was apocalyptic. I had been poetic before the war, but I suppose a grimness emerged during my time in the Wehrmacht. My mind was hardly ever cluttered with thoughts of the supernatural and imaginary horrors; in fact, they were actively suppressed by my family. While I had a fairly religious upbringing, I would not say that I was ever a superstitious sort.

It's difficult for me to relate much of what occurred in that war. I still see so much in my mind; these memories haunt me like vengeful apparitions. I am grateful in my conscience that I was never a Nazi, but I suppose that all my countrymen share that collective guilt to some degree.

I saw so many men die and remember so many horrid things, yet one memory still comes back to me, for I still question its existence. Now, I had already explained that I was under much mental duress, as were others in my company. We were starved and fatigued and were not in the proper state of mind, this I admit to. I confess that I am surprised that I am able to relate these memories with such clarity, but they are difficult to *forget*.

I have never harbored any fears of the supernatural and tales of ghosts and monsters, though they were often told in my country, were of little interest to me. The fear I felt now was real and not imagined and yet I felt like some lost child in the wilderness.

I crouched to catch my breath in the night and watched as my breaths dropped and froze on my uniform, the cold something unbearable. At times, I gripped my rifle for support, but the cold metal in my hands was no comfort.

I'm not sure how far I had traveled, for in a war, the sounds of combat are never shut out. I could see through the darkness that there was a clearing ahead and I could smell the smoke of what must have been a massive offensive. I recognized the scent of death as well as the burnt powder of spent shells and neared it with trepidation. My rifle was readied and I struggled through the snow, which was getting thinner, but at times had reached my knees. My limbs felt numb and I hoped that someone would be there that could provide food and comfort. Images of food and drink appeared imprinted in my mind, along with the comfort of my fellow man.

As I drew nearer the spot at the edge of the forest, a light emitted from the ground, which I assumed was the fire from a pit or the smoldering ruin of an exploded shell. There was nothing to accompany my labored breathing save for the howling wind and the crunch of my footsteps against the snow and the hardened ground. I began to panic. What if I found the enemy there? What if they were to capture me?

I pondered these questions for a moment, but my frozen state would not permit me to stay idle and I reached the edge of the forest and looked down over the pit.

It was like a massive crater, surrounded by flames and varying debris. This place had obviously been shelled, but there was so sign of life. I was too afraid to shout out for anybody, knowing that if I was heard by the wrong party, I would be dead.

I looked over the side and knelt down in the frozen dirt, thankful for the warmth, but not the sight that greeted me. Inside the crater were several bodies, all dead and spread out across the floor of the earth.

My eyes were much better back then and I could tell from the distance that these had been SS men. As I looked around, I realized this had been some sort of encampment. It was strange to see, really. I stepped over the edge and worked my way down and realized that the crater I was peering into was dug away, yet I saw no machines nearby. Now, I knew this ground was frozen and I knew that it would take many explosives to make such a hole, so I was confused.

The remnants of tents were flapping in the wind, torn and burnt. The flag of the swastika also was flapping, trying to free its frayed self from its flag pole. It was a peculiar place and it felt so strange. I looked over some of the bodies, to see if I recognized any of them, but I did not. Nor did I see any signs that these men had even been engaged in combat. Where were the bullet wounds, the shrapnel? I did find some with such injuries, but they were further from the pit and, to the best of my knowledge, were self-inflicted.

I found one man left in a tent, dead of course. He had been a major and in his hand was his pistol and in his head, a small red hole. This was a macabre sight and at first, I fancied that these men had taken their own lives, fearful of the advancing Russian army, but I knew the SS and they would never adhere to such cowardice.

Some others had weapons beside them, but there were hardly any shell casings found and it was evident that a fight had occurred. I thought that perhaps the ambush had been so perfect that they were overtaken during rest or during a meal, but this appeared to not be the case, either. I feared the Russians, but I was but a common foot soldier. These were the very best men that Germany had to offer and here they were dead and mangled. What had become of these men and why were they here in this state?

Even in my frozen condition, I was filled with questions and I searched for the answers, even in the dark. The camp had a few tents and a guideline that led to a small structure erected from stone and looking ancient near where the bodies of the men lie. It stood in its own crater and appeared to have been excavated. It was a strange square building, like the prayer huts that you may find in some of the rural villages nestled in the mountains, except it was much older, more ancient than Christianity.

I approached it with a torch that I lit from the flames of the pit. It was a stick wrapped in a torn fragment of one of the tents and came across a fantastic image. There was the swastika in bright red, drawn across the front of the structure and rather crudely. It looked as if it were written in *blood*.

Below it were drawings, almost like those you would see in the pyramids of Egypt. They depicted people attacking other people, with great yellow orbs emitting from their eyes and mouths. A dark figure, not quite a man, presided over them and other strange and indecipherable things spotted the background, lost to time. They resembled to my eyes, the demons and vampires of the ancient monasteries that I had seen in Romania, though these portraits were so obscured and rough that it was difficult for me to determine exactly what they were meant to be.

I stepped to touch the decayed wall, when I noticed a body at my feet. I nearly screamed when I saw the man's face, his eyes open, mouth agape. He was an older man and not dressed in the uniform of the SS. Rather, he looked like some sort of scientist or doctor, as he was clad in white, though covered in bloodstains. His hands were red and when I knelt down to examine them, I realized that they were covered in his own blood and that he had most likely drawn the symbol of the swastika over the wall.

The eyes of the dead are what haunt the mind of the soldier the most after the war. Philosophers suggest that the eyes contain the most power of any individual and in them are carved the soul of man. I had seen many dead and open eyes across Europe, empty lost souls. Most looked onward towards Heaven, as if to ask, "Why am I to die?"

This man's eyes showed something more. It was true fear. I had known it from experience. This man had witnessed something quite terrible before he fell and it was terrible to see. I closed his eyes with my cold hands, trembling as I touched the clammy flesh of the dead man. Tears filled my own eyes as I thought of this man's life and what horrible end came to them and my own comrades behind me. Some anger burned inside me, a resentment towards our leaders and this waste of manpower. Why were these men not there to help us when we needed them so? Why were they being sent on some camping trip, while our troops were being slaughtered in the thousands?

I looked for identification on the dead man before the structure, but found none on his person. I went to look for papers, hopefully something to alert me of what this place was and who these men were. Why were they conducting such an expedition so close to the front?

I was ignorant of archaeology at this time, but I now believe that is what the site was. It was some sort of excavation and if the SS were involved, then it must have been of some significance.

We knew that some of our leaders believed in the occult. It was sometimes joked about on the field that Himmler chased just as many ghosts as he did Jews. Of course, we dare not speak so loudly, for even in jest, the Nazis were not to be trifled with. Now, I took it lightly, for I did not believe in such things, as I had already mentioned.

Most of the papers were scattered about the remnants of the camp and the few I found were nearly indecipherable to my uneducated eyes, but a few were still legible and they disclosed some information about what they were working on. I saw several words that I did not understand, perhaps they were Latin or some other more ancient dead language. As I said, I was ignorant of such things and could only surmise that this had been an excavation and one of military importance. I read a few and found that this was some sort of holy location, but not of any religion I recognized. For the time being, the fear of the advancing and unstoppable Russian forces remained in the back of my mind, as I pondered this new and macabre mystery. It was rumored that the SS were interested in the occult, though most laughed this off as being just rumors. Of course, we know that many in the high command did believe in such strange things and it was more than possible that this place was designated as a place of significance by Himmler, he who believed our race to be destined by God.

I gathered a few of the papers and read them beside the pit, where a number of dead soldiers lay. One paper went on about some kind of gateway and suggested that it was somewhere in Russia, I'm assuming the location that I was at. Another had a small map and various red circles marked strategically across Europe, suggesting that there were other expeditions like this one.

Many important papers were missing or too difficult to decipher, especially in my state of mind, but what I could fathom was that this was top secret information and nothing that a common soldier like I should be reading.

I wished that I was not here. If I could lift myself and fly, I would have flown away to my home with my Mother and Father, away from this hellish pit and Godforsaken country with its inhuman soldiers and appalling weather.

For the first time in my life, I felt another fear, one rooted in childhood. It was a cold fear of something unnatural and monstrous. This world was strange enough and I was so alone, like one who was imprisoned in a cemetery with the dead, so I was alone in a world of death and madness.

My mind drifted from the troubles behind me and I knelt beside the pit of the dead and warmed my hands by the jutting flames. I closed my eyes and tried not to think of death and wondered if these men had gone mad and that maybe I was mad as well.

I'm not sure how long I sat by the pit warming myself or how long my eyes were closed to the world, but something made me open them. I heard a sound coming from within the pit and looked to see the sad figures of dead men. I counted them and realized there were two dozen of them. Two dozen more men that would never see families again. My tears were spent and it was useless for me to waste more energy on these souls.

Just then, at that moment, as I turned my head, some of the men in the pit began to twitch!

Now I was concerned, as I was startled and thought that maybe they were alive. However, I could tell from the unnatural positions of their prostrate and frozen forms that they had been dead a long time. It was perplexing, to say the least and I stood up and considered my actions, whether to jump in the pit or turn to run.

I saw their hands began to move: first the fingers and then the wrists. This was followed by a jerkiness of the feet and movement of the trunk when finally they opened their eyes. I do not intend for you to believe all of what I relate here, but as God as my judge, these men opened their eyes and a bright yellow light emitted from them.

They emitted from those orbs like the ray of an electric flashlight. There were no pupils, just this horrible, shining light and when they opened their mouths, another light emitted from them, just like in the painting on the old wall I had found. I backed away from the pit and could see them move, but not like living men do. Rather, they *levitated* from the ground and a sound was heard that I cannot accurately describe, except as a high-pitched mew like no animal I've ever heard on this earth.

My mind was conflicted as to what to do and I searched for my rifle, ready to defend myself against whatever force controlled these "men."

I backed away from the pit slowly as the flames grew intensely and the earth inside it cracked and split like in an earthquake, though only in the damned pit and nowhere else. My rifle was placed against my shoulder and I readied myself for whatever horrible thing might come to attack me, when I heard a shuffling sound behind me.

I turned around and looked into the dead face of an officer, the same one who had taken his own life in the tent, that red frozen hole in the side of his head, the blood cold.

He bore a blank expression at first, but a turn of his head and it became twisted and strange. He smiled at me, but it was not a pleasant expression. It was something loathsome and inhuman, almost animal-like in nature, his teeth protruding over his lip, his stance crouched and ready to pounce, looking like some jungle cat. I aimed and fired at him with my Mauser rifle and in my delirium, not one shot halted his slow process towards me. Never did I think of shooting one of my own men, especially an officer, but I was not certain he was even a *man* anymore.

I turned and ran towards where I found the excavated wall, trying to run past it, when a great rumble was heard behind me, like something within the earth. By now, I could see the bodies of the men in the pit floating above the fire and staring at me, the great light of their eyes shining down upon me. A low cracking sound was heard, but nothing mechanical, rather organic in nature, like the snapping of celery. Something appeared from within the pit and all the men who were dead now stood on the frozen earth and stared at me. They each raised their arms in unison as if to give the Nazi salute, but instead they pointed at me and opened their mouths and a noise emitted like no man could make. I screamed so loud, I was certain the Russians would shoot me down, but how could they not hear all this?

Whatever was rising from the pit was huge in structure and fearsome in shape, not quite a man and not quite a beast. It was draped in shadows and only the flicker of the flames gave any shape to its form. Was this what we were trying to reach? Was this what they were after?

I dropped my rifle and ran blindly into the darkness of the winter night, not daring to look behind me, tears frozen on my

180

cheeks as I did so. The cracking of the earth grew and I could feel them behind me, coming closer and closer.

Just then, the sun began to rise over the horizon ever slowly and soon an orange tint overtook the blackness of the evening sky and little by little, the light became master.

When I had gained enough distance, I did look back, but saw nothing. There were no men, no terrible thing behind me. I half expected to see that black shape in the painting on the wall, but instead saw only the ruins of a camp and the faint flicker of flame. Our flag swayed gently in the breeze.

I dared not return and took off running, for how long, I know not. Eventually, I found our lines again.

When I told my story, few were interested. They had all heard the ravings of madmen across the front and had their fill. I was sent to a hospital, for I was sick and covered in patches of frostbite, which I did recover from. Our company was squandered and we were now in full retreat. This would be the beginning of the end and I never did mention my cowardice and I saw very few from my old outfit.

It took me many months before I could rejoin my unit, however meager we were by the following year. Our country was in shambles and we were paying the price for global domination. The homeland was but a ruin and many of my family and loved ones would succumb to the disease of nationalism by force.

Later, I was deployed again in France. Shortly before I surrendered to the American army, I queried about the expedition and discovered that there *was* a special detachment of men working on some site on the Russian front and elsewhere in Europe. I wish I had saved those papers I found, but I was not even sure if it had been reality or some peculiar fantasy.

I never did find out what it was, but I did see that picture again, the one I described on that ancient wall. It was in a book about the occult, an old German text on the subject of ancient sorceries and beliefs.

A friend of mine knew of my account and lent me the decayed tome and he showed me an entry about a gateway that was said to be the stairway to the necropolis of *Azarien*. I never heard of the name before, but my friend said that it was an ancient God, long since abandoned by modern civilization. He said that this God was said to bestow great power from within the earth and strengthen those who believed in him, not just on earth, but in the afterlife. Hitler was not a religious man, but he did believe in the supernatural and the power of the will and destiny. Perhaps the story of a God that could promise such power on mortal men appealed to him, but there was a catch. If you believed in said God and unleashed him upon the soil of our world, he would and could, reverse said energy and use it to enslave those so greedy for its power. He suggested to me that maybe it was our *destiny* to lose and that we had fought on the side of evil and maybe there was some truth in what I said of my finding.

Of course, I do not believe in such things and have told myself that it was the work of an overtaxed mind, which *can* have the power to conjure up demons at will.

Certainly, I have been plagued by many such demons from that war for a great number of years and you know, as I have recalled many grisly stories for you about man's inhumanity. War is like a living Hell and I have to wonder how much worse the pit must be after having seen it all those years ago.

Though, I should add for curiosity's sake, that such a place as the temple they found in Russia, was meant to *punish* evil and release it upon men who practiced it here on Earth. That gateway must first be marked with a sign of the man's destruction.

The picture I saw in the book did not bear the mark of the swastika.

James is a mysterious recluse from the wild mountains of Pennsylvania. He has had a lifelong fascination with the macabre, being particularly keen to the Gothic masters. When he is not writing a new tale of terror, he often finds himself enjoying the solitude of nature or the darkened realm of the cinema.

Zombie Enforcement

By Spencer Carvalho

Zelda Carpenter walked into the rec room at the Zombie Enforcement Agency, East Coast Division.

During her training Zelda had learned that the Zombie Enforcement Agency was a secret government agency that dealt with zombie based threats. She learned that the zombie virus is a latent disease that is undetectable and incredibly rare. Less than one in a million people have it. It remains dormant during the person's life and only becomes active when they die. At that point the virus reanimates the corpse in order to spread. The first reanimated corpse becomes known as Patient Zero. While Patient Zero tends to be slow and shambling the people that Patient Zero infects maintain the same speed that they had before infection. When an incident occurs the Zombie Enforcement Agency is notified and they send agents to contain the threat.

Jack and Tyler were playing air hockey near the rec room's Christmas tree when they noticed some new agents walk in.

"Who's that?" asked Jack.

"I'm assuming you want to know who the attractive woman is," said Tyler. "Her name is Zelda."

"Zelda?" asked Jack. "Like the video game princess."

"Yeah I guess," said Tyler.

"That's awesome," said Jack.

"She's a former S.W.A.T. sniper," said Tyler.

"Ooh, a lady sniper," said Jack.

The leader of their base, Captain Henry Krunch, walked into the room.

"Jack, Tyler," said Captain Krunch. "This is Zelda. She'll be your new squad mate. She'll be replacing Kapoopski."

"Yes sir," said Tyler.

The captain left to deal with other matters. Zelda walked up to them.

"What happened to Kapoopski?" asked Zelda.

"He thought it would be a good idea to make a double barrel grenade launcher," said Tyler. "He was an idiot."

"He was a dreamer who dreamed too big," said Jack.

"We should probably do some drills together," said Tyler. "Later tonight we…"

An alarm went off throughout the building. Tyler sighed.

"Never mind," said Tyler.

"I'll get Spooky," said Jack.

Zelda followed Tyler down to the equipment room to suit up. Jack ran up to the barracks. He found Spooky sleeping. Jack shook him.

"Spooky," said Jack.

Spooky moaned.

"Tired or hung over?" asked Jack.

"Both," said Spooky.

"You can sleep on the plane," said Jack.

Spooky got up and followed Jack downstairs to the equipment room. While loading their gear Jack noticed Zelda grabbing some flares.

"Whoa hold on a second," said Jack. "Don't use flares. They look cool but you don't want to accidentally burn someone's house down. Just go with a flashlight. It works much better."

"It's true," said Tyler.

"Fine," said Zelda.

She grabbed a flashlight.

"You should also grab a silencer," said Jack. "You don't want hearing damage."

She grabbed a silencer. Spooky showed up carrying a blanket and put on his gear and grabbed a chainsaw. He also put on an armor plated face mask that looked like a hockey mask. This seemed strange to Zelda because no one else had a chainsaw. They ran to the hanger and got into the same cargo plane. They sat next to each other except for Spooky who climbed into the back of one of the Hummers that was loaded onto the cargo plane. It was a lime green Hummer.

"Why is it lime green?" asked Zelda.

"Camouflage is a waste of time with zombies," said Jack. "It's more useful to have something that we can find in the dark. We wanted something bright but we're required to use military colors so we went with lime green. We call it the 'Mystery Machine'."

The cargo plane door closed and it took off.

During her training Zelda learned that each Zombie Enforcement Agency base contained a company of eighty to two hundred and twenty-five agents. For each cargo plane they would split up into platoons of twenty-six to sixty-four agents and when they landed they would split up into squads of five to ten agents.

"Who else is on our team?" asked Zelda.

"Wheeler," said Jack.

Jack nodded to a guy sitting in the driver's seat of the Mystery Machine. Zelda saw him on the base earlier. He stood out because he was in a wheelchair.

"Why do you have a disabled driver?" asked Zelda.

"Do you know what's the most important trait for a good driver?" asked Jack. "That he does not get out of the vehicle."

Zelda thought about that for a few seconds. She then turned back to Jack.

"What's your story?" asked Zelda.

"There's only two things you need to know about me," said Jack. "One, I'm awesome. Two, I'm incredibly humble. And three, I'm bad at counting."

Zelda laughed. She looked at Tyler.

"What about you?" asked Zelda.

"I used to be in the army," said Tyler. "Now I kill zombies."

"There's more to the story than that," said Jack. "He was probably the last soldier to get discharged because of Don't Ask,

Don't Tell. Less than a month after they discharged him they repealed that rule. Their loss, our gain."

"Were you military too?" asked Zelda.

"Not exactly," said Jack. "I was more of a…"

"He played paintball," said Tyler.

"Don't undersell me," said Jack. "I was a paintball champion. I have trophies."

She looked at his weapons.

"You don't have an assault rifle," said Zelda. "You just have pistols. Why's that?"

"I'm a marksman," said Jack. "I'm all about precision. Instead of firing off a bunch of rounds all willy-nilly I use one bullet per target, all head shots. The key is balance. I use two equally weighted pistols, one in each hand. It keeps my body in balance. It's all about balance."

Eventually they reached their location of Pittsburgh, Pennsylvania. The captain spoke over the intercom.

"We'll be landing in a few minutes. Get in your vehicles now."

There were a variety of military vehicles. Jack, Tyler, and Zelda got in the Mystery Machine. Tyler sat in the passenger's seat.

"We had it modified," said Tyler. "It's electric, environmentally friendly and very quiet. We also have a mini fridge in the divider and we keep extra weapons in the back underneath where Spooky's sleeping."

Zelda noticed that the driver's seat had been modified for a disabled driver.

"Any questions?" asked Jack.

"Yes," said Zelda. "Did you name the Hummer after the van from Scooby Doo?"

"Yes," said Jack.

The cargo plane landed in an airfield. As soon as the plane stopped the cargo hatch opened. The captain's voice came on the radios of all the military vehicles.

"Rollout," said Captain Krunch.

The vehicles left through the back of the cargo plane.

186

Pittsburgh was a lot colder than where they were stationed. Wheeler turned up the heat.

"I hate the cold," said Jack.

They made a convoy that sped nonstop to the town of Pittsburgh. They reached a bridge and saw that there was already a perimeter around the town.

Zelda had learned in training that the Zombie Enforcement Agents formed a perimeter around the infected area. Then other agents would go into the infected area to kill the zombies and rescue the human survivors.

As the Mystery Machine crossed the bridge, they saw a sign listing the population.

"I bet that number is a lot lower now," said Jack.

The Mystery Machine pulled to a stop near Main Street. Main Street was lit up with bright Christmas decorations. They got out of the hummer. It was nighttime but there was still power so they didn't need to use their flashlights.

"Safety's off," said Wheeler. "It's zombie killing time."

"I really hate the cold," said Jack. "The one good thing about winter missions is if it's around Christmas time then you get the added lights from all the Christmas decorations. Plus it reminds me of Gremlins."

"Great movie," said Tyler.

Another Hummer stopped near them. Chad and his squad got out.

"So how do you guys want to do this?" asked Zelda. "Your team takes one side of the street and we take the other?"

"Stay out of our way," said Chad,

Chad's group walked past them without saying anything.

"That's rude," said Zelda. "It's also stupid. We should be working as a team."

"That was Chad," said Jack. "He's a jerk and an idiot. Check this out."

Jack and Zelda watched Chad's team work. They moved up to the building on the right. They knocked the door down with a battering ram and quickly moved into the building.

"That's stupid," said Jack. "That's what you shouldn't do. We'll take the building on the left."

Zelda climbed up onto the Mystery Machine. She set up her sniper rifle. She had it pointed at the door. Tyler raised his assault rifle.

"I'll open the door," said Jack.

Jack walked up to the door and used his auto key.

Zelda remembered that an auto key was a device that could open any lock. It was a small metal cylinder about the size of a bottle of pepper spray.

Jack opened the door and quickly moved back with his pistols raised. Nothing ran out. Jack leaned in.

"Hey zombies!" yelled Jack. "Why don't you run towards us like stupid mindless monsters and make it easy for us to kill you?"

Jack backed up and took a knee beside Tyler. Zelda had her sniper rifle pointed at the doorway. They could hear a sound coming from the building. Zombies ran out. They ran out quickly and were shot quickly. Between the pistols and assault rifle the furthest any of the zombies made it was three feet. There were four dead zombies on the ground. They waited a few seconds to see if there were any more but there weren't. Jack got up. It all happened so quickly that Zelda didn't even shoot. She wasn't sure if anyone noticed. Jack looked at her.

"How're you doing?" asked Jack. "Feel good?"

"I'm fine," said Zelda.

"Good," said Jack. "Some people have a hard time with this."

"Reloading," said Tyler.

Tyler reloaded.

"How about next time we pour some water in front of the doorway, give it time to freeze, and when the zombies run out they'll slide all over the place," said Jack.

"So you want to make them faster and more erratic?" asked Tyler.

"Never mind," said Jack.

"Zelda, cover the doorway," said Tyler. "Jack and I will clear out the building and check for survivors."

Jack and Tyler moved towards the doorway with their weapons raised. Jack leaned his head into the doorway.

"Hey, human survivors! We're here to help you so don't shoot us! Stay where you are! We'll come to you and get you to safety! Just a reminder, don't shoot us! It would be very rude!"

Jack and Tyler went into the building. They searched every room but couldn't find any survivors. After a few minutes of searching they went back outside.

"Any trouble while we were gone?" asked Jack.

"Nope," said Zelda.

They moved on to the next building. They repeated the same process but no zombies came running out. Jack and Tyler proceeded into the building to search for survivors. While they were inside Zelda noticed something out of the corner of her eye. She turned her head and positioned her sniper rifle to her right. She saw a lone figure walking down the street. She spoke over her headset.

"There is activity out here," said Zelda.

"How many?" asked Tyler.

"One," said Zelda.

"Then take it out," said Tyler. "Fire at will."

Zelda lowered her head behind the scope and saw a young girl covered in blood. She was staggering around. It was such a strange sight that she just watched her stagger around. Zelda found it fascinating. Jack's voice came over the headset.

"Make sure it's a zombie first."

"I'm pretty sure it's a zombie," said Zelda.

"Pretty sure," said Jack. "Pretty sure. How about you become positive before you put a bullet in its head?"

"Hey, are you human?" asked Zelda.

The zombie turned toward her and started running in her direction. Zelda waited for it to get closer and then took the shot. It was a perfect headshot. She then turned back to the doorway and noticed Jack and Tyler on the second story with their weapons pointed out the window covering her.

"I've got this," said Zelda.

"Just making sure," said Jack.

When they went back into the building and could no longer see her Zelda smiled. Wheeler rolled down his window.

"Congratulations on your first zombie kill," said Wheeler.

189

"Thanks," said Zelda.

Jack and Tyler cleared the building and then moved on to the next one. Wheeler spoke to them over their headsets.

"I've just heard that there's a group of survivors at a vet's clinic near here," said Wheeler. "Hurry up."

Jack and Tyler quickly got into the Mystery Machine.

"What about clearing the buildings?" asked Zelda.

"We can do that later," said Tyler. "Rescuing human survivors is priority number one."

They got in and quickly made their way to the vet's clinic. There were cars parked in random spots by the entrance. Jack and Tyler went in. The first door was no problem but the second door was barricaded. It was a glass door so Jack could see the items barricading it and he could also see people inside. Jack knocked on the window.

"Hello," said Jack. "We're here to rescue you."

Jack could see a man with a rifle. Jack changed the clips in his pistols. He switched out his live rounds for rubber bullets in case the human survivors needed to be subdued.

"How do we know you're not crazy?" asked the man with the rifle.

"Because I'm talking to you," said Jack. "I'm not crazy. I promise."

Some people inside removed the items barricading the door. The man with the rifle didn't help. Jack and Tyler got in and looked around. There were seven people.

"Is this everyone?" asked Jack.

"Yes," said a guy in a white coat.

"Aren't there any guys like us here?" asked Jack.

"They were here but then they left," said White Coat.

"They just left you guys here?" asked Jack. "Those jackasses. It was probably Chad. He's such a douche. Was the guy's name Chad?"

"He didn't say his name," said White Coat.

"Did he look like a Chad?" asked Jack.

"I guess," said White Coat.

"Stupid Chad," said Jack.

"What's going on?" asked the man with the rifle.

"Well, first you're going to lower that rifle," said Tyler. The man lowered his rifle.

"It's empty anyways," said the man with the rifle.

"Who are you guys?" asked White Coat.

"The CDC," said Tyler

The Zombie Enforcement Agents were taught during their training to tell people that they were part of the CDC. It made an effective cover because most people had no idea what the CDC actually did. They were also taught to tell people that it was a rabies outbreak because zombies would make people panic and panicked people acted stupidly. The Zombie Enforcement Agency had no problem hiding the existence of zombies from the general public because the Agency made deals with the six conglomerates that owned over ninety-five percent of all U.S. media.

"There is no need to panic," said Tyler. "We just have a small rabies outbreak. We will get you to safety."

"It's not rabies," said White Coat. "I'm a vet. I've dealt with rabies before. This is nothing like rabies."

Jack and Tyler were quiet. The people in the vet's clinic stared at them.

"Well, it's uh, you know," said Jack. "It's like really bad rabies. It's super rabies."

The Zombie Enforcement Agency's medical truck pulled up outside. Zelda spoke over her headset.

"The medical truck is here."

During her training Zelda learned that the medical trucks were used to help the human survivors. The drivers for the medical trucks were under strict orders not to leave their vehicles. The field agents were supposed to escort the human survivors to the medical trucks.

"All that matters is that we'll get you to safety," said Tyler. "Is this the whole group?"

"No," said White Coat. "Jenny's in the back. She was injured."

Jack looked at Tyler.

"You secure Jenny," said Jack. "I'll get these people to the medical truck."

Jack turned to the crowd.

"The white truck outside with the red cross symbol on it will keep you safe," said Jack. "There are medical personnel inside that will check you to see if you need any medical care. I'm going to escort you to the truck. Follow me."

Jack switched his clips from rubber bullets back to live rounds. He spoke over his headset.

"Zelda, I'm coming out. I have a group with me. I'm going to get them to the medical truck."

Jack went out into the parking lot with the group behind him. They were almost to the medical truck when a large group of zombies ran out from behind the medical truck. They saw Jack and his group of human survivors and ran towards them. Zelda was out of position and wasn't able to get any of the zombies in her line of sight. Jack raised his pistols.

"Behind me!" yelled Jack.

Some of the human survivors moved behind Jack while others stayed where they were frozen in fear. Jack started firing both pistols. Every bullet hit a zombie and every shot was a head shot. They kept coming at him. His pistols held eight bullets each. He fired all sixteen rounds but there were still two zombies left. The two remaining zombies ran towards Jack with their arms raised out and their mouths open. He dropped one of his guns as he reached for another ammo clip. He reloaded and fired two more rounds into the last two zombies who were close enough to land at his feet.

Zelda ran up to Jack holding her sidearm.

"I couldn't get a shot," said Zelda.

Jack looked around to make sure the human survivors were all right and that none of them had run off.

"We should get these people in the medical truck," said Jack. "The gunfire might attract more of them."

Jack picked up his pistol and reloaded it. Zelda helped Jack get the human survivors into the medical truck. Before Jack and Zelda could finish loading all the human survivors into the medical truck Tyler came out carrying Jenny. She had her wrists and ankles tied together with a gag in her mouth.

"She's close to turning," said Tyler.

He carried her onto the medical truck.

"What's going to happen to her?" asked Zelda.

"She'll probably turn into one," said Tyler.

"Let's get back to work," said Jack.

During her training, Zelda learned that there was no known cure for the zombie virus. All the human survivors were placed into different medical compartments so that they would not infect each other. The doctors on board the medical trucks would take samples from the infected in order to gather more data regarding the zombie virus in the hopes that someday they would find a cure.

The squad went back to clearing houses. They started working on the houses near them instead of going back to Main Street. While Jack and Tyler were clearing a house Zelda reached down and knocked on Wheeler's window. Wheeler rolled it down.

"What is it?" asked Wheeler.

"Do you have any guns?" asked Zelda.

"No," said Wheeler. "I don't carry any guns."

"What's it like not having a weapon?"

"I drive a four-ton death machine," said Wheeler. "I don't use guns but I definitely have a weapon."

Jack and Tyler were clearing out a home when they noticed something. Jack spoke over the headset.

"We may have a problem here," said Jack. "The guy who lived here was really into fitness. There's a lot of exercise equipment and the pictures of him show that he's huge. He looks like a bodybuilder. Also, we found a lot of steroids. If he's still human we're fine, but if he's turned then we could be dealing with a Heavy."

Zelda remembered learning that the zombie virus had strange effects when mixed with certain body altering chemicals. If a person had a large amount of steroids in their system when they turned into a zombie then the zombie virus accelerated the effects of the steroids and caused a mutation. It caused the person to become larger, stronger, and more aggressive. Their skin also became thicker, which made it harder to bring them down. These kinds of zombies were referred to as Heavies.

"Wheeler, warn the other agents," said Tyler. "Make sure to tell them where we are because the Heavy shouldn't be too far from this residence."

"Guys," said Zelda. "I think I see it."

Zelda saw a large hulking creature. She had trouble seeing it because it was very dark out, but she was able to tell that it was wearing a Santa outfit.

The Heavy saw Zelda and started rampaging towards her. She fired but it kept charging. She reloaded and fired again; this time she shot its kneecap. She hoped that would slow it down, but the Heavy kept charging. She abandoned her sniper rifle and pulled out her sidearm and then backed off the Mystery Machine while firing. She backed up towards the direction of the house while firing at the Heavy's head. She was aiming for its eyes but it was moving its head around a lot and she kept missing. Jack and Tyler ran out and they all started firing at its head. Tyler had his assault rifle on full auto and fired his entire clip at the Heavy's head. One of the bullets the trio was firing managed to hit one of the Heavy's eyes. That slowed him down for a second but it also made him madder. He yelled in anger. Wheeler honked the horn. The Heavy turned toward the noise.

"Look out," said Wheeler.

The Mystery Machine ran into the Heavy. The impact knocked it to the ground and the Mystery Machine continued forward and got stuck on top of the Heavy. It was thrashing its arms around wildly. It was trying to hit the vehicle and then started trying to lift it off of him. Then they heard the sound of a chainsaw. Spooky ran out from the back of the Mystery Machine with his face mask on and his chainsaw ready. He ran around to the front and brought the chainsaw down on the Heavy's head. There were a lot of blood and bone fragments spewing into the air. The chainsaw had trouble working its way through the Heavy's thick head but he eventually split it in two. When it was over Wheeler backed the Mystery Machine off the Heavy. Spooky lifted off his face mask to admire his work. Jack, Tyler, and Zelda moved in to get a better look at the dead Heavy.

"You picked a good time to wake up," said Jack.

"Wheeler couldn't keep it steady," said Spooky. "It was all bumpy. Anyways, what did I miss? Who's she?"

"That's Zelda," said Jack. "She's a sniper."

Zelda waved. Spooky waved back.

"Did I just kill Santa Claus?" asked Spooky.

"Zombie Santa Claus," said Jack.

"What's next?" asked Spooky.

"Well, now that you're awake you can help us finish killing all the zombies," said Tyler.

Spooky smiled.

"Groovy," said Spooky.

Spooky got into the back of the Mystery Machine. Wheeler rolled down his window.

"I told you I had a weapon," said Wheeler. "Four-ton death machine."

They went back to Main Street. Chad and his squad were still there. Jack was going over to call Chad a douche for leaving the human survivors unattended. He also had a snowball attack planned. Before Jack could speak they heard a screech.

"What's that?" asked Zelda.

"That's a Speeder," said Jack.

Steroids weren't the only chemicals that mutated the zombie virus. Meth also had strange effects. If a person had methamphetamines in their system when they got infected with the zombie virus, then they became faster. Their movement also became strangely erratic and they would screech like an animal in pain. They would also fidget and scratch to the point where they would grind their fingertips down to the bone leaving sharp points. Speeders were considered to be the most dangerous of the zombie mutations.

Chad and his team perked up at the idea of taking out a Speeder.

"Zelda, move toward the screech," said Chad. "When it starts to chase you, run back to us and lure it into a trap."

"How very brave of you to volunteer her," said Jack. "Why don't you be the human bait?"

"She's the new guy," said Chad. "That means she gets the crap job."

"That's stupid," said Jack. "And you're stupid."

Chad stood upright.

"What did you say to me?" asked Chad.

"I called you stupid because you are," said Jack. "You want to get yourself killed, that's fine. If you get your squad mates killed then… where is the rest of your squad?"

Jack looked around and only saw three of Chad's squad mates.

"We had casualties," said Chad.

"You started off with seven people," said Jack. "Now you're down to four. Three agents died? How did three agents die? They're zombies. They're stupid and you guys have guns. How the hell do you lose three agents to zombies?"

"It doesn't matter," said Chad.

"You guys suck, you know that?" said Jack. "You guys want to go after the Speeder, go ahead. We'll finish clearing Main Street looking for survivors."

"We already cleared out these buildings," said one of the guys from Chad's squad.

"What's your name?" asked Tyler.

"Bruce."

"How many survivors were there?" asked Tyler.

"Not many," said Bruce. "One of them said that people were seeking shelter at the high school near here."

"I guess we're headed to the high school," said Jack.

They started to get into the Mystery Machine.

"A large group of people," said Chad. "That's sounds like a good spot to look for the Speeder."

Chad and his squad got in their Hummer. Both squads made their way to the high school. When they got there, Zelda got in position on top of The Mystery Machine while the guys made their way to the door. They all aimed their guns while Jack opened the door and propped it open. He was about to yell into the high school to draw out the zombies when Chad and his squad moved into the building. Jack and Tyler stared at each other for a second.

"These guys are idiots," said Jack. "No wonder they keep dying."

Jack, Tyler, and Spooky followed Chad and his squad inside.

"These guys don't even have silencers," said Tyler.

"Let's keep our distance," said Jack. "I don't want any hearing damage."

Chad and his squad advanced through the halls. Three zombies ran towards them. Chad's squad fired many bullets and managed to kill them.

"What the hell are you guys doing?" asked Jack. "Do you guys have your assault rifles on full auto?"

"Yes," said Bruce.

"Morons," said Jack.

Jack walked away in frustration.

"You don't need to keep those on full auto," said Tyler. "Keep them on single shot. You'll reload less. You only need one or two shots to take down a zombie. Just keep that thing around eye level and you'll be fine."

"Except for zombie children," said Jack. "I hate zombie children. They are so creepy. Oh, and zombie midgets. Or zombie little people. I'm not sure what the correct term is."

Bruce turned his assault rifle from full auto to single shot. He was the only one. They continued through the high school. They quickly moved through the hallways. When they passed a classroom with an open door a zombie ran out and attacked one of the guys on Chad's squad. Jack shot the zombie in the head.

"Are you okay?" asked Tyler.

"It bit me," said the agent.

"You guys really need to cover each other better," said Jack. "You should…"

The infected agent shot himself in the head.

"Why did he do that?" asked Jack. "He had maybe a few more hours before he would have turned. Also he may have gotten lucky and been immune."

"Coward," said Spooky.

They heard a Speeder screech inside the school.

"It's here," said Chad.

"We need to find the survivors," said Tyler. "If there are any."

"Where do we look?" asked Bruce.

"Either the auditorium or the teacher's lounge," said Jack.

"We'll split up," said Chad. "You guys take the auditorium while my team takes the teacher's lounge."

"That's a stupid idea," said Jack. "Splitting up is dumb. There's strength in numbers. We should stick… actually I don't like being around you so I'm okay with splitting up. See ya."

Jack, Tyler, and Spooky left. They eventually found the auditorium. The doors were chained shut.

"I think we have some bolt cutters in the Mystery Machine," said Tyler.

Spooky started up his chainsaw and cut through the chains. He then kicked open the doors. The room was filled with zombies. The zombies looked at the agents.

"I need the practice," said Spooky. "Thin the herd."

Spooky ran forward and started killing the zombies. Jack and Tyler started killing some of the zombies around Spooky so he wouldn't get overwhelmed.

Zelda and Wheeler waited outside in the parking lot. They could hear the chainsaw over the radio.

"Cold up there?" asked Wheeler.

"Freezing," said Zelda. "The roof's pretty warm though."

Zelda looked around at the empty parking lot.

"We're missing all the fun," said Zelda.

"We have very different ideas of fun," said Wheeler.

"What's the deal with Spooky?" asked Zelda. "Why does he use a chainsaw?"

"Before he joined the agency he used to make chainsaw ice sculptures."

"Really?"

"His ice dolphins were beautiful."

Inside Spooky finished killing the zombies. He turned his chainsaw off. Jack walked in.

"Are there any human survivors hidden in this auditorium?" asked Jack.

There was no response.

"Just checking," said Jack. "Do you think Chad's dead yet?"

At the teacher's lounge Chad kicked open the door. He and Bruce went inside while the other squad member, Jonathan Redshirt, covered them from the hallway. Chad and Bruce carefully checked the teachers' lounge but couldn't find anything. Redshirt noticed something out of the corner of his eye. A Speeder ran through the hallway on his right. He quickly turned and started firing at it. He missed it and ran off after it eager to prove himself to his teammates.

"Where's he going?" asked Bruce.

Redshirt fired as he started to turn the corner. He did a lot of damage to the corner because he had his rifle on full auto. Right as he turned the corner he ran out of bullets. He stopped and went wide eyed as he saw the Speeder looking at him. Redshirt started to change out his clip but before he could finish the Speeder slashed his throat. Its sharp, bony fingers cut his throat open spilling blood down his chest. The Speeder ran off before Chad and Bruce were able to get to him. Bruce bent down to check Redshirt's pulse as Chad ran off after the Speeder.

"What about Redshirt?" asked Bruce.

Chad didn't say anything. He just kept running.

As Jonathan Redshirt laid there bleeding to death his last thoughts were about how Jack warned him about not wasting bullets. Then he died

Tyler saw the Speeder run by.

"Speeder," said Tyler.

They saw Chad chasing after it. Jack, Tyler, and Spooky ran after them. Tyler got on the radio.

"He's coming your way," said Tyler.

In the parking lot, Zelda got ready. The Speeder ran out the door and got shot in the chest. The shot hurt it but it wasn't enough to kill it. It ran in her direction. She had trouble getting it in her line of sight because of its erratic movements. She took a deep breath and fired. The shot grazed the Speeder's head. It was nearly at the Mystery Machine when Wheeler turned on the headlights. The Speeder couldn't see but kept running and jumped. As the Speeder ran onto the hood Zelda rolled off onto the snow landing on her feet. The Speeder ran onto the roof and started slashing blindly. Zelda pulled out her sidearm. She aimed at its head and had it in her sights when a hail of bullets flew by. Bullets hit the Speeder, the Mystery Machine, and Zelda. The impact knocked her to the ground. Chad was firing his assault rifle on full auto in their direction. Some of the bullets actually managed to hit the Speeder, but none of them were kill shots. Chad ran out of bullets and started to reload his clip as the Speeder jumped off the roof of the Mystery Machine. Wheeler watched helplessly as it moved toward Zelda. The Speeder's mouth was open and it held its sharp, bony fingers out. There was no remorse or humanity left in its eyes, only anger remained. The Speeder lunged at Zelda and she blew its head off with her sidearm. The other agents ran over to her.

"You shot me," said Zelda.

"Accident," said Chad.

"Are you okay?" asked Jack.

"I'm fine," said Zelda. "I think."

She checked herself. They looked around the snow to see if there were any red spots.

"The vest stopped the bullet," said Zelda.

She got up. Jack turned to Chad.

"You idiot," said Jack.

"Shut up," said Chad. "It was an accident."

"No," said Jack. "It was careless. The people on your squad keep dying because you're stupid and careless."

"I should punch you right in the face," said Chad.

"I should shoot you right in the face," said Jack. "If we tussle we're doing it with bullets, not fists."

"You're not worth it," said Chad.

Chad walked away back to his Hummer.

"He didn't even say sorry," said Spooky.

Wheeler rolled down his window. "I just checked with the others over the radio. This place is pretty much cleared out. It's over." They all smiled. Tyler looked at Zelda.

"Congratulations," said Tyler. "You survived your first mission. Plus, you killed a Speeder."

"Yay," said Zelda.

Jack looked over at Chad. He was standing near his hummer. Bruce walked out of the building and started talking to

Chad. Jack couldn't hear them but he watched intently. Jack changed out his ammo clip.

"What are you doing?" asked Tyler.

"Loading the rubber bullets," said Jack.

He aimed his pistol across the parking lot and shot Chad in the testicles with a rubber bullet. They laughed as Chad rolled on the ground in pain. Bruce also laughed.

"We should probably leave," said Tyler. "Let's get out of here."

"I'm going back to sleep," said Spooky.

Spooky climbed into the back of the Mystery Machine and went back to sleep. They all got in and drove off. Dawn was approaching as Wheeler drove them up to the top of a hill. He parked up there so they could all see what the town looked like in the daylight.

"Hopefully you ruptured one of them," said Zelda.

They all laughed.

Spencer Carvalho has written short stories for various literary magazines and anthologies. His stories have appeared in literary magazines like the Barcelona Review, Mused, Inner Sins, Aphelion, Fever Dreams Ezine, eRomance, eFantasy, *and* eScifi. *His stories have appeared in the anthologies* Certain Circuits Volume 1, Another Wild West, Remembrances of Wars Past: A War Veteran's Anthology, *and* Tales of the Undead- Suffer Eternal: Volume 3.

The Festival of Nydogun

By Carl Thomas Fox

Every year, on December twenty-first, the Winter Solstice, they gathered on the beach, waiting for dawn.

Waiting for the new dawn.

For centuries, the blodveidimenn had gathered on this small rocky beach in Iceland for the sacred rite they held every Winter Solstice, awaiting for the coming of the dagangadur, the Daywalker. After all, in recent history, they became known as vampires, and they cannot abide sunlight. For centuries, they gathered here, fasting for the length of the longest night, waiting for the dawn where, amongst the ashes of other fallen vampires, the dagangadur would emerge, and bring in a new race who could venture into the sunlight.

They returned to this rocky beach for one reason. This was where their race originated.

Thousands of years ago, during the Ice Age where there was little sun on a small island, known by the natives as Dokksvidi, a group of humans evolved differently. They became accustomed to the dark, their senses sharpening. With little food, and no crops to grow in the darkness, these humans fed on the blood of animals that lived on the island. As they fed, they took in many of the attributes of the predatory creatures they hunted, becoming more animalistic, enhanced strength, flexibility and durability, as well as developing their fangs. Furthermore, as the creatures they fought and hunted were predators, the animals fought back. The blodveidimenn adapted to this, leading to them having accelerated healing.

For centuries, the blodveidimenn lived on their island, separate from other humans. But then the volcano erupted from beneath them, shattering their island. The blodveidimenn were forced to leave, rushing out on wooden canoes to southern lands as their world fell in fire and water.

Upon reaching the southern lands, they came across normal humans, and they saw how different they were. The blodveidimenn found they were at least four times stronger and faster than these southern humans. The southern humans were blind in the darkness, whereas the blodveidimenn saw as clear as day. Humans could only hear a few feet, the blodveidimenn could hear miles away, and focus individual sounds. Humans had lost the animal instincts of recognising through scents, whilst the blodveidimenn could follow scents for miles, recognising individual scents. Finally, their lifespans. The blodveidimenn were not immortal, like most vampiric lore would eventually say. No, they just had longer lifespans, aging ten times slower. In addition, disease and decay never touched them and even though they could suffer injury, they healed instantly. This made killing them difficult.

For these reasons, as well as their quick learning and heightened intelligence, the blodveidimenn considered themselves as superiors, with humans as their main prey. Genetically, they were similar enough for the nutrients of human blood to benefit them, but separated enough that it was not cannibalism.

However, there was one way the weaker humans had an advantage.

The sunlight.

Humans could walk in the sunlight unaffected by it. In fact, the humans seemed to thrive in the sunlight. But the sunlight burnt the flesh of a blodveidimenn and blinded them. It burnt the flesh, causing sores and blisters filled with a pus that poisoned their blood, killing them within moments. Because they evolved in darkness, the blodveidimenn had to remain in the darkness.

Nonetheless, with their vast intellect, they were able to mix into human society. In addition, they found that their children acted much like the humans. On their island, they thought they aged quickly to adulthood, experiencing violent and painful growing pains when their hunger for blood reached grand heights. Amongst the humans, the blodveidimenn saw that their young aged at the same rate as humans. During puberty, usually when no longer needing mother's milk, the hunger for blood started and sent them into a death-like state, to emerge perfect. Amongst the humans, the children were integrated, to live as humans, to learn what they could before the blood hunger started.

However, they found another means of reproduction. When they fed on human blood, they were nourished. But when a human fed on their blood, they entered a violent fever, from which they died of. During their 'death', the superior blood mutated the inferior body to survive, allowing the individual to rise as one of them. They could use integrated coverts who could move unseen. However, these mutated blodveidimenn could not reproduce through sexual conduct, only the transfer of blood.

Armed with this knowledge, the blodveidimenn moved through the world, wishing to enslave the humans. But they had limitations. Blodveidimenn could not survive in sunlight, yet humans could move in darkness and light. Also, because of their shorter lifespan, the humans reproduced faster. Several human generations could spring up in one blodveidimenn lifetime. With this limitation, no matter how hard they tried, the blodveidimenn could never outnumber the humans.

For centuries, the blodveidimenn wandered through the human world, living amongst them in the darkness, feeding. Trying to increase their numbers, relying on the transfer of blood more than birthing children, choosing humans who already considered themselves above other humans, but not with a superiority complex. No convert, or blodur as they were called, should ever rise and take control. Only the pure blood elders, none as blodfaedd, could rule, and they were decreasing in numbers.

It was the sun that was their main downfall. Even though they could walk during an overcast day, the blodveidimenn were still afraid of the daylight. That was when, two thousand years ago, one of the blodfaedd elders had a vision. A dream of a blodveidimenn rising from the burnt remains of others, untouched by sunlight. The coming of the dagangadur. In his vision, he saw how it was done, and so was born the Festival of Nydogun.

Every December twenty-first, on the longest night, they all gathered on a beach, waiting for sunrise. As time grew on, the volcano that destroyed their home forged a new land that would soon become Iceland, but known as Radasteyjan to them. Seeing this as holy ground, they returned to this new forming land, gathering on a rocky beach. The idea was simple. All had to fast throughout the longest night, a sacrifice for themselves, and be brave enough to endure the sunlight. If any feared, if any wished to leave, they could. They were never shunned, and were always welcome to return the following year. But the idea was very basic for all to follow: fast on the longest night and be brave enough to wait for the sun. Of course, hundreds died in the sunlight, and no dagangadur rose.

These were the thoughts passing through Henry's mind as he stood on the beach, watching the festivities going on. The hundreds of blodveidimenn gathering, moving in groups, talking in the Icelandic language that was their native tongue. At a glance, they were just people of various backgrounds, but Henry knew who they really were, and why they were here, on a cold snowy night, the waves crashing and spraying against the giant rocks of the beach. Standing in a large group near the far end, were a group of robed figures. The elders, the last of the blodfaedd, who ruled over all blodveidimenn and governed the Festival every year. It was clear enough to Henry that not all the elders believed, because they obviously ran before the sunrise, seeing as they return every year.

Henry was a nonbeliever, and he secretly mocked all those who believed in the coming on the dagangadur. The only reason he came was because of his maker.

Fifty years before, Henry Barrow was a successful author of horror stories. What made him unique was his explicit descriptions of torture, and how he captured the suffering and pain of the victims. There was a reason for this; Henry was a murderer. Paying for the services of prostitutes, female and male, he had his way with them, only to bind them and torture them for days in a secret house he had in the countryside. As he tortured them, in different ways, he recorded as much as information as he could, using it for his work.

For this reason, a female blodveidimenn by the name of Raudurmaer came to him. She introduced herself by the human name she was using, Bridget Porter, and allowed Henry to bind and torture her. Stripping her of her red clothes, he tortured her for days, but no matter what he did, he could never break her. Seeing he was growing exhausted, Raudurmaer broke free and moved to him. With him in his weakened state, she laid him down, riding him as she drank his blood, biting her own tongue, letting it flow into him.

Of course, Henry turned into a blodveidimenn. She gave him the name of Dokkord, telling him they were now the last two members of the Ungurdauda clan. Her maker was the last elder of the clan, all of whom died during a Festival. She was the only survivor, surviving because she fled. However, she swore an oath, to rebuild the clan and await the coming of the dagangadur. Therefore, being infatuated with his maker, Henry came every year with her, escaping just before the sunrise. However, there was one promise she couldn't keep. Being the last of her clan, and not a blodfaedd, she could not rebuild the clan. Only an elder could. Therefore, as the elders were concerned, the Ungurdauda clan was dead.

"Are you all right, Dokkord?" said a voice, bringing Henry out of his thoughts.

Turning around, Henry found himself looking at Raudurmaer, dressed in a thick red fur coat. She always spoke to him in English, for he had never been able to understand the language. Nonetheless, as was custom, she always referred to him as his blodveidimenn name.

"Yeah, I'm fine," Henry replied. "Just deep in thought. How far into it are we?"

"About halfway. The elder is coming up to speak."

As all blodveidimenn gathered, an elder stood up and started speaking, but of course with Henry unable to understand.

"Velkomid braedur og systur. Eins og alltaf, vid erum saman komin, a Radasteyjan, ad bida komu Nydogun. Tru pin og

forn mun hjalpa koma fram i dagangadur, gerir ad verkum ad uppfylla orlog sin og stjorna heiminum.

"Nu hofum vid sampykkt um midja nott, og morg ykkar hafa verid. Sumir hafa fluid, ofaer um ad pola, en vid munum ekki fordast pa. Nu erum vid ad byrja ad Helgiathofn af Freistingum."

Although Henry did not understand, he knew that the Helgiathofn af Freistingum was a test. A test to see if those who had not fled yet could endure a torturous act of temptation.

From a nearby car, the elders dragged out a large barrel and a group of four humans, screaming and pleading. Showing no compassion, the elders strung the humans up on a piece of scaffolding above the barrel by the feet, and slit their throats. The blood cascaded out from the gaping wounds, filling the barrels. From the moment the first drop of blood touched the air, several blodveidimenn rushed at it, lapping the blood. As soon as they tasted it, all sense returning to them, they left the beach, ashamed of failing so easily. Many others fought the urge, starving, snarling furiously as the blood filled and the humans died.

During the Helgiathofn af Freistingum, Raudurmaer turned away from the sight, burying her head into Henry's body.

"God, I always hate this part. The barbaric nature of it, the inhumanity. Torturing us with those fresh humans and fresh blood."

Wishing to comfort her, Henry wrapped his arms around her, wishing to keep her safe. He knew the torment of starvation. Ten years ago, the slayers had captured him and held him hostage for a month, starving him. The rage, the delirium, the pain. It drove him to near madness. Especially as one had been cut when they captured him, and two of the slayers were women, each having their bleeds during his incarceration. If Raudurmaer hadn't come, he would have been a raging, skeletal beast.

Pushing the thoughts aside, feeling his hunger raging in him, Henry focused on Raudurmaer's blonde hair, lined with the falling snow, as he held her closer to his chest. He then glanced at his watch. Another nine hours to go until sunrise.

"Dokkord," she sighed, remaining buried in the softness of his winter coat, "I know you don't believe in any of this, but please don't check your watch."

"Sorry," Henry replied with a grin. "Just keeping an eye on the time to keep you safe."

Raudurmaer looked up and, with a gingerly smile, reached down for Henry's crotch. Even in the cold, her touch always made his blood pump.

"I know that is not why you want to go," she said in a husky voice, pressing harder. "Tell you what; I will make you a deal. Let us wait until the prayer. It always ends an hour before sunrise, for those who don't believe to still have time to leave. We will go then. I saw a small hostel along the coast. We will go there, have a feast on the teenagers there, and you can do whatever you want with me."

"Sounds good to me," Henry replied with a smile, leaning down to kiss her.

Time seemed to move a little faster as the two lovers hugged and kissed. With the excitement of what they were soon to do, they could not help but grope each other. The snow continued to fall, becoming heavy enough to blanket the jagged rocks of the beach. What was left of the blood in the barrel had cooled enough so the blood collected in it, looking like a strawberry ice cone.

With the human bodies no longer needed, they were put into a blazing bonfire, which many of the blodveidimenn gathered around to stay warm.

It was now time for the prayer, marking the near completion of the festival. One of the elders stood up and started speaking, not that Henry understood a word of it.

"Regin sem gaf okkur lif."

"Gefa okkur ljos," all chanted in return, and would do so with every sentence. This was the only part Henry had learned: 'give us the light'.

"Regin sem gaf okkur blod."

"Gefa okkur ljos."

"Vid pjonar myrkri spyrja um eitt."

"Gefa okkur ljos."

"Gefa okkur ljos og gera okkur oll," everyone, and the elders, said in unison.

He was so hungry, and deeply focused on the beauty in his arms, that Henry did not notice until it was too late. A sound invading his ears. No one realised it until it was too late.

From the darkness of the night, which none could focus on because of the bonfire's glare, an army of trucks burst onto the beach. With a flick of switches, powerful sun lamps came on, burning any blodveidimenn they came across. They all ran, screaming in fear and pain. Mercilessly, those on board the trucks fired guns and crossbows, mowing several down to their death.

"Vigi!" an elder roared in rage. *"Drepa pa! Drepa alla menn!"*

The order was clear. Enraged by the slayers attacking on their holy night, when all were cold, starving and weak, the blodveidimenn rushed and fought back. Wishing to keep Raudurmaer safe, Henry hid her behind a rock and rushed to help the others. The blodveidimenn fought and killed as mercilessly as the slayers; corpses littered the snow-lined beach. Some of the trucks had blades on the front, impaling some of the blodveidimenn. As the trucks drove, they were dragged along the rocky ground, shredding them apart as they screamed.

However, as the fighting and slaughter of both sides continued, Henry heard something that made his blood boil. A scream, and it was a scream he knew. Turning around, he watched in horror as a slayer was driving a spear into Raudurmaer's heart, twisting the spear so her breasts wrapped around the spear. Blood spurted from her mouth, she was dying.

Roaring in rage, Henry charged at the slayer, leaping into the air as he did so. He leapt with so much force that the two landed in the sea. Able to hold his breath, Henry remained underwater, holding the slayer against the sandy seabed. The man tried fighting back, clawing at Henry's arms, the cold salty air entering his mouth. He wriggled and twisted, trying to get free, but the hands holding him were too strong, and the eyes looking down at him were filled with rage.

Soon, the man stopped struggling.

Satisfied with his kill, Henry emerged from the water and looked at five slayers, standing at the beach edge. Judging by the corpses all over the place, Henry and these five slayers were all that were left.

Enraged, Henry charged at the humans. For some reason, they did not fight back; something had caught them by surprise. No matter, Henry used the advantage, mercilessly snapping necks, until only one remained. By this time, sense returned to Henry. He needed to feed.

Baring his fangs, Henry approached the terrified slayer, a girl no more than nineteen. Fear filled her as Henry's shadow loomed over her.

"Non, il n'est pas possible," she started crying.

"What's not possible?" Henry snarled, understanding French.

That was when he noticed his shadow was looming over her. When he noticed the confused humans were looking behind him, allowing Henry to slaughter them. Slowly, Henry turned around, his hand instantly rising to shield his eyes. On the horizon of the writhing ocean, through clouds that were breaking apart, Henry fund himself looking at a bright, glaring orb of yellow white.

The sun.

It was not blinding him. Looking down at his other hand, Henry saw he was not burning. He was standing there, in the sunlight, whilst he heard and smelt the other blodveidimenn in the beach burning. He did it: endured starvation throughout the Winter Solstice, rising from corpses and ashes.

He was the dagangadur.

But he was also hungry.

Behind him, he heard the slayer trying to run. Filled with so much hunger, Henry bound into the air, landing on top of the pleading girl. Holding her down, Henry bit down into her neck, enjoying the rush of warm blood, feeling his strength raging through him.

Satisfied, Henry stood up and walked over to the burning remains of Raudurmaer. Filled with dismay, he caressed her cheek. Even in death she still looked beautiful.

If only she could see him, the dagangadur. It was now time to start a new age, and bring in the dagblodveidimenn. But first, there was something he had to do. Something he was meant to do with her. Enjoying the warm sunlight in his face, Henry proceeded down the coast, heading towards a certain hostel.

Living in Swansea, South Wales, Carl lives with his fiancée, Samantha Smith, and their two daughters Amelia and Nevaeh. Carl works as a teaching assistant in the Reception area of a Primary School, in which he runs a creative writing club to help children write stories.

A Pagan with a deep interest in the occult and ancient mythologies, Carl uses this as much of this as he can in his writing. All the stories he has written, and the others he is planning to write, over a hundred, will all be part of what is known as the Wellworlds mythology. A singular mythology that all work focuses on, almost mirroring the Norse idea of Yggdrasil, the tree that all worlds are connected to. This is a life-long work that he is deeply focused on.

If you wish to read one of Carl Fox's novels, he had placed it on Facebook a while back. It is called The Wolf God, *a horror novel about werewolves searching for the final solution. You can find him on Facebook at carl.fox.5454@facebook.com.*

The Lonely Road

By Guy Burtenshaw

The first day of winter, and Miles Rhodes found himself
standing in the center of the road staring ahead into the darkness.
Even though it was minus five with a threat of snow in the air,
Miles felt far from cold. He was wrapped in three long-sleeved T-
shirts, a thick woolen jumper and a ski jacket. He was trembling,
but not from the cold.

The road that led from the university to the town was
usually empty at two o'clock in the morning, particularly early on
a Wednesday morning, but the old single lane road that wound
through the countryside was always empty, not just of cars but
also of life.

He had only been at the university for three months when
someone had told him about the road, and he soon learned that
the road had a legendary reputation going back as far as the
university had existed. The university was not an old institution.
It had only been built in 1954, but the road had been there much
longer. It had once led from the town out to a village, but the
village had been demolished along with its manor to make way
for the university campus. Several people claimed to have seen
ghostly apparitions on the road and there were other stories of
students getting lost on their way back from town and never
being seen again.

Miles did not believe in ghosts, and he most definitely did
not believe that anyone had ever gone missing, never to be seen
again. If students had been going missing, it would have made
the news, and he could not see how anyone could possibly get

lost on a single stretch of road. All you had to do was put one foot in front of the other and keep going in a straight line. He did believe that students returning from a drunken night on the town might have thought they had seen shapes drifting around in the dark and stumbled around lost for a few hours, but nothing more.

Now that he stood at the start of the road on the edge of the campus staring into the dark, he did not want to step one foot further. He had never been dared to do anything before, but he had been drinking and the dare had been made. All he had to do was walk the two miles along the road starting when the clock above the university library struck two. There was an ancient inn at the other end of the road called the Sargeson Inn, and if he made it he felt that he would be accepted into the higher levels of university life. There was also a wager at stake, and that involved a large amount of alcohol.

He shuddered as the bell struck two. The silence that followed felt hollow, but he did not really have any choice. There were three years of university to go, and he was not about to let anyone slam the door in his face.

"Here goes," he said to himself and started walking.

The first few steps were easy, but then the cold kicked in and with it rushed the realization of what he was doing. It was dark and the old road was a truly lonely place. He did not believe in the myths that had built up around the road, but if anything did happen there would be no one to find him until it was too late. He had his mobile phone with him, but the battery was flat. If he slipped and fell and broke his leg, hypothermia would probably kill him before anyone even thought of sending out a search party to see where he had got to, and that was if they all did not assume that he had just lost his nerve and gone back to the halls for the night.

An owl hooted and he almost turned back, but he supposed it dispelled one of the myths. There was life somewhere on the road. He pushed on, trying to calculate in his mind how long it would take him to reach the other end of the road if he continued walking at a brisk pace. It was only two miles, and he knew that he could run a mile in less than five minutes. He guessed that even if he walked slowly he could complete the walk in less than half an hour.

Miles managed to walk at a brisk pace for a good fifteen minutes before a few snowflakes gently drifted down around him. A few snowflakes would not have posed any problem, but the snowfall soon stared getting heavier until the road surface became indistinguishable from the verges on either side with a blanket of snow covering everything.

He slowed down, not wanting to slip. He was only wearing flat-bottomed shoes with no grip whatsoever. The only blessing that he could see from the snow was that it made it easier to see where he was walking. Instead of complete darkness, there was a murky grey hint to his surroundings. It reminded him of a scene from a film he had recently seen. He could not remember what the film had been called, but he did remember that the outcome for the male in that film had not been good.

He wished that he had brought his iPod with him. A little music would have made the time pass quicker and helped him along. His favorite band was Iron Maiden, and he started humming Phantom of the Opera, but stopped at the sound of a badger growling. He hoped it was a badger growling, because he could not think of anything else that would make such a growling sound.

He looked about, wondering whether anyone was watching him. He would not put it past some of the people he had met over the past few weeks to trail him all the way, perhaps harass him with strange noises and snigger at his reaction. He told himself to ignore anything that did not sound like an owl, a fox, or a badger.

After about ten minutes of walking, he stopped and looked back. The road disappeared into a mist of swirling snow. Looking forward again he squinted his eyes, trying to see through the falling snow. He thought he would have been able to see the lights from the town, but all he could see was snow. Something dashed across the road ahead of him.

He realized he was holding his breath and forced himself to start breathing again. It had just been a dark shape, too big to

215

be a fox. He blinked a few times. He was getting tired and was not even sure whether he had even seen anything it was so fast.

"I saw you," he shouted.

He tried lifting his arm to look at his watch, but it was hidden beneath his coat. He supposed it did not matter what the time was. If he kept going, the walk would not take too much longer.

He started forward more quickly, wanting to get to the end of the road. The cold was biting into his face. He was sure that he was past the halfway mark. If he had not been, he told himself that he would have turned around and gone back to the halls and to hell with the dare. Other doors would open, and three years really was not that long.

Something growled to his left. He stopped. There was a cluster of trees along the side of the lane. He stared into the trunks waiting for movement. He thought he saw something, but he was not certain.

"I can still see you," he shouted.

He wished that he had brought a torch with him. He would have been able to look amongst the trees and see who, if anyone outside of his imagination, was lurking there. He did not feel scared about the presence of someone amongst the trees. The only people that knew he would be on the road were his fellow students. No one else would be out on the road in the middle of the night in the freezing cold.

"Are you going to follow me all the way?" he yelled.

Miles smiled to himself and started running, and once he had started, he did not know why he had not run from the start. He would have been at the Sargeson Inn already downing shots.

Something dashed out from the trees in front, taking him by surprise, and he lost his footing. He tried to correct himself and his feet slipped sideways and down he went, hard onto the snow-covered road, his right knee slamming down onto his left calf. The pain was sudden and intense and seemed to suck the air out of his lungs.

He looked up expecting to see the empty road leading into the swirling snow, but there was a dark figure standing in the middle of the road no more than thirty feet away. The face was in darkness, but he could feel the eyes boring into him.

"Good one," Miles shouted, wondering whether he would be able to restrain himself from punching his lights out when he got back onto his feet. The pain in his calf was slowly subsiding, but the last thing he wanted was for the muscles to start cramping.

As he stood he looked along the road. The figure had gone. He looked about, but there was no sign of movement anywhere. He had only looked away for a second and could not see how they could have hidden themselves in such a short amount of time.

He looked towards the trees by the side of the road and felt that enough was enough. All he wanted to do was get to the end of the road, have a strong drink and then go back to the halls and sleep.

He limped towards the dark mass of trees and stopped. There was a steep bank leading up to the trees. He paused a moment unsure of whether he should just ignore them, or take them by surprise.

He sidestepped up the bank, the snow making the climb much easier than he had anticipated, and took hold of a branch to steady himself. Slowly he made his way around the tree expecting to see the figure, but as he passed between the trees he could not see anyone. He made his way past the trees where the ground dropped down and he ran into an iron fence.

"What the…"

It was a fairly large fence about seven feet tall, and as he looked through the iron columns he could clearly see that the fence surrounded a small cemetery. The graves were marked with substantial stone monuments and he assumed that it had once belonged to the old manor house that had been demolished when the university had been built in the fifties.

He made his way along the fence and found the gate. It was open and he felt that he knew where his antagonist was hiding: amongst the tombs. The gate was half open and he pushed it further. He thought he could make out slight dips in the snow, but nothing that looked large enough to have been made by a person, although it was still snowing and any tracks would quickly be covered.

The sound of his feet crunching into the snow seemed loud in the still of the night. A layer of snow about two inches thick had built up on the tops of the tombs and a fine layer was clinging to the inscriptions that had been chiseled into the stone.

The iron fence surrounded a square plot of about thirty feet by thirty feet, and the largest tomb stood in its center. The others were shaped like large stone chests. The centerpiece, which he assumed was the oldest, stood about five feet tall and was topped with a stone urn, adding a further four feet. It all seemed excessive for a grave hidden behind a cluster of trees on a road that would struggle even to be described as a backwater. He supposed the graves had been there longer than the trees, and the road would have once been the only way to and from town.

He walked over to the large tomb and wiped the snow away from the inscription. He squinted his eyes, trying to read what it said, then pulled his cigarette lighter from his pocket, struck the flint, and held the small flame out:

I am the way into the city of woe
I am the way into eternal pain
I am the way to go among the lost

He recognized the quote from Dante's *Inferno*, but could not see any name or dates. He had wiped the snow away, expecting to see the name of the person or persons that rested beneath the stone, and had hoped to see a date, but the quote was all that he could see.

He walked around the tomb, but on the other three sides there was nothing, just a smooth surface. His mind turned back to the figure he had seen in the road and he looked about at the smaller tombs.

"Come out, come out, wherever you are."

He wished that he had a padlock on him. He would lock the gate and see who was missing when he got to the inn.

He had hoped that someone would stand up from behind one of the tombs. He scooped a handful of snow from the top of

218

the tomb and compacted it into a ball ready to throw, but no one appeared. He dropped the snowball to the ground by his feet.

He shivered, and he knew that it was not from the cold. He turned to leave and found that the gate was closed. He expected to see a padlock securing the gate, but there was not, although he did see that the only footprints in the snow were his own.

He walked to the gate and took hold of the bars and pulled. Something touched his right shoulder and he spun around and came face to face with an old man. The face was gaunt and haggard, the eyes sunken and dark. There were patches of hair across a mottled head.

Miles stepped back, repulsed, and saw that the man's clothes were little more than old rags hanging from an emaciated body. He felt back for the gate not wanting to turn his back on the man. He curled his fingers around an iron column and pulled, his anxiety intensifying as the gate refused to move.

The man raised his hand and reached out towards him; Miles' eyes fixed on the bony fingers, cringing in anticipation of being touched by something that resembled a living cadaver.

"Feed," the man said, the man's lips barely parting to release the strained word.

The fingers pushed painfully into his stomach and he pushed the man hard in the chest, knocking him over. Behind him were other people. He counted six, all in a similar deathly state.

"Feed." He could not tell which of the persons had said the word, but the intent felt very real.

He turned and pulled hard, the snow around the base of the gate hindering movement, but only momentarily. Hands clasped his arms and tugged. He pulled his arms free and fell out of the burial ground, landing heavily on his hands and knees. He quickly turned over ready to defend himself. There was no one there.

He saw footprints in the snow from the people that had tried to accost him, but of the people themselves, there was no other trace. He looked about him and saw something dark lying on the snow by his feet. Reaching forward, he took hold of it and saw that it was the pointed iron spike from the top of one of the iron columns that stood either side of the gate. He looked up and saw where it had broken off, presumably from rust.

He got to his feet, clambered up to the cluster of trees and made his way back to the road, falling down the bank and onto the road. When he got back onto his feet again, he started walking, his hand clutched tightly around the iron spike, scanning the way ahead; glancing back every few yards.

Someone jumped out from behind a tree to his left and he thrust the spike at them and started running. After about twenty yards he stopped and looked back, expecting the road to be empty. A dark shape was slumped on the ground. He waited for it to move, and when it did not, he slowly started walking towards it.

He held the spike up and touched the tip. It looked like blood. He stopped and stood, staring at the dark shape on the road. He turned around, paranoid, and when he looked back at the body someone was crouched down next to it. It looked up and even through the snow and darkness he could see a smile on the face of the cadaverous man he had pushed over.

Miles wanted to turn and run, but he felt frozen to the spot. He watched as the man started pulling the body up the bank and into the darkness of the trees. He stood staring for what felt like an eternity. Something growled close by, and he was no longer so sure that it was only a badger. There were other creatures in the night, and he was not certain what noises they would make. The only thing he was sure of was that all animals feed, and to feed, other animals must die.

He turned and started running, throwing the iron spike towards the bank as he went, his calf throbbing with every stride, but he did not stop until he reached the door of the Sargeson Inn. Before entering he looked back towards the start of the old road. Obscured in darkness and snow, if he had not just endured its length, he would never have guessed there was anything there.

He pushed the old oak door and entered, his skin tingling as the warm air surrounded him. The door slammed closed behind and he jumped.

He looked about the room and could not see anyone anywhere. He held his breath and listened for the sound of voices. He knew he was in the right place. There was only one Sargeson Inn, and the door had not been locked, so there had to be people about.

From the room was quite small with a low oak ceiling and lit by a log fire burning in a large stone fireplace to his left. The bar was by the back wall. As he approached the bar, he sniffed at the air. There was the aroma of ale and cigarette smoke. There was a telephone attached to the wall behind the bar. His wallet was in his pocket, and there was no way he was going to walk back the way he had arrived when a taxi could drive him back to the halls.

Miles walked through the door to the left of the bar, his stomach feeling as though it was trying to tie itself into a knot, the knot tightening with each step.

From the moment the figure had appeared on the road, the night had felt wrong. He felt as though reality had somehow shifted, but he knew he was wide-awake. He bit painfully on his tongue to prove the fact.

Stairs led up, and the voices drifted down from above. The only relief he could find was that the stairs led up and not down.

As he put his right foot on the first step, he paused. An image of an angry landlord appearing at the top of the stairs with a baseball bat filled his head. Any other country and the angry landlord might have a gun. The only positive he could manage was that he could outrun a baseball bat.

He continued up, his heart rate quickening with every creak the old oak stairs emitted, and at the top of the stairs he found a closed door. He could not make out what was being said, but the voices were coming from the other side of the door. He reached out and pushed.

As the door swung open, he faced a wall of darkness, but more unsettling was the sudden silence. He felt inside for a light switch, but only found the rough surface of the wall. Something grabbed his hand and he yelled. The room became flooded with light and a group of people he recognized all started laughing at him.

"Thought you'd given up," a girl he recognized as Vanessa said.

"I had a pony on not seeing you until Monday," a boy he recognized as Michael to her left said.

Miles just stared at them as his pulse slowly returned to normal. Had he really just walked two miles in the dark and freezing cold, just so that he could be friends with these people?

"It was only two miles," Miles said and suddenly felt very self-conscious about the blood on his hand.

"Where's Rachael?" Vanessa asked.

"Rachael?" Miles asked confused.

"You were taking so long, she went out to see where you were."

"I didn't see anyone." He thought of the people amongst the tombs, and then thought of the figure that he had stabbed with the iron spike. The figure that he had seen being dragged into the darkness.

"Is that blood on your hand?" Michael asked.

Miles raised his hand and looked at the blood smeared across his fingers, and then back at Michael and Vanessa. The others had returned to drinking, which showed how little significance the dare had really been to them. All they wanted to do was spend the next three years drinking and whiling away the time until they had to set foot in the real world.

"Nose bleed," Miles told them. "The cold weather does that sometimes. Where does a freezing cold undergraduate get a drink around here?"

Miles hoped that Rachael would show up on the campus on Monday morning, but he doubted it would happen. He had a terrible feeling that Rachael would be reported missing, and he had an even worse feeling that the police would be paying him a visit very soon. His parents had suggested that he take a year out before university. He thought that he might be postponing his studies for twelve months and travelling abroad.

Miles wanted to scrub the blood from his fingers, and while he was scrubbing the blood from his hands he would decide whether to return for a drink or call for a taxi. He had been wearing gloves, so his prints would not be on the spike, but the cold would do a wonderful job at preserving the blood on its tip. If – when – the police searched the area, they would be sure to

222

find it, and he would be not just their number one suspect but their only suspect. He knew people had been sent down for life even if a body was never found.

He shivered as the raspy voice calling feed passed through his mind. He did not think anyone would be finding a body.

He knew he needed to get the spike, take it to the end of a long pier and let the corrosive seawater do its work. He would also be burning his clothes, but he would not be setting foot on the road until the sun had well and truly risen. Whatever had dragged the body away might even have done him a favor.

"Drink," Vanessa said bringing him out of his thoughts with a sudden jolt.

He turned his head and saw that Vanessa was holding a tumbler of what looked like whisky. He took it and poured the liquid down his throat and grimaced as it hit his stomach.

"Thirsty?" Michael asked as he approached.

"Cold," Miles responded. "I suppose everyone here had to walk the lonely road."

"Technically true," Vanessa said.

"Technically?" Miles queried, wondering whether he could get another drink.

"Rachael started the walk and ran back to the halls as soon as she heard a twig snap, but then she didn't have the advantage of the snow. There wasn't even any moonlight that night. Not even her shadow to keep her company. Some people are cats and some are mice. Rachael was a mouse. Ran back to the city of woe."

"Back to eternal pain," Michael added.

"Among the lost," Miles said as he felt the blood drain from his face. "Dante's Inferno."

"Another drink," Vanessa offered and smiled. "A toast to winter."

Miles found himself wondering whether anyone else had turned and run from the road. He had a feeling that if they ever had, they never got as far as graduation.

Guy Burtenshaw lives in a small town in southern England and has been writing horror stories for many years. He has published several horror novels, a collection of short stories as well as short stories in various magazines and anthologies, and also writes murder mystery novels under the pseudonym G D Shaw.

Candles Against the Dark

By Sylvia McIvers

"The snows lay outside these many days," declared Nana Irena, "and the sun does not shine properly. You must put a color in your cheeks."

"Mom! Tell Nana that I don't have to eat tomatoes if I don't want to."

"The wisdom of many years I hold, but does the child wish to listen?"

"Mooom!"

Mom looked up from chopping peppers for dinner. She has grey eyes and wavy brown hair like mine, but hers falls gently past her chin while mine is twisted into a fat bun. I've been polishing Nana's menorah, erasing a year's worth of green coloring from the copper candelabra. Hair full of polish? Yuck.

Arguing with Nana is a waste of breath, but Mom tries, for me.

"Nana Irena, stop teasing my little girl." Mom flipped chicken cutlets frying in their hot pan. They sizzled almost loud enough to cover Nana's sniff. Mom quietly put cherry tomatoes in a small bowl near the salad. Whoever wanted could eat. Who didn't want... Words weren't the only way to win an argument. Mom's great. And she's chopping anise, which makes salad taste like licorice.

Still – "I'm not little." Annoyance put extra vigor in my arm as I rubbed the hollows of the copper flowers, where green patina grew extra thick. Patina. That sounds expensive, but Mom says it just means a thin layer of dirt.

"Rena eats enough healthy food," Mom continued chopping without missing a beat, "to skip eating vegetables she doesn't like. You don't have to worry about her not getting enough nutrients to grow nice and tall."

Not as if Nana ever ate enough nutrients. She's hardly taller than me.

"I know you listen to nutrition shows on the radio, but not everything there is … accurate. Also, please don't to listen to political programs with Mina around, she remembers the most unfortunate words."

If I had used those words when I was four, you'd have washed my mouth with soap.

"You can listen to some nice music programs instead. We bought that new radio especially so you can switch between AM and FM yourself."

"Be proud of the child. Even when she is angry at her Nana, she works hard on the menorah. She should have a treat."

"What do you have in mind, Nana?" Mom asked, rinsing her knife in the sink.

I held my breath. Nana's ideas can be very old-fashioned.

"After I tell Mina her bedtime story, perhaps Rena would like to watch the television with her Nana. Or she can operate the video machine which is too complicated for these old hands. Or perhaps she would like to hear one of the family stories."

"About one of the other Irenas and Renas? You bet." I grinned as I rinsed off the polish under warm water, arguments forgotten. Maybe I had grown a little old for stories – I'll be fouteen in the summer – but I liked hearing my name in the starring role.

"Very good. I will call Mina to wash up for dinner."

Nana Irena turned, her ruffled brown skirt swinging around her knees, and walked out of the kitchen. She missed the center of the doorway, and her left arm slid smoothly through the doorpost. She'd be embarrassed if she knew, and I laughed.

"What's the joke?" Flipping hot chicken onto a plate took both eyes, so Mom missed Nana's little episode.

"Nana looks so solid, in her red peasant blouse, and a kerchief over her hair. She even has little golden birds embroidered on her slippers. It's funny to see her walk through walls like she was the kind of ghost no one can see." I washed the last traces of polish off the menorah.

"Not everyone can see her," Mom said in her This Is Important You Better Listen voice. "Only family, and we don't talk about her."

"Only family and whoever holds this." I rubbed the menorah dry with a soft rag. "Nana died while she held it in her lap, and she's been haunting it ever since. That's why this heirloom is so important for our family."

"Yes." Mom put the cutting board away.

"So can I take it to school tomorrow?"

"Can you – Rena Lightner, surely you realize that 'haunt' plus 'heirloom' means keep it home."

"Ms. Brown wants us to bring in a winter holiday item that's been in the family for more than a generation. Stupid Current Events class. She was careful not to mention a specific holiday, but you know what? Everyone will bring in tree ornaments, the bigger the better. What do we have? A dreidel you played with as a kid? Booorrrrring. A jug of oil that burns for eight nights and never grows empty? Oh, wait, we don't actually have one of those. Only one miraculous oil jug ever existed, way back when the Hanukah story took place. What should I bring?"

Mom opened her mouth to answer me, and shut it again. Took a deep breath. Let it out. She leaned back against the counter and rubbed her forehead. She always says that the kitchen has warm colors, like the honey-brown cabinets and reddish brown counters, to encourage calm conversations. Maybe that's why Mom didn't blow her stack. I rubbed the already dry menorah to keep from biting my nails. I'm totally not nervous. At all.

"Hanukah doesn't lend itself to long-term ornaments, Rena. Oil and candles are only used once. Holiday food, ditto. Rena, maybe you can bring Grandma Molly's recipe card, and I'll help you fry up a batch of latkes?"

227

The oily potato pancakes were delicious, but... "They only taste good hot, and I can't reheat them."

"Maybe you can bring a new box of the colored candles we use every year."

Mom's eyebrows rose and fell, saying You Love This Idea. Or maybe, Play Along Because I Don't Have A Better Idea. My eyebrows pulled in, and said You Must Be Kidding. I kept right on rubbing the menorah. Maybe a genie would pop out with an idea. No, our menorah already has a ghost.

"Jimmy Higgins down the block brought in old fairy lights class last year."

"Everyone laughed at him. He told me."

"Hanukah starts tomorrow night at sundown."

"School's over before then!"

"We can't risk it getting lost or stolen."

"You think I'll be careless?"

Mom's nose started doing that I Am Taking Deep Breaths and Being Reasonable thing. "We need the menorah on the windowsill, where it's been every Hanukah since we moved into this house. And we'll need it when my family comes to our Hanukah dinner Saturday night. It's been on our family's windowsills for centuries, honey. If anything goes wrong..."

"It won't!" I put down the menorah. I might squeeze it too tightly, and bend the branches by mistake. Would that show Mom how responsible I am? "I saved Styrofoam egg cartons to line a box, so it will be nice and padded. You'll see, I won't let it get a scratch!"

"Is this why you've shined it up so nice?"

I felt my cheeks heat up. My hands twisting the cotton rag. "It's hard. I'm the only Jewish kid in my class. At least last year Judy went to school here, but her family moved to New York."

Mom frowned. "We're not moving. Plenty of Jews live right here."

"Not in my class. Please can I bring the menorah? I'll take real good care of it."

"But honey. If you take it to school, Nana Irena will come along. Anyone who touches it will see her."

"I can put it in a clear plastic bag, so no one touches it by mistake. Brittany Swire said she'll do that with her angel ornament, because the paint started to flake off. Please, Mom!"

"You've really thought of everything. I'm impressed."

"So I can bring it?"

"I need to think about this some more. Here come Nana and Mina, and I hear Dad's car coming up the driveway. Set the table, now, and don't discuss this over the meal."

Morning. Mom sipped her coffee as I jiggled in front of my cereal bowl.

Finally, she said, "Bring in. I won't give you the 'be careful' speech, because you know it already."

"Lock it in my locker unless I'm actually using it," I sing-songed. "Don't let it out of my sight. Don't let anyone touch it, don't drop it, don't leave it on the bus, don't leave it in school. Don't throw it off the roof, don't flush it down the toilet, don't trade it for a lollypop."

Mom's eyes crinkled, and Mina's mouth moved as she memorized this new rule.

"And?"

"Don't let anyone hear me talking to Nana. You're the best, Mom!"

I sat near Olga Khanaeva on the bus. We've been friends since first grade, when she was jealous of my grey eyes and I was jealous of her thick black curls and pointy chin. Mutual admiration really helps people though the first day of big-kid school. Nana looked at the noisy kids bouncing around the bus, muttered "Unruly rascals," and flickered out of sight. Olga and I continued our discussion of Olga's new step-mother and older step-brothers. Olga had cried on my shoulder through the divorce two years ago, and moaned as her father dated one loser after another. The step-mom seemed not completely awful. She laid down reasonable house rules, and didn't favor her own kids too often. Olga didn't give me permission to visit yet. Her step-brothers were mean, and she hung out at my place the way she did since her parents started splitting up.

Olga tells me everything. I wish I could tell her about Nana, but I'm not allowed.

In school, I clicked the lock shut on the menorah: No one steals Nana.

Math. Science. English. Lunch. The mystery meat made me wish my family kept kosher, so I'd have a steady excuse to bring my own food. Finally, I tucked the menorah back into my book bag and hurried to Current Events. Nana whispered after me, all the way to my seat. Olga hurried from her locker, and shoulder-bumped me for luck.

"Why do you sit in the back row, child? Surely scholarly children sit in front, where the teacher sees their faces."

"Not in this class, Nana."

I suddenly felt grateful that I sat in the last seat of my row. I could whisper secretly to Nana, standing beside me in all translucent. Hah. My English teacher gave me an A for this vocabulary sentence from one of Nana's stories: In a strange building, with only one grandchild to give her strength, the ghost grew weak, and more translucent.

Right after Olga sat down in front of me, Ms. Brown clumped to the front of the classroom, unbuttoning her dull pink cardigan. She called for a volunteer to start the show and tell. She called it demonstrations and informative speeches, but that didn't fool anyone. Brittany jumped up, her perfect blond hair swishing past her shoulders. My long brown hair never swished. Her button-down blouse remained crisp. Mine had crumpled as I slouched through the day. Brittany always had something to boast about. She never had time to hear other people brag.

"Come up, Ms. Swire."

Brittany pranced to the front of the room carrying a big square box. She opened it, and foam peanuts spilled all over the floor. Ms. Brown didn't even frown. Teachers love that girl. With exaggerated care, she pulled out a ceramic figurine, complete with plastic bag.

"This little angel has been in my family since Mama turned five years old. See how its blue gown was rubbed clear off near the bottom? Mama said it's impossible to match the paint, since the statuette is so old. Anyone who wants to see it can come right up, but you can't hold it, because it's fragile."

All twenty seven of us stayed right in our seats. Brittany's smile went stiff as she realized no one intended to give her the chance to wail be careful, be careful. She tossed her hair and said, "None of you want to risk damaging Mama's angel? That's so thoughtful. Thank you very much!"

Her smile grew teeth, and she flounced back to her seat in the middle of the room. Olga and I never made faces at her back. Really never. Truth.

Olga didn't volunteer, but Ms. Brown said, "Ms. Khanaeva, would you care to demonstrate and inform next?" Why do teachers give orders in the form of a question? Olga walked to the big desk like a normal person, not a squirrel on a sugar high. Her stiff black curls and dark skin contrast sharply with Brittany's paleness, and her small brown paper bag sneered at Brittany's gigantic box. Kicking a few foam peanuts out of her way, my buddy turned to face the class. I sent her a thumbs up and a fierce grin, and she rolled her eyes at me. Chill, girlfriend. Got it covered.

"This icon of Saint Nicholas is not at all fragile, and you can pass it around as I speak." After twenty seconds, she ended with "Thank you for listening."

Head high, Olga marched back to her seat. Ms. Brown called another student. Most people spoke for less than a minute. People with smaller displays passed them around.

"Stop drawing in the notebook. The teacher looks right at you."

I looked up, pretending I had been paying attention all along.

"Ms. Lightner, please give us your demonstration and informative speech."

"Thanks," I hissed to Nana. I brought my box to the teacher's desk in the front of the room. When I turned to face the class, I squeaked my sneaker against an abandoned peanut. Loudly. Then I opened my box, took out a few filler egg cartons. Put them on desk, nice and neat. A few kids giggled, and some people darted glances at Brittany as I took out the plastic-wrapped menorah.

"For Hanukah, we light candles for eight nights." I tapped each branch, counting to eight. "This menorah is really old. It's been in my family for around four hundred years, passed from mother to daughter. There used to be a booklet with the name of the new owner inscribed as her mother handed it over. Unfortunately, it fell apart when my great-great-grandmother crossed the Atlantic. A lot of their luggage took damage due to the terrible conditions in steerage."

Nana nodded sadly. Her ghost-self had been as helpless against mildew as any of her living grandchildren.

"A family legend says this copper menorah belonged to an ancestress named Irena. Since then every first daughter, whether the mom inherited the menorah or not, is named Irena or Rena, in her memory."

Nana nodded again. She looked smug, just as she did at the end of every Irena story.

"I'd like to show it to all of you, since some of you may not have seen a menorah before. It's hardly fragile, though we have to be careful not to bend the branches. But, I spent an hour polishing it last night, so no fingerprints!"

Laughter rolled around the room. I took a deep breath. The classroom smelled of old linoleum, chalk dust and victory. In my politest voice, I asked Ms. Brown permission to walk up and down the aisles, so I can show and tell about my menorah.

The teacher pursed her mouth up to say no. Everyone started yelling that they wanted to see, they wanted to see. Ms. Brown gave the first real smile I ever saw from her.

"I'm proud of you all for taking this opportunity to expand your horizons. Yes, Ms. Lightner, you may demonstrate your menorah to everyone."

Does Ms. Brown even realize that more people are interested in snubbing Princess Brittany than expanding their horizons?

Nana followed me from seat to seat, careful not to walk through desks, though she stepped through a few knapsacks on the floor without noticing. I heard her skirt swishing just like

Brittany's hair. This child had dirt under his nails, such disrespect to the classroom. That one drew a lovely sketch of the menorah, have I made friends with her?

It was hard to hear my classmates' questions with the constant murmur, and I couldn't even ask Nana to be quiet. I didn't want to grit my teeth as I talked to people, because it might make me look as stuck-up as a certain other member of my class, who shall remain nameless. She makes a really good moral compass, though. Whatever direction she points? Do the opposite.

A few people hummed over the copper flowers, so thank goodness I had spent all that time cleaning the insides. ("Who can know that a modern young girl has an eye to see fine handiwork?") Others wanted to weigh the menorah on the palm of their hands. ("To what do they compare it? Did the child ever carry an axe, to know what an axe handle weighs?") It was heavier than most of them expected. ("Did the child expect a hollow plastic pipe?") Only two people asked me why we use a menorah for Hanukah. ("An intelligent mind, my child, make friends with this one.") One asked if we have family dinners on Hanukah, and I said sure, my mom's parents and her brother's family were coming over to our place on Saturday night. They'd even bring their silver menorahs, and we'd all light the colored candles in the same room.

When I reached Olga's seat, I saw my box and egg cartons on her desk. I offered her a small smile in thanks. She winked, and asked how we lit the menorah, though she already knew. I explained, loudly, that we'd light one candle tonight and one more each night until all eight branches had a candle.

"You mean your holiday lasts for over a week?" Huge eyes painted fake astonishment on Olga's face. I bit back a laugh. I have the best pal a girl could want.

"That's right," I said, all nice and serious. We have this Q & A every year. Usually over hot cocoa or painting our toenails in outrageous colors, but this is good too.

"Is that like the Twelve Days of Christmas?"

"I don't know. We don't celebrate Christmas in my religion."

The classroom exploded. Not celebrate? Were we atheists or something? Were we anti-American? No presents under the tree? ("Pagan nonsense.") Everyone in my class already knew I'm Jewish, but I guess no one really thought it through.

The boy sitting in front of Olga half stood from his seat. With astonished belligerence, he asked, "Didn't your parents tell you about Santa Claus?"

I fixed him with my most pitying stare. "Do you believe that a fat guy climbs down your chimney? Do you even have a chimney?"

He turned red. "Everyone tells kids about Santa!"

("Don't anger the gentiles, child, they outnumber us!")

"Sure they do," I answered over Nana's voice. "Then kids figure out that their parents lied. Meanwhile, they love the sainted fat guy for bringing them presents. When we get presents or Hanukah gelt, that's cash; we thank the actual giver. Not a mystical person who's just someone with a pillow up his shirt."

I walked up the last two aisles answering more questions about Santa than about the menorah. My heart did this weird fluttering thing, as I sat back down. My stomach squeezed up, too. Did my body think I was in trouble? Just last week in Social Studies, we learned about the pink monkey experiment.

The next kid was already talking. I kept seeing visions of monkeys, fur dyed pink, torn apart by their former friends. Friends didn't like when friends suddenly looked like strangers. But people aren't monkeys; people are OK with diversity. I had nothing to worry about.

Nana stood next to me, shaking her head. She looked worried enough for both of us.

On the bus home, Olga called her step-mom for permission to come to my house, saying "uh huh" and "OK, yeah" forever. I raised my eyebrows: Tell Me What's Going On Before I Explode From Curiosity, but she just waggled her fingers at me: Nothing Guaranteed Yet.

Olga flipped her phone shut. "I can come after I finish my homework and eat dinner, then I can come over for latkes."

She waved at me when I got off at my stop, and surprise! Mom reached the door at the same time as me, holding Mina's hand. Usually, Mom brings Mina home from playgroup an hour before I get off the bus. Why come home so late right before Hanukah?

Mina shouted, "Guess what! The car broke and I sat on top of the trunk until the tow truck dragged our car to the fixer shop!"

"The garage told me," Mom said, "that the five year warranty expired last week and I could have expected a breakdown within the month. How am I going to prepare everything before your dad comes home?"

As Mom unlocked the door, I grabbed Mina's hand and pulled her aside as Mom charged, coat and all, into the kitchen.

"Let's stay out of Mom's way," I said as I wrestled with the knot on Mina's scarf. Who tied little kids into woolly knots?

"Perhaps slower fingers are best for such a task."

I hung up my own coat as Nana helped Mina. "Why don't you color in your new Hanukah book, so we can all look at the pictures after we light the menorahs?"

Mina ran off. I bit my lip: I'm Not Sure What To Do. Tell Mom that Olga is coming over, or tell Olga not to come?

"You are distressed, child. When a mother must hurry, the child should not stand under her feet. A helpful daughter might line the window with foil paper and lay out the menorahs. Know that your mother's heart filled with hours of worry, and worry has birthed anger. Shaky anger loves to scold. Do not be the target."

By the time Dad came home, I had lined the window with foil, put a box of matches, and arranged candles in the menorahs. I even managed to set the table without triggering a scolding.

After dinner, Mom said sure Olga could come over, hadn't she been here the last two Hanukahs?

Mina piped up, "She probably knows all the blessings by heart. I do too!"

With a small laugh, Mom said, "I know she doesn't get on with her brothers. She can come to the party on Saturday night, too."

For the party, Mom and I bought Hanukah themed paper plates, napkins, and cups, and a plastic tablecloth spangled with menorahs. Mina and I set the table as Mom flipped potato latkes in hot oil. I was under strict instructions not to eat any before the relatives all had some. Really, did Mom think I have no manners? Nana laughed when she saw me spinning each dreidel before putting it in the center of a plate. She spun a few herself – not bad for an old ghost! She is stronger and more coordinated already, just from anticipating more family coming over.

The folding table near the wall held plates of donuts, which Mom only ever bought for The Holiday of Oil. I filled one bowl with chocolate coins covered in gold foil, and another with shiny new pennies. The adults would distribute real Hanukah gelt later, but the kids could play dreidel with pennies as soon as they came. We finished setting up just before Grandpa and Grandma rang the bell. Her name is Irena, like Mom and Nana. Some family traditions cause a stupid amount of confusion.

Mina and I ran to hug and kiss them. While Mina checked Grandpa's pocket for candy, I helped hang up coats, glad it wasn't raining or snowing. I hate hauling heavy, dripping coats into the bathroom to drip. Uncle David and Aunt Miriam came in then, with their kids Irena, age ten, Mikey, six, and Pearl, four.

"It should be my job to put candles in the menorah," announced Mina, "because my birthday is on the last day of Hanukah, and I was named after the menorah."

Nana Irena beamed at the little brat, but Grandma said, "We light with oil, sweetie. You can choose which color candle Grandpa lights the wicks with."

"You can put my menorah on the sill," smiled Uncle David, "but Pearl always sets up my candles."

Now I was really glad I had polished Nana's menorah so well. Grandpa's silver menorah shone brighter than the New Year's ball over Times Square, with flowers and swirls all along the branches. Uncle David's menorah is all smooth lines, but it towers over the rest. Kid-sized menorahs are simpler, except for Pearl's with eight Disney characters holding the candles. Whoops! While I was thinking, Mina finished her menorah and starting putting candles in mine!

236

"Wrong colors," I said, and took them out. I can put in my own candles, thank you very much. When I'm all grown up, I'll have to be polite and let the children do it for me. My eyebrows pull together: I don't want to share, you future kids!

Candles done, the little kids grabbed dreidels and pennies, plopped down on the floor near the window. They'd play until the grow-ups were ready to light the menorahs. Then we'd all sing the holiday songs, and eat. Kids on the floor or grown-ups chatting on the couch: who I should join? Would I rather be the youngest grown-up or the oldest kid? Dither, dither.

The doorbell rang.

Olga! She came in with a swirl of frosty air, and three people yelled, "Shut the door!" Taking off her coat, my friend asked, "Am I too late to gamble with the Hanukah top?"

"The what?"

"The top, the top!" She made a twist and spin motion with her fingers.

"Oh, the dreidel. Sure, we're just starting up a game. Grab some pennies."

Olga settled onto her knees between me and Irena. She held the dreidel, rubbing the Hebrew letters the four sides. "Do I remember the rules? This letter with one foot is gimel, guh, grab the whole pot. Then everyone puts in ten pennies and the game goes on. This square letter is hei, huh, half the pot is yours. The letter with branches is shin, shuh, shove half your pennies into the pot. This skinny letter is nun, nuh, nothing happens this turn. Right?"

"Right," said Mikey, bouncing in place. "Let's start already."

"I'm youngest, I'm first!" announced Pearl.

Nana sat between little Mina and Pearl, petting their hair and telling of her very first grandchild. "My son had married already nine years, and no children came."

Pearl grabbed her dreidel and spun. "Shin! Do I really have to put pennies in?"

As she slid one shiny penny at a time, Nana said, "Everyone in the village whispered that they should divorce and marry other people while they could still have children. Suddenly my son went to the wood carver and asked him to make a cradle. Oh, the gossip! The son born in Irena's old age would place a grandchild in her arms! You children play at gambling – the men made bets if such an old woman would live to see the child."

Why did Nana tell her story now? We three older grandchildren heard it a thousand times. The two four-year-olds had to concentrate on the game, and Olga couldn't even see her.

Olga spun a nun, nothing, and groaned. I spun a gimel, grab. I laughed and everyone else groaned as we all slid ten pennies into the pot.

"The child was born, and I helped as much as much as my old, liver-spotted hands could manage. My daughter in law had no mother and no sisters, and there were no women but me to help with the little girl."

"Hei, half! Look how much I got!" Mikey wiggled happily.

"Can I trade dreidels?" Olga frowned at her orange one. "It gave me three nuns in a row. Maybe that gold one will have better luck. Aaaaand, gimel – grab! But Mikey just took half, so there isn't much left."

"Better than nothing," I said as I spun a shin, shove. Olga helped me groan over the bad luck, while her wrinkled eyebrows and half smile said, Better Luck Next Time.

Pearl spun her wooden dreidel, and Nana kept talking. "On the third day of the holiday, as I scraped wax off the menorah, I felt a gentle heaviness overtake my arms, my legs, my hands. I put the precious copper menorah in my lap, and curled my fingers between its branches. A great light shone, although it was night."

"Shin!" Mina's shoulders drooped. "But I only have seven pennies, do I still have to put in half?"

"Yup," I answered. "Three for the pot, four stay with you. Better hope no one gets a gimel before you grab some more pennies, or you'll be... out!"

Mina groaned long and loud, then jumped up and grabbed some chocolate coins to console herself. Before dinner! I had never been allowed to do that.

"There stood my righteous mother, holding out her arms for me. She did not wear the wrinkled face she died with. Youth and joy graced her, as they did when I was as young as Mina."

"Hei, half. Look, Minah, I got your pennies. Can I give some back to you?"

"Nice thought, Olga, but no. My turn. Can I borrow that gold dreidel? It seems to have all the luck."

"'Come with me, my child, the angels await with silver trumpets, to escort you.'"

"'But the child,' I said. 'There is to one to help but me.'"

"'It is time,' said my mother, with the same stern voice I remembered from when I wanted sweets before my dinner." Nana flicked the empty foil in front of Mina.

I held my breath, and glanced at Olga. Had she noticed the foil moving by itself? No, she stared intently as Mikey shoved pennies into the pot. Then Irena got a shin, shove, and put even more pennies in the pot. Olga took the lucky gold dreidel, and what do you know? She got a shin, too!

"Come on, gold! What happened to that streak of gimels?"

Mikey laughed. "Dreidels don't remember from one spin to the next."

My turn. Everyone, including me, was down to eight or nine pennies. If I won this pot with a gimel, I'd win the game.

"No matter how long we argued, I did not change my mind. Mama could not give me orders anymore, and the child needed her Nana's help. My mother gave me a sad look, and stepped backward toward the light. 'You must choose before the gate to the next world closes. What face will you wear? How old will you be? Choose wisely, for when the light fades, you will remain as you are.'"

I held the gold dreidel to lips, trying to taste the luck. But Olga had just lost. Maybe the gold's luck was used up.

"I remembered myself at forty, strong and joyous, with my only child pulling at my skirts. My arms must be strong for my family, not like the crone who only sat and rocked the cradle."

I rummaged through the box of dreidels. Which looked lucky? Not the green, not the blue...

"I remembered also the day my dear husband asked me if I would choose a divorce on our tenth anniversary with no children. I did not want anyone else's children, and if the good Lord did not choose to send any to us, I would stay all the same. Oh, the smile he gave me then! It was worth a dozen children."

Maybe this dreidel, silver as a menorah, would win me the pot.

"He bought me this red blouse and brown skirt with red embroidery to wear only in the house, for a modest woman did not wear red in public. I chose to wear it among my children's children for eternity."

My fingers closed around a copper colored dreidel, like Nana's menorah. I rubbed the plastic, brought it to my lips.

"Of course I look substantial. How else can a Nana help take care of the children? My ghost arms are strong. My hair is a rich brown, though I cover it just as I did when I first married."

I set the copper dreidel on the smooth wooden floor, held the stem between two fingers.

"At first, I walked through walls. A shame, an embarrassment! I learned to be more careful. A ghost who does not know what is solid should never hold a baby. The young mama could hardly see me, though she saw the cradle rock, she saw the baby lifted into my rocker and stop crying as someone patted his back. My son insisted he smelled his mama, as I had been in his youth. At last they realized I had remained when the light shone and the angels awaited me."

The dreidel spun and spun. The six of us stared as if we played for diamonds, not pennies.

"My son told his wife not to worry. Had his mama ever ill-wished them? I was not strong enough to talk, at first. When a second child was born, I grew stronger. With the third, I was visible, and my joy sang to the children."

The dreidel slowed, wobbled, fell on its side. Gimel. I pumped my fist in victory. The pile of pennies had grown so big from all the shins, everyone shoving their pennies into the middle, that I couldn't pull it to me with both hands. Olga snickered and lent a hand, scraping pennies along the floor. Mina and Olga sniffled a little at losing, and consoled themselves that at least neither of them had won over the other, best friends forever.

I'd be grateful if they didn't fight with each other all night.

Before we could start a new game, the grown-ups came to the window. Time to light the colored candles! Grandpa recited the blessings, then used one red candle to light the wicks floating in oil. Then Dad chanted the blessings and lit his candles. After Mom lit the copper menorah, everyone else had their turn. When the last Menorah was lit, we sang the Hanukah songs celebrating a victory from when the Greek Empire ruled the world.

Food! The latkes had cooled enough to eat – though I liked them hot enough to almost burn my tongue. We passed around a platter of chicken in apricot sauce and sesame seeds. Cole slaw, cucumber salad, and a tossed salad left almost no room in my plate for the chocolate coins I saved for dessert. Nana passed by my seat, and said all that salad adds a color to my cheeks, but I couldn't answer. Olga was telling me how her stepbrothers had hidden girly presents and wrapping paper in their closet, which she had found totally by accident as she searched for her snow boots.

"Do you think they wanted to buy presents for me? Or will they be mad because their mom made them spend their own money on a stupid stepsister?"

"That's an important difference," I agreed. "Did you buy them anything?"

"Music from their favorite bands – and earphones."

I felt my cheeks stretch in a grin. "Maybe you'll all become a happy family after all."

Olga squirmed, shrugged. "Too much, too fast. I miss my mom."

I tried to think of a new topic, when the doorbell chimed. Mom excused herself from the table and went to the front door.

"Flower delivery," we heard, then the lock snicking open.

"On a Saturday night?" Olga wondered.

241

"Just because the stars came out at four thirty, doesn't mean six o'clock is night."

Mom backed into the room, hands rigid in front of her.

Two guys followed, wearing wooly hat to their eyebrows and scarves over their noses. One held a long flower box. The other held a gun.

"Everyone sit tight. No one has to get hurt! Put your jewelry, wallets, and watches in the nice lady's collection plate."

The gunman swung his gun between us. The other man opened his flower box and took out a sack. Walked to the window sill. Snuffed the candles. Grandma started to cry, then stifled her sobs. My eyes opened too wide to cry. Olga, too. Little Mina and Pearl stared open mouthed.

Mom picked up a clean plate with shaking hands, came to me. Her eyes said, Don't make him hurt you. I dropped my earrings onto the picture of dreidels and gelt. Mom walked around the table. Rings, bracelets, necklaces, all jumbled together like a weird jewelry box. The gentle jingle was the only sound – almost.

"Who interrupts our holiday! Is this an ancient village? My family did not abandon the homeland to find the same corruption here!"

"Sssh." Mom tried to soothe Nana, because what could a dead granny do against a gun?

Olga whispered 'no, no' behind her teeth.

I arched my eyebrows at her: What's Wrong Besides The Obvious?

Barely moving her lips, she said, "That's Jared's hat – green with gold stars – my stepbrother."

"Might not be him." I didn't move my lips, either. "We don't see his face at all." Still, my stomach turned. How could anyone in Olga's family rob my family?

The green-hatted thief – Jared? – wrapped Grandpa's menorah in a towel and stuffed it into his sack.

Mom started walking back to the thief at the doorway, but his gun waved her back to the table. "Children's jewelry."

"It's plastic! Why?"

242

The gun waved. Because I said so.

Mina screamed when Mom told her to drop her hearts necklace in the plate. Pearl, too. Mom just took the necklaces.

Green-hat had trouble jamming Uncle David's huge menorah into his sack. Gun-guy snickered. Aunt Miriam started to cry, quietly, like Grandma. Green-hat finally jammed the branches into the bag with the stem sticking out like a handle. He crammed our little menorahs in around that handle. It was like watching clowns piling into a tiny clown car, only less funny.

Gun-guy motioned Mom to pour the plate of jewelry into the flower box. All our pretty things, tangled like trash! I bared my teeth at the man. He didn't even look in my direction. I was too little, too helpless.

Nana seemed helpless, too. "Not my menorah!"

"Who said that?" Green-hat glared at the table, copper menorah in hand.

We all sat quiet. Mina and Pearl put their hands over their mouths. Uncle David squeezed his teeth together tight enough for me to hear the squeak.

Nana said, "Put it down!"

Green-hat focused on Nana. "Sit down, old lady."

"His voice." Olga grabbed my wrist, eyes so wide I thought they'd fall out. I was too scared to yelp.

"That old lady," said gun-guy, drumming his fingers on the flower box. "is sitting down blubbing."

"Her!" Green-hat pointed with the copper menorah.

"No one's there. Hurry up."

Green-hat slowly put the copper menorah into the sack. As soon as his fingers lost contact with it, he stared wildly from side to side. "Where did she go?"

Olga hiccupped. "Not Jared's voice. His hat, not his voice."

"Who?" The gunman's eyes flicked around, but of course he saw everyone sitting quietly.

"The old lady disappeared."

"There was no old lady. Are you on drugs?"

Nana took a deep breath. She took a few steps toward Green-hat and her copper menorah.

"Not him, Nana," I whispered.

Nana glided to my seat. Did her legs move? Was she acting like a no-body ghost?

"Why, child?"

I whispered without moving my lips. "If you grab your menorah, gun-guy will hurt us. Can you take away the gun?"

"No. But many movies I have seen on the television. When the gun spits out all of its bullets, heroes tackle the bad men." Nana looked significantly at Dad and Uncle David, who gulped and nodded.

Nana rolled her shoulders, and stalked toward the gun-guy. She grabbed his wrist and pointed it at the ceiling. Green-hat shouted words I couldn't understand. Olga, fingers still wrapped around my wrist, pulled me almost into her lap. Mom, her back to the wall, clenched her fists. Mom and Aunt Miriam stopped whimpering. Our heroes tensed, ready to jump up and rush the bad guy.

Screaming, gun-guy tried to pull his hand down. Nana held on. She squeezed the trigger, sending bullets into the ceiling.

I shivered. My room was directly overhead. Would I find bullets in my bed?

The gun clicked – no more bullets. My sweet, gentle Nana, with her silly, old fashioned way of talking, slammed the gunman's head into the wall. He slid down in a heap, not moving.

Nana cried out, "Save my menorah!"

Dad and Uncle David jumped up so fast their heavy wooden chairs fell over. The noise made Green-hat drop his sack. It was almost funny how fast they took him down. Did Dad get into fights as a kid? Uncle David took off his belt and buckled Green-hat's arms behind his back. Yanked off his hat.

I jumped up. "That's Brittany Swire's brother! What are you doing here?"

"When Brittany told me you have this holiday with big silver and copper pieces, she didn't say you have this weird stuff, too! What is wrong with this house?"

I jammed my knuckles into my mouth. Brittany had turned my family, my holiday, into pink monkeys. Nana had been right to worry.

244

"Nothing," said Dad. "I'm calling the cops."

Brittany's brother tried to break loose, but Dad sat on his legs. Uncle David went to comforted Aunt Miriam and Grandma.

Olga still held me close, but her fingers loosened. "Tell me what's going on."

I gulped. Did I have permission? At this point, did I need permission? Time to think… "Can it wait until Grandma stops crying?"

Olga looked at her, head on the table right near all the chicken bones. "Before I go home."

"Agreed."

After the groggy gunman and Brittany's brother were hauled off, after everyone gave their statements, after the police and finger-printers left, I sat on my bed with Olga. Took a deep breath. "I don't know where to start."

"Start with whatever attacked the gunman."

"Nana Irena."

"The grandmother crying at the table?"

"Not exactly." I petted the copper branches in my lap. Nana nodded encouragement. "The grandmother who stayed with the family for the last four hundred years. Want to meet her?"

Olga leaned back: Girl's Gone Crazy.

I felt a smile pulling at the corners of my lips, but forced my voice to stay serious. Would my best pal hear the difference between amused laughter and crazy cackling? "Hold this."

Nana walked to the doorway, started humming a lullaby.

"The menorah you brought to school?"

"Just take it."

The line between her eyebrows said, I know it's a trick. How much will it hurt? Still, she closed her fingers around Nana's heirloom. Her eyes jerked to the door to see who was humming. There was Nana's familiar kerchief, red blouse, and brown skirt with red embroidery.

"Who's that?"

"Nana. Remember the family legend I told in school? When Nana Irena died, she sort of stuck around."

Olga's mouth opened, closed, opened, stayed that way.

Nana stopped humming. "A bad ghost I am not. My son's wife was an orphan. Who would help her? My son was not home all through the day, and the poor woman was exhausted. What kind of Nana leaves a baby like that? So I stayed. There was always a new baby to help. Today I helped against those thieves. Do you not have your lovely locket back?"

A shaky hand patted that very locket. "It has my mom and dad's wedding picture. I don't know why I'm keeping the stupid thing; they're never getting back together."

Nana shrugged. "Nothing lasts forever. Hold tight to the good memories, child. Now I will go so you may speak."

"So. A ghost attacked the gunman before your dad attacked Brittany's brother."

"You're taking this pretty calmly." Was that a good sign? Or was she just winding up for a total screamfest?

"You know what worried me?"

My eyebrows said, Tell Me Everything.

"I thought you'd hate me forever because my stepbrother robbed you. I thought my dad would get divorced again. Instead, the stepmom said I could stay the night because you need a friend's company! I thought my whole life was wrecked. Now Brittany's life can be wrecked. A ghost? Pffft."

I started laughing, with just a hint of cackle. "Best friends forever?"

"Cross my heart and hope to die."

"From the world until the world, Amen."

Olga fell asleep first. I watched her curly black hair spread across the pillow. My BFF just met the family ghost, and it didn't scare her hair white. She'd eat in the kitchen with us tomorrow, and I'd put the menorah there in case she and Nana wanted to talk.

Sylvia McIvers lives in New York. She writes whatever the voices in her head tell her to write; this story, for instance, was dictated by Nana Irena. Sadly, there isn't enough time in the day to write all the stories that demand to be written. While waiting their turn, the voices have extended conversations among themselves about world peace, and how to go about joining a reality TV show when one does not exist in reality.

Sylvia is writing a novel exploring what was happening in the world while Snow White grew up in the palace, and what the local witch thought of having a royal princess dumped in her bailiwick.

Due to an unfortunate typo, Sylvia misunderstood the imperative for writers to accumulate cats, and so she has an extensive collection of real and virtual hats. Imagine her delight in Googling hatnip, and finding several amusing hat sites.

She can be contacted at sylviamcivers@gmail.com.

www.ingramcontent.com/pod-product-compliance
Lightning Source LLC
Chambersburg PA
CBHW060543260626
47161CB00003B/1031